Bring Me Home

Also by Alan Titchmarsh

FICTION

Mr MacGregor

The Last Lighthouse Keeper

Animal Instincts

Only Dad

Rosie

Love and Dr Devon

Folly

The Haunting

NON-FICTION

Tales from Titchmarsh

Knave of Spades

Nobbut a Lad

Trowel and Error

England, Our England

Fill My Stocking

Alan Titchmarsh's Favourite Gardens

Gardeners' World Complete Book of Gardening

The Gardener's Year

British Isles: A Natural History

The Nature of Britain

The Kitchen Gardener

How to be a Gardener

My Secret Garden

Alan Titchmarsh

Bring Me Home

First published in Great Britain in 2014 by Hodder & Stoughton
An Hachette UK company

1

A CIP catalogue record for this title is available from the British Library

Hardback ISBN 978 0 340 93691 7
Trade Paperback ISBN 978 0 340 93692 4
eBook ISBN 978 1 444 72171 3

Printed and bound by CPI Group (UK) Ltd, Croydon, CR0 4YY

Hodder & Stoughton policy is to use papers that are natural, renewable and recyclable products and made from wood grown in sustainable forests. The logging and manufacturing processes are expected to conform to the environmental regulations of the country of origin.

Hodder & Stoughton Ltd
338 Euston Road
London NW1 3BH

www.hodder.co.uk

For Daphne Flora and Zachary Theo with love

‘Life is a series of episodes – sometimes with long periods of relative inactivity between. But it is a mistake to assume that the *status quo* will remain, however settled that period of life seems to have become, for there are always surprises around the corner – and always a good supply of spanners to be tossed in the works, often by unseen hands.’

Tom Derwent, *Travails with My Aunt*, 1975

I

Castle Sodhail

June 2000

'It takes patience to appreciate domestic bliss; volatile spirits prefer unhappiness.'

George Santayana, *The Life of Reason*, 1905

'You really are the perfect family, aren't you?'

Charlie Stuart was, for a fleeting moment, unsure whether to take the remark as a sarcastic assessment of the current state of his domestic life or as an innocent and kindly meant compliment. But registering the fact that the bearer of this dubiously couched commendation was a woman whose capacity for tact had, for the entire duration of her seventy years, been notable only for its absence, the situation pointed – somewhat surprisingly – to the latter. Nessie Mackintosh was a middle-aged divorcee who managed, by virtue of brass neck and a certain native insouciance, to appear at every village house party, in spite of the fact that few hosts could ever remember having invited her. She specialised in offering frank and candid appraisals as to the current state – emotional, financial and political – of every resident of the broad scattering of houses, large and small, that constituted her domain. This Sunday lunchtime she was behaving true to form.

'I'm sorry?' Charlie enquired, by way of clarification.

'Well, Mr Stuart, just look at them. Every girl happily married; and to such eligible young men.'

Struggling to avoid choking on his glass of modestly priced Sancerre, the father of the three brides who were scattered about the large hall did his best to avoid baulking at Nessie's less than accurate description of his sons-in-law.

'Well, I suppose . . .'

'A banker, a lawyer and a farmer. All necessities covered,' she continued.

'Now there's only the boy.'

That was true enough. Charlie glanced across the room to where his son and heir stood, chatting to three other 'eligible' young women who seemed entranced by his company. It was at moments like this that he was tempted to intervene and warn them what they might be letting themselves in for.

'Yes. Only Rory.' He was lost in reverie for a moment, unsure whether to be jealous of his son's ability with the opposite sex or sympathetic to the likely outcome of the day, bearing in mind the events of the morning.

'But boys will be boys, won't they?'

The trite, if ostensibly inoffensive, remark was the last straw. Fearing that unless he extricated himself from the company of the judge of his current domestic state he might commit if not another crime then certainly an unfortunate lapse of diplomacy, he murmured, 'Will you excuse me for a moment; I think I need to fill some glasses.' Nodding briefly at the unsuspecting source of his irritation, Charlie snaked through the assembled throng. Considering that there were now enough bodies between himself and the tiresome woman to affect some degree of camouflage, he made for the heavy oak door that was wedged open and slipped out onto the gravel drive. It was a June day; not a particularly pleasant one. The sky evinced little in the way of azure blue, preferring instead to opt for a more appropriate pale grey. Appropriate to his mood at least; but then to match that he needed thunder clouds and torrential rain. At this rate he might find his wish coming true.

He crossed to a lichen-encrusted bench under an ancient yew tree, flopped down and drained the last of the wine in his glass before leaning back and listening to the gentle murmur of voices from within the castle. It had been his for thirty years now – every grey stone and every strip of ancient mortar his to love and to cherish till death . . . well, there was no need to go there. Not again.

The events of the morning – events for which he was to blame – seemed to block out any kind of future. He half wished that he could change places with Rory, who seemed far more capable of a phlegmatic view of life; far more willing to accept what fate threw at him and to deal with things one step at a time. That had been his own approach, until that morning.

He looked up at the castellations and turrets that stood out ever darker against the leaden sky. What had they seen in the last hundred-and-sixty years? Worse situations than the one that faced him now?

Charlie shuddered involuntarily and lowered his eyes to the milling throng who were now spilling out of the vast oak door and onto the powdered granite drive of the castle. They were laughing, most of them, happily lubricated by the passable Sancerre and unremarkable Merlot. He should be there really, thanking them for coming, wishing them well. But the girls would do that, along with their 'eligible' husbands. Eligible! He winced, and watched as they bade their guests farewell: Ellie, the eldest one, slender as a willow wand, her blonde hair brushing the shoulders of her smartly tailored jacket; her husband Archie, the banker, at her shoulder, smiling that knowing smile of his. It had always irritated Charlie. Well, once he had found out what Archie was really up to, anyway. An overheard phone-call, in which he was brokering some deal that was clearly of dubious legality, had left Charlie in little doubt as to his modus operandi.

On the other side of the door, Lucy, the middle of the three girls, who looked most like her mother, stood with her arm through that of her farmer husband, Richard – his cheeks as ruddy as those expected of a man who worked the land, his tweed suit the texture of steel wool and of a shade of green that would enable him to blend into the moorland and disappear from view – something he seemed to infinitely prefer to the agonies of being in company.

And where was Sarah? Charlie scanned the eddying throng to spot her, and then saw her being pulled out of the front door by Rory, intent on introducing her to the lucky girl – plucked from the trio – of whom his son was clearly enamoured. This was obviously the chosen one; the one whose future was about to be blighted. Rory would have wanted Sarah's approval; as twins they seldom operated independently. Charlie had wondered at first why Rory had given his approval to Sarah's marrying Nick – a high-flying lawyer whose sorties overseas would keep him away from her for half the year at least, until the obvious struck him – that Sarah would be closer to Rory that way and perhaps more reliant on him.

There was no sign of Nick today. Bangkok, Sarah had said, and her father had, once again, feared the worst.

'The perfect family.' The words echoed in his head. It was a particularly hollow echo. With one daughter married to a man Charlie considered an absentee shit of the first order, another to a pleasant but pathologically shy and monosyllabic farmer, and a third to a banker who steered a perilous course that teetered between litigation and corruption, 'perfection' was not the word that sprang most readily to mind. As Rory patted the bottom of his latest inamorata by way of farewell, it retreated even further. But they were his children and Charlie loved them in spite of it all. Loved them and vowed to take care of them, come what may.

Charlie leaned back on the bench, trailing his sleeve as he did so in a pile of fresh pigeon droppings. 'Shit!' he muttered. Then the particularly apposite nature of his exclamation struck him and he let out a bitter laugh. It was enough to attract the attention of his youngest daughter.

'Daddy,' called out Sarah. 'Come and say goodbye to your guests.' Sheepishly he rose from the bench and did his best to wipe from his sleeve the foul-smelling residue. He failed in his attempt, succeeding only in covering his hand with the astonishing quantity of glutinous muck.

Before he could warn her off, Nessie Mackintosh came forward to grasp his hand by way of gratitude for a lunchtime that had added immeasurably to her level of local intelligence. Try as he might to avoid manual contact, her single-minded intention triumphed and full contact was signalled by a soft squelching sound. She seemed oblivious to the aural and tactile qualities of the handshake – both of which combined to prevent Charlie saying anything at all by way of farewell. Instead, he simply stared at her with his mouth slightly open, as Nessie veered off down the drive with all the navigational skill of a learner driver on an icy road. The Sancerre had clearly taken effect.

Waving at the last of the departing guests, and aware that his hand was in dire need of highly perfumed soap and extremely hot water, Charlie turned towards the house. What should have been a feeling of relief at the departure of several dozen guests simply brought closer the impending revelation. Lunch would be welcomed, certainly; he could do with something other than wine inside him. But then would come the moment of truth.

They were all here now, except the errant Nick. Six out of seven was as much as he could expect nowadays; to get them all in the same place at the same time was nigh on impossible. Well, Sarah could pass on to Bangkok the news that he was about to impart to his children and two of their respective spouses. What would be their reaction, he had no idea. He had absolutely no previous experience of being a father who had to inform his children that the man they regarded as their reliable and unadventurous parent had done something which was likely to bring their world crashing about their heads. He had put off the evil moment for as long as he could. But the time had arrived when he had little alternative but to put them in the picture, before events themselves – and others who would relish the role – made his position all too clear.

He walked steadily towards the door, then stopped and looked up at the sky. Several seconds passed before he did something quite out of character: he was a man not given to dramatic gesture, but on this occasion he raised his arm and with considerable force threw his glass at the wall of the castle and watched it smash into little pieces.

For a moment he stared as the shards of glass plummeted from the unyielding granite. Then he buttoned his jacket and walked indoors.

2

The Highlands
The Past

'History is not what you thought. *It is what you can remember.*'

W.C. Sellar and R.J. Yeatman, *1066 and All That*, 1930

Scottish castles are thick on the ground and, in most cases, in an advanced stage of ruin, but regardless of their state of repair they are, almost without exception, the stuff of legend and folklore, of curses and gruesome deaths. It was a disappointment then to Charlie's father, Angus Stuart, to discover that the castle he inherited on the death of his own father in 1940, at the age of just sixteen, was singularly devoid of both history and bloodcurdling legend. Built in 1840 as a shooting lodge and left to the Stuarts in 1920 by a grateful former employer, it stood on a small but robust promontory that pushed tentatively out into the chilly waters of Loch Sodhail, referred to by the family for as long as anyone could remember as 'Loch Sod-all' – a reference to the singular lack of activity on the part of the local population, which numbered less than a hundred and whose appetite for culture and society was on a par with that of a closed religious order.

The correct pronunciation is 'Loch Soul'. To cynics in the region the name was regarded as ironic; to others an acceptance of simple fact.

For centuries the population of the scattered crofts and the Highland village which took its name from the loch itself, had been a hive of inactivity, until some enterprising energy company had come up with the idea of damming the downstream end of Loch Sodhail and using it as a source of hydro-electric power.

Had the locals been possessed of the merest fraction of the energy which it was predicted that the new hydro-electric plant would produce, they might well have objected on the grounds of despoliation of the countryside, the presence of some rare midge, or the removal of the livelihoods of local crofters. As it transpired, they grumbled and muttered to themselves but in the end settled for moving their sheep higher up the mountain. Had the rare-midge route been an option, it is doubtful that any of them would have cared. Except for Angus Stuart.

But one man's voice – even if he is the man who lives in the local castle and owns a couple of thousand acres of windswept moorland – is no match for a multinational conglomerate with seemingly limitless funds. Angus was young; too young, they said, to be given the charge of the local castle. He was also inexperienced in the ways of high finance – inexperienced in the ways of almost everything – and even if he had been blessed with greater years and more influence it is doubtful whether he would have succeeded in preventing the advance of 'progress'. His inheritance did absolve him from serving in the war, even if the estate's contribution to the country's rural economy was minimal. His absence, it was judged, would have had a detrimental effect on what ranked as agriculture in this part of Scotland. With the end of the war came progress, or what passed for it.

Since its construction in the 1950s, the Loch Sodhail dam had fulfilled its role as a power source in the Highlands and the locals – many of them too young to remember the whimpers that passed for protests in the years immediately after the war – had come to accept the high concrete edifice, over which ran the narrow road from one side of the loch to the other, as being as much a part of the local scenery as the heather-clad mountains and the dense plantations of Scots pine that ran down to the rim of the water.

Castle Sodhail itself was high enough above the waterline to survive the inundation, even if its demesnes – such as they were – were reduced by a third.

'S'only lawn,' was the verdict of the factor, who regarded the arrival of the earth movers and pile drivers with no more than a passing interest. Within a year he had retired to a flat overlooking the Firth of Lorn in Oban.

Angus, for all his youth, was a pragmatist, not an idealist. Moping about past events was, he considered, a waste of time and energy. He set about turning around the estate, and at the tender age of twenty-two he married Fortune Murdoch, daughter of a crofter and the sister of a local ghillie. Fresh-faced and energetic, Fortune could have been daunted at the scale of the dwelling over which she would now preside, having been brought up in a two-bedroom cottage. Instead, she embraced the challenges and idiosyncrasies of castle life and brought to Sodhail a warmth and liveliness that even the dourest locals had to confess was an improvement on the previous atmosphere of the castle, where the temperature had been on a par with the waters of the loch. Angus's father, Old Rory, had considered two logs on the hall fire to be bordering on profligacy.

With Fortune at his side, Angus began a programme of improvements for Sodhail. He built up a highly thought-of shoot, replenished salmon stocks in the loch and, as cottages became available, renovated them and turned them into holiday lets. It was not a move that endeared him particularly to the locals, but as he himself pointed out, there were few children prepared to take on the work of their fathers when such cottages became empty. As an alternative to dereliction, the holiday-cottage route would at least keep the properties in good order.

The process also caused considerable concern at the bank, whose manager took a degree of convincing that anyone from the soft south, or even the Scottish borders, would want to journey this far north to catch a fish or shoot a grouse when they could do so in greater comfort many miles closer to home. And anyway, who had money to spend on holidays so soon after a war?

For several years Angus and Fortune lived hand to mouth in three rooms of the draughty castle, but by the time Charlie arrived on the scene in 1950 matters had improved and the bank manager, as well as managing funds, occasionally managed what passed for a smile. Not with any great frequency, but enough to let the Stuarts know that they were safe for the time being.

At his mother's knee, and at his uncle the ghillie's side, Charlie learnt the ways of the Highlands and of its wildlife – of the strange sounds of the capercaillie and the plaintive cry of the curlew, of the roar of the stag and the mewing of the buzzard. They became, to him, as familiar as traffic noise to a child of the city. And so it came as a blow when his parents decided that having been schooled in the three 'r's at the local primary, courtesy of Mistress Lang, he should be sent south to complete his education. On learning of his fate, the boy ran away. Not for long. Just for an afternoon. Sitting on a granite boulder high above the loch, he watched the wind as it made ripples on the surface of the water – icy cold even in summer. As he gazed at a golden eagle wheeling across the sky, tears stung his eyes and he bit his lip, the better to stop them flowing down his cheeks. This was where he was meant to be. Where he had always been. Why should he have to leave? As the sun dipped behind the mountain ridge, a chill breeze sprang up. Beginning to shiver, Charlie got up from his perch above the land of his forefathers – well, two of them at least – and deftly made his way down the narrow track, sculpted by the feet of deer and sheep. He knew it every bit as well as the path that ran from the door of the castle to the loch.

Rubbing the sleeve of his coarse-knit sweater across his eyes, to remove any evidence of his anguish, he slipped through the side door of the castle and up the back staircase that led to the oak-panelled landing. His bedroom lay at the far end – its tall mullioned windows overlooking the loch and the mountains beyond. He knelt on the window-seat, his face so close to the thick and heavy curtains that he could smell their familiar dust-laden aroma. It was a scent he knew well; the secure scent of home. Only when the light had faded and the sky had turned purple did he creep downstairs into the sitting room where his parents sat in front of the fire – Angus smoking his pipe and poring over the pages of the *Ross-shire Journal* and his mother quietly knitting. She looked up as he entered the room. His father did not. At ten years old, going on eleven, Charlie knew what was expected of him. Of the proposed trip to Inverness he said not a word but sat, instead, with his back to his mother's chair, watching the sparks from the logs in the vast grate soar up the chimney and into the night air.

It was June – a favourite time in the Highlands, but still chilly enough in the evenings for a fire. There were but three months left before he would be sent away to school. He would make the most of it. He would not cry. He would not moan. He would take what life offered and be a man, even if he was only ten, going on eleven.

He walked over to the bookcase, took down the large morocco-bound atlas of Great Britain and began his search for Inverness.

3

Castle Sodhail

August 1960

'Type of the wise who soar, but never roam;
True to the kindred points of Heaven and Home!'
William Wordsworth, 'To a Skylark', 1827

Charlie had always thought that Murdo Murdoch was a strange name, but then he had also thought that his mother's name, Fortune, was odd, too. Especially since she hadn't really got one. They had a castle, yes; but not much in the way of money to go with it – or so his mother said. Murdo was Charlie's mother's brother, but being a local ghillie meant that to Charlie he was a friend as much as an uncle, someone who could – and would – show him how to catch a fish, how to stalk a deer and how to get close to almost anything that walked, flew or swam. Murdo's wife was a great support, too – always aproned, it seemed, and always ready to push a piece of cake or a slice of pie in front of him when he arrived, famished, from walking on the moors. Murdo and Mrs Murdo had no children of their own, and as a result, Charlie was always treated as the son they never had.

There was barely a week left now before Charlie was due to leave. The moors had turned a dusky purple and he was out with Murdo for one last time before being packed off in the battered old Land Rover that would take him to Egglestone Academy in far distant Inverness. He was not impressed by the sound of the establishment, nor with the prospect of being in the company of a hundred and twenty other boys. And away from all this – away from the moors and the mountains and the castle.

'You'll get used to it. Aye; it'll be the making of you,' instructed Murdo. They were sitting in a small, clinker-built rowing boat twenty yards out into the loch. The ghillie looked about him, scrutinising the insect life before prising open his box of flies and selecting something suitable for the season and the time of day. It was early August. He pulled out a particularly lurid fly whose plumage was a mixture of orange and yellow, murmuring to himself, 'This should do.'

Charlie watched as Murdo deftly knotted the fly to the end of the line. 'What is it?' he asked.

'It's one of my own,' muttered Murdo, without looking up.

'What's it called?'

'I don't know that I've given it a name yet. Only made it yesterday, from yon golden pheasant in the pen at the lodge.'

'What *will* you call it?'

Murdo snapped the line taut a couple of times to check that the knot was secure, then, with the pair of short-bladed scissors that dangled on a piece of elastic from the breast-pocket button of his sleeveless khaki jacket, he snipped off the loose end. As the scissors sprang back, he looked at Charlie.

'I'll call it "Lucky Charlie" . . . if you are.'

Charlie grinned, forgetting for a moment that times like this would be thin on the ground for the next few years.

Murdo handed Charlie the rod. 'Go on then; cast yer line.'

For a ten-year-old, Charlie's casting was unusually proficient, but then he had been handling a rod almost since he had been able to walk. A short one at first – Murdo had had it made especially for him – and then longer ones as he grew. Now he was able to handle a ten-foot rod with natural ease, Spey casting and double Spey casting when the occasion warranted.

Murdo watched as the lad spun the line out across the water, and let his own mind wander over the times they had spent fishing and deer stalking over the years. The boy was eager to learn; a natural countryman at ease outdoors and with nature, though he seemed reluctant ever to carry a gun, except for clay pigeon shooting at which he proved surprisingly adept. Only on the Glorious Twelfth would he agree to take a peg at the start of the grouse season; fearful that a refusal would incur the wrath of his father and be regarded as bad form by the other guns. Watching wildlife seemed to suit him more than killing it, fish excepted. He didn't seem to mind that. 'It's all right as long as we eat them, Murdo, isn't it?'

'Aye; I cannae argue wi' that,' was the ghillie's inevitable reply.

The fish seemed not to be biting. Cast after cast yielded nothing. As Charlie played out his fly, Murdo would slowly ease the boat forward with the oars, confident in the accuracy of his charge's aim, and unafraid of a wayward hook. His confidence was not misplaced. Charlie's action was automatic; rare in one so young. In this, if nothing else, the boy had an easy confidence. He was about to turn and admit to Murdo that the fly would have to be called something else, when a pull and the scream of line leaving reel signalled success.

'Let it go,' murmured Murdo habitually, knowing that in reality the boy needed no instruction on how to land a salmon.

He watched as Charlie pointed his rod in the direction of the as-yet-unseen fish, and leaned back in the boat to enjoy the moment.

Charlie alternated between reeling in when the line went slack and letting it shriek out again when the fish sped off through the water. Fifteen minutes later, Murdo lowered the landing net over the side of the boat and scooped up the gleaming salmon. 'A cock: a twelve pounder. Your ma will be pleased. Sunday tea.'

Charlie sported a wide grin. 'It's a good one, isn't it?'

'Aye, it's none bad,' admitted Murdo, who was extracting the hook from the undershot jaw of the two-and-a-half-foot fish. 'None bad at all.'

With the fish safely in the bottom of the boat and the rod stowed, the two began the short journey back to shore, Murdo pulling on the oars and Charlie sitting on the plank seat just in front of the transom.

'Dad says they might let us fish at school occasionally.'

'No reason why not. Plenty of places around there. Loch Ness for a start.'

'Big fish?'

'Aye. Apart from yon monster. Not sure what he weighs. You'll catch a fourteen pounder there though. Twenty-two pounder caught not long ago in the River Moriston, they say. Very big fish . . .'

Charlie looked thoughtful. He was silent for a while and then said, as levelly as he could, 'I'll miss you, Murdo.'

The ghillie pulled harder on his oars. 'Och, you'll be back soon enough. There's holidays. They'll come around sooner than ye think.'

Charlie fell silent again. There was no sound except the gentle play of water on oars; Murdo was an accomplished boatman. Tentatively he asked the older man, 'What do you think I should do?' Then, seeing the puzzled look on Murdo's face, 'About the future, I mean.'

Murdo did not look up from his rowing. 'Och, the future is a long way off. You can let that take care of itself for now.'

Charlie persisted. 'But I need to think, don't I? To work out what I want to do?'

'Aye. But there's nae rush.'

The stream-of-consciousness conversation continued. 'Dad would like me to take over here, wouldn't he?'

'One day.' Then, muttering under his breath, 'There's naebody else.'

'That's what I want to do. To be laird.'

The ghillie adopted a cautionary tone. 'That's a lot of responsibility. You sure you're up to it?'

'Not yet. But I will be.'

'Well, you just bide yer time. It'll all happen soon enough.'

The boy fell silent, and the rest of the brief passage to shore was without conversation.

As the bottom of the boat crunched into the pebbles, Charlie jumped out of the boat, took the painter as a matter of habit and tied it to a rusty metal ring secured to a large boulder. The knot tied, he patted the boulder and turned to Murdo. 'All safe,' he said.

Murdo stepped out of the boat into the shallow water with rod, net and fish in hand. For a moment, the two looked at each other, but then a voice distracted them and they turned as one to look in the direction from which it came.

'Well done! It looks a whopper!'

Charlie grinned at his mother, who stood at the top of the narrow jetty that ran from the grass in front of the castle, down into the water.

'Aye,' confirmed Murdo. 'A decent fish.'

'What did you use?' asked Fortune Stuart.

Charlie looked towards Murdo for confirmation. The ghillie nodded, and Charlie turned back to his mother.

'Lucky Charlie,' he said.

* * *

The following week he left for Inverness. His mother waved him off from the castle door, and Charlie waved back from the passenger seat of the Land Rover, unaware that he would never see her again.

4

Egglestone Academy, Inverness

1965

'I and the public know
What all schoolchildren learn,
Those to whom evil is done
Do evil in return.'
W.H. Auden, 'September 1, 1939', 1940

It took Charlie Stuart a full two years to get over his mother's death. A heart attack they said; sudden and without any warning. In truth, he would never get over it completely, but after two years of being away from home, with only the brief holidays offering any kind of respite, a certain steeliness crept into his heart; a toughening of spirit borne of necessity. While not an exact replica of Dotheboys Hall, Egglestone Academy was founded on ancient Scottish stones and ancient Scottish traditions. Cold showers, cold meals and cold hearts were thicker on the ground than Charlie had been used to. At first he would confide in Murdo on his return visits to Sodhail, but finding the old man less and less willing to listen to his tales of woe, he began to keep things to himself, with a slow dawning of realisation that unless he found in himself some inner reserves of strength, then the trials of life would grind him down.

His relationship with his father had never been especially close. Angus Stuart had an estate to manage; an estate that needed much of his time and most of his energy. He had come to rely on Murdo when it came to keeping an eye on the lad, and for all his dour sensibilities, Murdo Murdoch took pleasure in watching Charlie grow up. The relationship between father and son was not in any way improved by the arrival on the scene of Charlotte Niven.

The locals were surprised. No one imagined that Angus Stuart really noticed other women, and while Fortune was alive he certainly never looked in their direction. But three years to the day since her death (a fact not lost on Murdo, who set his jaw at the unfortunate coincidence of dates), Charlotte moved into Castle Sodhail and took over the role of mistress of the house.

Angus had met her on a rare – and reluctant – visit to Edinburgh. He had been looking for furniture and found himself inveigled by some acquaintances into attending a drinks party. She was everything Fortune was not: extrovert, impetuous and the life and soul of any party. And she seemed to like parties. Whenever she appeared, Murdo made himself scarce, disappearing into the distance like the proverbial Scotch mist. As far as Charlie was concerned, his overriding feeling was one of bewilderment: that his father could even consider replacing his mother with another woman, and that when the unthinkable happened and he did, that this loud, mercurial and apparently insensitive harridan should be his choice.

School holidays, once looked forward to with feverish excitement and relief, became something to be dreaded. Charlie would try to find an excuse not to go home, but then found himself pulled back by the moors and the castle itself. How could he forgo them, even if being among them meant being in close proximity to the stepmother he so reviled?

On one occasion his father took him to one side. He was fourteen years old and becoming aware of women and the unforeseen effects they could have on men – and boys. Angus called him into his study in the tower at the eastern corner of the castle. 'Sit down,' he said, curtly.

Charlie did as he was bid and clenched his fists, nervously.

His father did not look at him at first. Instead, he gazed out of the narrow mullioned window towards the moors.

'I know it's not easy for you. Having someone come to live here who seems to be replacing your mother.' He paused for what seemed like an age, then carried on. 'It's not easy for me, either. I was very fond of your mother. There will never be another woman like her . . .'

Charlie felt himself colouring up; partly out of anger and partly embarrassment. He had never heard his father talk like this before; was unsure he wanted to now. He would far rather let events take their course and keep well out of the way, avoiding any kind of personal involvement; any kind of 'heart to heart' with the father who, up to this point in his life, had confided very little to him in the way of personal feelings, other than the triumph of catching a fish or shooting a stag.

His father turned to face him now. 'You may not like Charlotte very much, but she's a good woman. Good for me . . .'

Charlie found it hard to meet his father's eye; unwilling to listen to this unwanted confession, which was making him increasingly uncomfortable.

'Maybe when you're older you'll understand,' his father continued.

Oh God! thought Charlie, *this is getting worse.*

'There's a lot to do here, and I don't want to do it on my own. You're away at school, Murdo isn't getting any younger . . .'

'And Murdo doesn't like her either,' Charlie wanted to say. But he bit his lip and kept silent.

'There's no way that Charlotte can ever replace your mother. We will not get married. Not yet. But—' He hesitated, tapped at the stone sill of the narrow window and then turned to face his son. 'I enjoy her company. She lifts me out of myself. Running the estate doesn't get any easier, and I'm not getting any younger.'

The predictability of the conversation engendered in Charlie a feeling of revulsion and disappointment. Whatever else his father had been while he was growing up, he was still a figure to be admired – the laird; the man in charge of the estate. The boss. Now he was talking as though he were a spent force: a man who could not go on alone. It was all rather pathetic.

'I need her support. I enjoy her company . . .'

There floated into Charlie's mind the image of the Duke of Windsor and the abdication speech. They had covered it just a few weeks ago in a history lesson. Now it seemed that the history lesson was repeating itself. He tried his best not to look sullen, but failed. The Duke of Windsor, Charlie had decided, was a weak man, and weakness was something he had never had cause to attribute to his father. His anger was mingled with a deep sense of disillusionment.

Seeing his expression, a note of impatience crept into his father's voice. 'I'm afraid you'll have to get used to the situation,' he said. 'It's not going to change. Charlotte is here to stay and you'll have to make the best of it.'

Any faint measure of sympathy that Charlie might have conjured forth, had he made the effort, was extinguished by his father's apparent intransigence. Fine. If that was the way he wanted it, then that was the way it would be.

'Can I go now?' he asked.

His father sighed. 'I'd really rather you made the best of it, Charlie. It's not the end of the world. I do still want you to take over this place. One day.'

One day, thought Charlie. *When will that be? And will she still be around when I do?*

His reverie was broken by the shrill sound of Charlotte's voice echoing up the spiral stone staircase that led to his father's study.

'Lunch, you two! Come on, break it up; it's on the table. Soup. And you know how quickly it gets cold in this place!'

Charlie was grateful in a way that the summons absolved him from having to articulate any sentiments to his father. Instead, he got up from the chair and walked across the small room towards the door. As he passed, Angus caught hold of his son's arm and turned him so that they stood face to face.

Unable to avoid eye contact, Charlie stared hard at his father. The older man displayed a look of steely determination. Quite softly and distinctly Angus said, 'Don't make trouble; that's all. If you do, I'll never forgive you.'

5

Egglestone Academy, Inverness

March 1967

'For there is nothing more likely to make a man turn against his father than the arrival upon the scene of a woman who is not his mother.'

Tom Derwent, *Wedded Bliss*, 1977

'Going home for Easter?'

The voice seemed but a distant echo, and Charlie would have ignored it had it not repeated the question more insistently and at greater volume.

'I said, *are you going home for Easter*?'

Charlie looked up from his book and stared downwards in the direction of the voice. 'I suppose so.'

His companion smiled. 'You don't sound very enthusiastic.'

'No.'

'Is that because you're not or because you're lost in *Lady Chatterley*?'

Charlie closed the book and took his feet down from the table. 'I don't know what all the fuss is about.'

'Easter or *Lady Chatterley*?'

'Either. They're both overrated.'

'You're in good company then. Lawrence of Arabia didn't like it either.'

'Easter?'

'*Lady Chatterley*. Said the sex business wasn't worth the fuss; that he'd met only a handful of people who cared a biscuit for it.' Gordon Mackenzie remained prone, in front of the small fire that burned in the grate of their room at Egglestone Academy, his hands behind his head, his eyes riveted to the cobwebs that hung from the central bowl of a light fitting and its 40-watt bulb. They were in the sixth-form now, and that entitled them to a shared room, rather than a bed in a dormitory of a dozen boys, and a fire on Saturdays and Sundays – one coal scuttle to last the weekend.

Charlie walked towards the fire, carefully stepped over the supine form on the hearthrug, and prodded at the coals with the poker; they seemed reluctant to bestow upon the room's residents anything in the way of warmth; confining their activities to nothing more than a desultory smoulder.

'Cheap coal,' muttered Gordon. 'No point in expecting a blaze.'

Charlie grunted in reply.

Gordon got up from the floor and walked to the window. 'The weather's supposed to be getting better by next weekend. Sunny, the dear old weatherman says.'

Charlie looked at his room-mate quizzically, wondering how he came to be in possession of information that could only be gained from a television or radio, the luxury of which their spartan accommodation was plainly bereft.

'I was walking past Scottie's door and the forecast was on. I eavesdropped.'

'Lucky he didn't see you.'

'He did. He shut the door, but not before I saw what we're in for next weekend.'

'They're never accurate anyway. Not up here.'

Gordon sighed. 'There's no pleasing you, is there?'

The two had known each other for three years now. Gordon Mackenzie had arrived at Egglestone at the age of fourteen, his parents having moved further north in Scotland in order that Gordon's father should be nearer to his work with North Sea Gas. The boy was an affable sort, if bookish, and he and Charlie had got on well from the outset. After being cooped up with eleven other boys for five years, the chance to gain at least a modicum of privacy in their last two years at Egglestone had been welcomed by both of them.

Charlie could always rely on Gordon to chivvy him out of his dark introspection. He didn't mean to be morose; it was only when the holidays were imminent – the very time when he should be looking forward to going home to Sodhail – that his mood darkened. The prospect of family life, once so cherished, now seemed unremittingly bleak. How could things have changed so much? How could the one place he loved in the world more than any other, now loom over him like a lowering cloud?

He knew what it would be like. For the first day or two he would make a real effort to be polite. To fit in. To avoid rocking the boat. He had developed tactics for coping with the situation; he would be out for most of the day, on his own stalking deer or fishing with Murdo, when the ghillie could take a break from the day-to-day running of the estate, but he would have to come home in the evenings and sit through those interminable meals, watching his father fawning over Charlotte in a way that he had never done over Charlie's mother. God, how he hated it! Within a day or two he knew he would say something that caused his father to lose his temper. It happened every time.

He walked over to the window and dropped the paperback book into the waste bin.

'I wouldn't leave it there,' advised Gordon. 'Effie will take it straight to Scottie and then you'll be in for it.' He retrieved the dog-eared copy of *Lady Chatterley's Lover* from the bin, away from the prying eyes of the cleaner, and examined the inside of the front flap. 'Alex Jesmond is next on the list. Good God; he's had it twice already. Still, it is his book. I suppose he likes to keep an eye on it. I'll slip it to him at supper. Do you want to admit you haven't finished it?'

Charlie sighed. 'Better not. He thinks I'm enough of a wimp already.'

Gordon flopped into the battered armchair and drummed his fingers on the uncut moquette, which, thanks to hundreds of greasy palms being laid on it over the years, had been transformed into something resembling leather.

'You didn't find it a turn-on then?'

'A bit. But the language is so . . . old-fashioned. All that stuff about John Thomas. It made me laugh.'

'Well, that's something at least.'

'I do laugh sometimes,' protested Charlie. 'Just not when the holidays loom.'

'Why don't you come home with me?' asked Gordon. 'It's not exactly a castle, but Mum and Dad will be happy to have you. And at least you won't have to worry about saying the wrong thing at the wrong time.'

'No. It's kind of you to ask but I'd better go home. My dad's expecting me.'

Gordon looked thoughtful. He was a tall, lanky lad with a shock of dark hair and a body that seemed to fold up in all the wrong places – the direct opposite of the stocky-framed and fair-haired Charlie. Studious by nature, ever with his head in a book and a mind choc-full of quotable quotes, nothing much seemed to trouble him, and though he spoke rarely of his parents, Charlie envied him the even tenor, the normality, of his home life – even though it was something that could only be enjoyed during the school holidays. That Gordon should offer him the chance to share it at Easter was typical of his room-mate's kindness. Where other sixth-formers had been billeted with fiery-tempered, flame-headed Scots, or stuck-up impecunious scions of Borders gentry, Charlie had, at least, landed himself a good companion and one refreshingly free of mood swings. Unlike himself.

Charlie's conscience pricked him. 'Look, why don't *you* come home with *me*?'

Gordon's face betrayed his reluctance to partake of a week's holiday in a Scottish castle with a more than usually icy atmosphere.

'Oh, I know I make a fuss about it. But the place itself is great. Really special. And you've never seen it.' And then he felt a pang of guilt at refusing Gordon's own offer of accommodation. 'It's really good of you to ask me to your place but it's very small.' Then, fearful of having caused offence, which was not at all his intention: 'It's not really fair to expect your mother to keep making up a bed in the sitting room. It would put her to a lot of trouble.'

'Well yes, old chum, but . . .'

Charlie pressed him. 'You would like to come, wouldn't you? To see it, I mean? I've been droning on about it for all these years and you've no idea what it's really like.'

'Well, I'm not sure . . .' Gordon was clearly uneasy about the welcome he would be likely to encounter at Castle Sodhail.

'It will be fine if you're there. They'll both be well-behaved.' He saw Gordon hesitate, but before he could decline the offer Charlie continued: 'And I'll be on my best behaviour, too. If you're there I'll have plenty to occupy me and we can get out of the house as much as possible. There's fishing, deer stalking – not that I shoot, I just follow them and watch; it's fascinating – and climbing and . . . whatever you fancy doing. And Murdo's wife is a really good cook so we could eat with them, too – we don't have to dine in the castle every night. You'll like Murdo.'

'Won't your father mind? Doesn't he want you to himself?'

Charlie winced. 'Are you kidding? He likes me there because he knows that one day I'll have to take on the estate but he never really knows what to say to me. He'll be grateful for somebody else to talk to. Somebody to impress. And he's not a bad man, just . . .' At this point he found himself lost for words and realised that it was the first time he had drawn breath. The first time he had allowed Gordon to speak.

'Well, if you're sure . . . ?'

'Absolutely certain.'

Gordon shrugged. He found Charlie's childlike enthusiasm, even at the age of seventeen, almost impossible to resist. 'Right then, I'll call my parents and break it to them that they will have to do without me.'

'They won't mind, will they?'

The expression on Gordon's face showed that his parents would be unconcerned at his absence. 'Mum's not a brilliant cook and Dad likes to play golf. She'll be relieved that she can lunch every day with her girlfriends and spend the evenings in front of the telly. He'll spend the weekend at Troon.'

'Sorted, then?' asked Charlie.

'Sorted. In the words of your esteemed ancestors, "Sod-all, here we come".'

6

Castle Sodhail

Easter 1967

'To jealousy, nothing is more frightful than laughter.'
Francoise Sagan, *La Chamade*, 1965

Gordon Mackenzie was relieved that on this occasion at least the weatherman whom he had seen waving his hands across the Highlands of Scotland had been right. The weather was of tourist-brochure quality; the air clear and the light intensity high, with no sign, this early in the season, of even the most adventurous of midges. Mountains, crisp in outline against a pale blue sky, were reflected in the waters of Loch Sodhail like amiable giants in a looking glass. At eight o'clock in the morning no ripple disturbed the surface of the water, and the only thing visible in the cloudless sky was a soaring golden eagle some half a mile off.

Perched on the low wall that ran around the apron of drive in front of the castle, Gordon gazed down upon the water and murmured to himself, 'The man of wisdom delights in water; the man of humanity delights in mountains.'

'And which are you?'

Gordon, surprised at the interruption, rose to his feet, turning in the direction of the voice. 'Sorry!' he stammered. 'I didn't see you.'

'No reason why you should,' she said.

Gordon looked at the girl. She was around his own age, with fair hair that tumbled over her shoulders. Her face was bright and open, seemingly untroubled by the cares of the world. She wore leather boots and jodhpurs, a tweed jacket that had seen better days over a brown polo-necked sweater. In her hand she carried a riding crop. Gordon laughed involuntarily.

'What is it?' she asked.

'It's just . . .' He seemed reluctant to continue.

'Go on. What's so funny?'

'I was just thinking . . . well . . . you look like a girl in a Fred Astaire film.' A flushing of his cheeks betrayed his embarrassment.

The girl grinned. 'I'm very flattered. Ginger Rogers?'

'Yes. Or, er, Cyd Charisse.'

'Hmm. Legs not long enough, I'm afraid. Anyway, we've not been introduced.'

'No. But then neither had Fred . . .'

The girl came and sat on the wall beside him. 'So you like poetry?'

'Some, not all.'

'Who wrote that? About the mountains and the water?'

'Confucius.'

'Chinese?'

'Yes.'

'Did he say anything else? About the Scottish Highlands?'

'Not specifically. But there is a bit more . . .'

'Go on.'

Gordon cleared his throat. 'The man of wisdom is active; the man of humanity is tranquil. The man of wisdom enjoys happiness; the man of humanity enjoys long life.'

'Gosh. Clever you. Do you have to be one or the other or can you be both?'

Gordon looked embarrassed. 'Confucius didn't say.'

The girl offered him her hand. 'I'm Eleanor. I live over there.' She pointed to a clump of trees about a mile away on the other side of the loch. 'Not a castle I'm afraid, just a rather nice house. Where's Charlie? Having a lie-in?'

'Gone to get the rods. We're going out in the boat.' Gordon nodded in the direction of the rowing boat tied up at the end of the narrow wooden jetty that jutted out into the calm waters of the loch. 'Fishing.'

'This early? Goodness, you're keen.'

'Well, Charlie is.'

'Not you?'

Gordon shrugged. 'Oh, I don't mind.'

The girl frowned, then glanced back at the castle before picking up the conversation. 'How are things . . .' She paused. 'In there?'

Gordon shrugged again. 'OK.'

'Only OK?'

'It's a bit tense at times but . . . you know . . .'

Their conversation was interrupted by the emergence of Charlie from the door of the castle. 'Oh, hello! I wondered when you'd turn up,' he said.

The girl folded her arms and looked cross. 'Well, that's not very nice. You might look a bit more pleased to see me. It has been three months.'

'Sorry.' Charlie put on an expression of mock contrition. 'How lovely to see you, Eleanor; how have you been these long weeks that we've been parted?'

The girl regarded him with a disapproving frown. 'There's no need to go that far.'

Charlie turned to Gordon. 'You've met the Hon then?'

'Er . . . sorry?'

'The Honourable Eleanor Fitzallan of this parish. Sized you up already, has she?'

'Well, I—'

'Don't be horrible, Charlie. I don't even know his name. I gave him mine but he didn't give me his.'

Gordon looked embarrassed. 'Oh, sorry. How rude of me. Gordon Mackenzie. I'm at school with Charlie. In Inverness.'

The girl became arch now. 'I'd gathered that.'

Charlie sat next to Gordon, and patted the low wall beside him.

'Come and sit down and stop being so uppity,' he said to the girl.

'I'm not being uppity.'

Charlie tilted his head on one side and patted the wall again. With a sigh, the girl came and sat beside him. 'Do you want to come fishing?' he asked.

'No fear,' she replied. 'Anyway, I've ridden over on Dover and I want to walk him back in a while.'

Charlie glanced at the grey gelding tied to the fence fifty yards away. He was tearing at the first early blades of grass that pushed up alongside the stout oak posts.

Charlie and Eleanor had grown up together – she the daughter of an established Ross-shire family, long on history but short on funds, he the son of the local laird of similar financial standing. Their relationship was akin to that of brother and sister and the general tenor of their conversation betrayed as much. There was no shortage of teasing, regular spats that were over as quickly as they began, and periods of no contact at all when they were away at school – he in Inverness and she at some second-rank girls' establishment run by a moustachioed matron in Elgin.

Their respective parents had a cordial but not over-familiar relationship, but the arrival of Charlotte Niven on the scene had reduced their meagre ration of socialising to the barest minimum. Only Charlie and Eleanor kept the connection between the two families going on anything like a regular basis; the elders having found the once relaxed atmosphere transformed into one of mannered diplomacy.

Eleanor was the youngest of three children – an afterthought, she said – and the only girl. Her two brothers, ten and twelve years older, had flown the nest after university – one to work with Medicins Sans Frontières in Africa and the other to become a sheep farmer in New Zealand. If her parents had felt deserted by their sons, they never admitted to it. Their daughter, always headstrong and fiercely independent, was now seventeen, though she looked at least two years older. Charlie vacillated in his attitude towards her. There were times when he thought she was the biggest pain in the arse on the surface of the planet, and others when she was without doubt the greatest of companions. It all depended on her mood. And his. Today, things could go either way, though at this particular moment the 'pain in the arse' option appeared to be the more likely.

'Well, if you'd rather trot around on that old nag than come fishing, we'd better be off,' said Charlie, getting to his feet and handing a rod to Gordon.

'Just because you can't ride,' teased Eleanor.

'I can ride. I choose not to,' he retorted.

'Do you ride, Gordon?' she asked.

'Yes.'

Charlie looked taken aback. 'You? On a horse?'

Gordon nodded. 'Most holidays, when I'm home.'

'You never said. All these years. I mean . . . You don't look—'

'Like a horseman?'

'No. I mean you're all . . . gangly.'

Gordon gave one of his all-too-familiar shrugs.

'Perhaps we could go riding together?' offered Eleanor. 'When you're not going out with Horatio Nelson there in his little boat.'

Gordon beamed at her. 'That would be nice.'

Charlie looked from one of them to the other, and there was in his eyes the tell-tale sign of an emotion with which, in his short life, he had been relatively unfamiliar. Jealousy.

The atmosphere over supper that evening was more than usually strained. Charlotte was in a particularly dominant mood and Charlie found himself bruised by Gordon's encounter with Eleanor. He told himself it was stupid and pointless, but until now Eleanor had been someone he had always thought of as his own. Not in a physical or romantic sense. That kind of relationship with her he had never seriously considered, and he assumed that she was of the same mind. Oh, she was good-looking – pretty, even – but her familiarity and proximity to him in those early years of their lives had precluded thoughts of a deeply romantic nature. He was fond of her, but had never thought of her as anything other than the sister he did not have. And yet today . . . He felt, by turns, embarrassed and irritated at his state of mind. Why should he feel like this now? He had enjoyed brief encounters with girls over the past two or three years; nothing serious or lasting, but enough to awaken in him thoughts of a physical nature as well as emotional attachment. It was just that none of them had lasted the course. He brooded occasionally on whether that was his fault or theirs, but then something had always turned up – usually another girl – to prevent him dwelling on it for too long. He was young, after all, just seventeen; it was not as if it was important to find somebody yet – not for a long-term relationship anyway.

At the other end of the dining table, Gordon was discussing with Charlie's father the relative merits of Exmoor and Dartmoor ponies – a subject that left Charlie feeling that there was clearly a part of Gordon's life with which he had no affinity or connection. How could you know somebody for three years – share a room with them, even – and not know the simplest of things about them? Why had Gordon kept it to himself? It was not as if it were that important, or dramatic even; just a silly simple thing like riding a horse.

As he toyed with the salmon and cabbage on his plate, wondering at the wisdom of such a combination, Charlotte broke in on his thoughts with her penetrating voice.

'What's the matter with Charlie?' she enquired, as though asking the assembled company for their opinion.

Mindful of company, Charlie responded as politely as he could: 'Nothing. Just wondering what to do tomorrow.'

'Well, you're not spoilt for choice here, are you, with the loch, the mountains and the woods?'

There she went again, with her capacity for stating the obvious, thought Charlie. 'No,' spoken softly, under his breath, was the best response he could manage.

'Angus, darling. Charlie doesn't know what to do tomorrow and I was telling him that there really is no shortage of options. What do you think he should do?'

Charlie's father broke off from his conversation with Gordon and regarded his son with a look that seemed to combine pity with irritation.

Charlie noticed the expression and endeavoured to extricate himself from a situation that seemed to be getting increasingly out of hand. 'I'm not asking what I should do; I was just considering my options.'

'Doesn't that amount to the same thing?' snapped Charlotte.

'What does Gordon want to do?' asked Angus. He turned to Charlie's room-mate: 'I've a mare you can take out if you want to go riding. Charlie's not a keen horseman but I'm sure

Eleanor will be happy to go with you. She was out today with that gelding of hers.'

'Dover; yes, we saw him,' confirmed Gordon. 'I'd be happy to go, if you're sure you don't mind?'

Gordon was addressing Charlie's father, but then became aware that he might be overstepping the mark as far as his friend was concerned and, looking between father and son, did his best to make it clear that he wanted to upset neither of them.

'That's settled then. I'll have the horse saddled up for you in the morning and you can give Eleanor a ring and see if she's up for it.' Angus glanced at his watch. 'You can call her now if you like. It's not too late. You'll find her number on the pad in the hall by the phone – under Duncan Fitzallan. I should think she'll be glad of a change of company; Charlie and she seem to do nothing but bicker from what I can see, and Charlie and horses don't really get on very well, do they?'

Angus cast a look at his son, but the look was not returned. Charlie was manoeuvring a piece of salmon around his plate and wishing that he were anywhere else but right here, right now.

7

Creag Sodhail

Easter 1967

'Great things are done when Men & Mountains meet;
This is not Done by Jostling in the Street.'

William Blake, *Poems from Blake's Notebook*, 1807–1809

From the rock onto which he hauled himself, Charlie had a good view of the glen and the loch below. He was on his own, relieved that he no longer had to make polite conversation or feign interest in the day's plans formulated by Charlotte and his father for the entertainment of others.

The water of the loch sparkled in the morning light and the thin skein of mist that had skirted the mountain on his ascent had now melted away in the strengthening sun. The climb, as it always did, filled his lungs with fresh air and his heart with hope, however misplaced that optimism might sometimes seem to be. Perched on a massive lump of granite and sheltered from the wind, which seldom eased up here to less than a stiff breeze, his muscles began to relax. He leaned back against the heather-covered mound of peaty earth as the heaving of his chest began to subside. Still inhaling lungfuls of clear mountain air with the eagerness of a drowning sailor, he tilted back his head and allowed the sun to strike him full in the face. It was a sensation guaranteed to lift his spirits, to allow him, however briefly, to shed the burdens of the moment and simply luxuriate in the rawness of nature. The air was so pure that it stung his insides; the heather so sweet and sourly scented that it caused his head to reel. He clenched his fists around it, forcing the fibrous earth under his fingernails as though to anchor himself to his home territory in a world that seemed less reliable by the day.

From here, the war in Vietnam and, closer to home, the oil tanker that had run aground off the Cornish coast, seemed light years away. His father had muttered, over breakfast, of the formation of a new town in Buckinghamshire; a town that would be constructed on a grid system, with roads that would bisect each other at right angles. The prospect made him shudder. There were no right angles up here on Creag Sodhail, no right angles in nature except those created by nettle leaves alternately carried up the stem of the stinging herb. This place suited him better than the town; up here he could hear himself think (except when Charlotte was close by); up here on the mountain he could always be himself. He doubted that anyone could ever be themselves in a town like Milton Keynes. Daft name anyway – half poet, half economist.

Creag Sodhail, at 2,994 feet, was just six feet short of being a Munro and joining the 282 highest mountains in Scotland. There were times when this seemed poetic justice. In the same way that Castle Sodhail did not rank with the likes of Glamis and Cawdor in terms of notoriety and grandeur, so even its own mountain fell slightly short of joining the giants. But it mattered not to Charlie; it was lofty enough for him, and it was his – not to own, but to be a part of.

Breathing more easily now, he scoured the landscape below him for signs of Eleanor and Gordon, off on their 'pony trekking' expedition. He felt slightly ashamed of his attitude – Dover would not be described as a pony at around sixteen hands, and the mare offered to Gordon by Charlie's father was, at sixteen-two, a robust enough animal to allow a six-foot youth to sit astride her without looking absurd.

At first he could see nothing but a conspiracy of ravens clattering and chattering their way around a rocky outcrop halfway down the crag. He ran his eye along the shore of the loch and then caught sight of two moving specks. He pulled a small pair of binoculars from the pocket of his anorak, put them to his eyes and adjusted the focus. Yes; there they were, not one following the other, but side by side, proceeding at a gentle walking pace. They would stop every now and then and the girl would point something out to her companion. Charlie could imagine the conversation: 'That's where we live; we used to own all the land here once. Even Castle Sodhail, but that was given to Charlie's family years ago. The house and a few acres are all the Fitzallans have left now. I doubt that my great-grandfather would have given it all away if he'd known what lay in store . . .'

Whenever the subject came up, Charlie had to struggle not to feel guilty at his own family living in a more substantial dwelling than Eleanor's. But for a cruel twist of fate, she would be living in the castle and he . . . well, where would he be? Probably in some small croft, like Murdo, expected to follow his father in a penurious lifestyle.

He lowered the glasses and slipped them back into his pocket, struggling to maintain the optimism with which climbing Creag Sodhail would always imbue him. Having pinpointed his friends, and winced at the sight of the angular Gordon looking particularly odd astride a horse, he now found it difficult to take his eyes off them. How did it make him feel – really – this striking up of a friendship between Gordon and Eleanor? Why should it worry him? He was fond of both of them; to find that two of your friends got on with each other was a good thing, wasn't it? He should be feeling buoyed up that the circle had been widened; that the two people in the world for whom he felt the greatest fondness had appeared to hit it off so quickly. And then it struck him quite forcibly, how small was his own circle of friends. Of acquaintances he was not short; there were lots of them at Egglestone, but none whose company he would especially seek out. Was he odd? Was this normal? Aside from Eleanor and Gordon – and not forgetting Murdo – there were no others with whom he could share his thoughts. Even Murdo drew the line at talking too deeply about feelings. Charlie was sure he must have some, but whatever they were, Murdo succeeded in playing his cards so close to his chest that there was rarely a peek at their true colours.

As for his father . . . the increasing distance between them, borne of Charlie's mistrust of Charlotte, seemed to be widening by the day. Charlie did try to rub along with her, but instead of rubbing along, it invariably turned to rubbing her up the wrong way. Why could she not treat him as an adult human being, instead of an educationally sub-normal child? He knew that she had little experience of dealing with anyone younger than herself; that much was made abundantly clear by her attitude to anyone under the age of thirty, when she would adopt a form of language that would not seem out of place in a nursery school. This morning, true to form, she had upbraided him for not putting his knife and fork together on his plate at the end of breakfast. The fact that he had not finished eating seemed to have escaped her notice. Then she was off in her estate car to Fort William to look for scatter cushions and a coffee table to give the castle sitting room a more contemporary feel. Even Charlie's father had struggled to avoid arguing with her when she said that chocolate-brown walls would give a much more Sixties feel to the castle drawing room: 'It's not the Fifties any more Angus; we have to move with the times, even at Castle Sodhail.'

Charlie shuddered. What did it matter, up here, whether the walls of the castle drawing room were chocolate brown or primrose yellow, pillar-box red or cobalt blue? Up here the colours were true to nature; true to themselves.

Tired of his introspection and weary of not fitting in, he rose to his feet and made to descend the mountain. It was then that he realised that neither Gordon nor Eleanor were anywhere to be seen. They must have taken the route through the pinewood at the far end of the loch. Suddenly, and with a chilling realisation, he saw ahead of him a well of loneliness. Solitude was not something he had ever minded; it was something that was not simply comfortable but a state which, from time to time, he needed – time to be alone with his thoughts and feelings, to feel the balance of life. A chosen state that allowed him to put things in perspective. But this was different. He was not just a solitary being walking down a mountain, but an isolated soul without the prospect of any change in his current circumstances. The uncertain future that stretched ahead of him, while never before filling him with anything other than curiosity, seemed now to be nothing more than a terrifying void. How long would his father and Charlotte cling on to the castle? Would he be expected to take up residence there the moment he left school? There had been talk of university at the academy, but nothing had been settled. He must act, and act now, if his life were not to dwindle into some stagnant swamp that curtailed any ambition, any hunger for the future.

Instead of picking his way carefully between the chunks of granite, lodged on the side of the mountain by some prehistoric volcanic activity, he threw caution to the wind and loped down the side of the mountain as fast as his legs would take him. Not until he reached the gritty path that ran alongside the loch did he stop running. Bent double for lack of breath, and clutching at an old wooden finger-post for support, his lungs seemed on fire and his chest to heave as though it might burst open.

Gradually regaining his breath, and pulling himself upright on the lichen-encrusted post, he raised his eyes and read the legend it bore: 'NO THROUGH ROAD'. In his current frame of mind it seemed almost prophetic.

8

Egglestone Academy, Inverness
June 1968

'"What is he sent to school for? . . . If he'll only turn out a brave, helpful, truth-telling Englishman, and a gentleman, and a Christian, that's all I want," thought the squire.'

Thomas Hughes, *Tom Brown's School Days*, 1857

There was, in Charlie's breast, the faintest feeling of sadness as he intoned: 'The day is past and over, all thanks, O Lord, to thee', along with a hundred and twenty-three other boys, seventeen of whom would not pass this way again. The end-of-school assembly – Charlie's only trophy from the previous week's prizegiving a ten-shilling book token for coming top at spelling and a small and rather tarnished cup for the best dried and pressed flower collection – signified a more portentous end: that of the first chapter in his own life. It was not an especially impressive chapter, and these two modest mementoes of his literary and botanical prowess were not something that he would find himself boasting about. Angus had looked slightly embarrassed at his son's lack of achievement, while Charlotte had been more concerned with a small mark on her pleated white skirt.

Pushing both token and trophy into the side of the cabin trunk that stood by the door of their shared room, Charlie pulled off the throttling tie, shed the now shapeless blazer whose elbows had seen off more leather patches than a pirate's eye, and slumped down on the bed. Gordon, whose belongings were strewn about the place as though his own trunk had exploded, stood gazing at the scene of devastation, scratching his head.

'You'll have to start somewhere,' muttered Charlie.

'Yes, but where?'

'Anywhere. We've only got half an hour before we have to be out.'

The words he spoke brought home to him the finality of it. Out. The end. But then another beginning. Of what? Charlie rolled on to his stomach and gazed across the room to where Gordon was leaning on the jamb of the open door. 'Are you going straight home?' Charlie asked.

'Yes. It's Mum's fiftieth birthday party. How about you?'

Charlie was silent for a moment, then he said: 'I have to go to a wedding breakfast.'

'What?' Gordon looked puzzled.

'Dad and Charlotte got married this morning. I have to go to a wedding breakfast tonight.'

'Isn't that a bit of a contradiction in terms? A wedding breakfast – at night?'

'That's what they call it, apparently, regardless of the time of day.'

Gordon looked serious as he declaimed, 'I chose my wife, as she did her wedding gown, not for a fine glossy surface, but such qualities as would wear well.'

'Who said that?'

'Oliver Goldsmith – *The Vicar of Wakefield* – don't you remember?'

'I don't remember anything like that; you're the one with the quotations. That's probably why you got into Oxford. Your brain is the size of a football – I think mine's about as big as a pea. And you're right about Charlotte, too. She seems to be wearing well and she's certainly lasting the course . . .'

'Why didn't you tell me they were getting married?'

'Didn't want to ruin the end of term,' confessed Charlie.

'God, I don't envy you. Who else is going? To the breakfast, I mean.'

'Well, Murdo won't be there, that's for sure. Or Mrs Murdo. Dad was tactful enough not to invite them.'

'Is Murdo still smarting? Hasn't he got over it yet?'

'I think he's got over Dad being in a relationship with somebody else; I just don't think he's got over Charlotte.'

'Who has?' muttered Gordon. Then, trying to lighten the mood, 'But there'll be others there, won't there?'

'There'll be a few of Charlotte's friends. She doesn't have many in the village, but she'll invite some from further afield I suppose. And I think the Fitzallans will come. Out of politeness.'

'And Eleanor?'

'I don't know.'

There was an uneasy silence between them. Then Charlie asked, 'Do you still write to her?'

Gordon made to make light of it. 'Yes. Now and then, you know.'

'Do you fancy her?'

Gordon looked up. 'Does it matter?'

Charlie shrugged. 'Only asking.'

'Well . . . she's very nice. We talk about things . . . you know. Not that I've heard from her for a while.'

'When was the last time?'

'I can't remember.' Gordon was attempting to pile clothes into the trunk now, hoping that the interrogation would be short lived. 'Anyway, why this sudden interest? You haven't asked about her for months.'

Charlie slid off the bed and walked to the window. He didn't speak for a while, but watched the steady stream of school leavers and parents as they carried crates and cases, trunks and cardboard boxes out to the assorted Ford Cortinas, Hillman Imps and more serviceable estate cars that lined the rough and curving drive of the academy.

He mused on what they would find when they got to their respective homes – normality, he imagined. Whatever that was. Then he turned to Gordon and with an apologetic note in his voice said, 'I didn't mean to sound . . . you know . . .'

'Bitter?'

Charlie smiled. 'Oh . . . I don't know. Just jealous, I suppose.'

'What of? There's no earthly need, you know. Nothing's happened. We just swap letters now and again.'

Charlie fidgeted for a moment and then asked, 'Have you ever . . . I mean, not necessarily with Eleanor . . . but have you ever . . . well . . . done it?'

Gordon looked surprised. 'I say—'

'I know, only . . .'

'Have *you*?' asked Gordon.

Charlie, looking embarrassed, developed a sudden fascination with the pattern on the threadbare carpet, which he traced out with the toes of his left foot. 'No. I mean, not properly.'

'Improperly then?' Gordon grinned, relieved at the chance of lightening the tone of conversation.

Charlie continued to look sheepish. 'Not even that. I had a bit of a fumble with one of the girls at that disco we had at the end of last term. Behind the curtains. French kissing and . . . you know . . . putting my hand up her blouse, but other than that . . .'

'It didn't go any further?'

'I got my face slapped. It put me off a bit.'

'I say, you're easily deflected aren't you? And why bring it up now? You've hardly mentioned it in three . . . no . . . four years.'

Charlie looked at Gordon accusingly. 'There was nothing *to* mention. Not a single thing. Well, other than the quick fumble. And that wasn't something I was going to go round broadcasting. Not in front of the likes of Alex Jesmond, who's had every bird this side of Glasgow if we're to believe what he claims.'

'And do you?'

'Not really, but you know what I mean. It's not the sort of thing I felt I could talk about. Even to you, since you seemed to be able to chat so easily to Eleanor.'

'Look, Charlie, most chaps are lucky if they manage a quick grope behind the bike sheds – just like you did, except that yours was behind the curtains. This "Swinging Sixties" lark is something that's happening in London, Glasgow and Edinburgh. It certainly isn't happening up here – not that I can see at any rate. We're only eighteen. There's still plenty of time to sow our wild oats – provided we're careful.'

'That's funny,' said Charlie.

'What is?'

'I've never heard you talk about sex, either.'

'No,' said Gordon. He looked pensive for a moment, then said, almost to himself: 'Unlike Alex Jesmond. He never talks about anything else.' Then he shook off his momentary introspection. 'My dad reckons that those who talk about it most, do it least.'

Charlie looked surprised. 'You've talked to your dad about it?'

Gordon lobbed a final armful of assorted belongings into the trunk, flipped down the lid and sat on it, the better to compress the contents and allow the latches to be fastened. 'Oh, you know – the fatherly talk. I'm not sure who was more embarrassed: him or me. I wasn't certain whether I was meant to know anything at all and if I should feign complete shock at what he was describing, and it was quite clear that he was unsure just how far to go. We declared a sort of truce when we got to rubber johnnies; I nodded a lot and looked knowing, just to signify that he didn't have to describe how to put one on.'

Charlie laughed. 'I can't imagine my dad ever telling me the facts of life. But then, having been surrounded by animals, I suppose he assumes that if I don't know now I never will.'

Gordon winked. 'He could always have asked Charlotte to take you on one side.'

'Don't ruin our last moments together by mentioning that woman. You know she's had a fountain built outside the castle?'

'A fountain? At Sodhail?'

'Yup. Right in the middle of the drive. I tell you, it looks like something off *Sunday Night at the London Palladium*.'

'You mean, your dad let her put it there?'

Charlie sighed. 'He simply can't say "no" to her.'

'What . . . ever?'

'Well, he did put his foot down at buying her an E-type Jag.'

'That's something then.'

'Yes. He got her an Austin 1100 instead. A posh one.'

Gordon grinned. 'It will be interesting to see how that survives in the Highlands. Cattle grids and salt spray a speciality.'

With finality he clicked the latches on the trunk and stood up. 'There we are then. All done. Are you up for a jar before we go? Now that we're legal?'

Charlie glanced at his watch. 'Just the one. The Austin 1100 is picking me up at six.'

* * *

Their conversation in the John of Gaunt, opening its doors just as they arrived, was of a valedictory nature. The first pint went down with some speed, as did the second. They were on their third, swearing undying allegiance and promising to meet up before the year was out, when their conversation was interrupted by the entrance of the school caretaker, a small man with a shuffling gait and a scruffy moustache. He was an Irishman, known to the pupils of Egglestone Academy, for some long-forgotten reason, as Taffy O'Connor.

'Mr Stuart?'

Charlie looked round and noticed the discomfited figure who was addressing him. 'Mr O'Connor. What is it?'

The little man in the cigarette-ash-dusted navy-blue suit looked nervous. 'There's someone enquiring for you.'

Charlie glanced at his watch. 'Shit, it's half past six. She'll be going spare.'

'A young lady in a dark green and cream Austin 1100 Vanden Plas is asking if you were ready. She said you were expecting a lift. I've helped her load the trunk onto the back seat. It wasn't easy. '

Charlie grinned at the fullness of Taffy's vehicular description, pushed his still half-full glass away from him and slid off the bar stool. Assuming that the huffing and puffing were intended to demonstrate the degree of effort that Taffy had put into the loading of the car, and the assiduousness of his care and attention born of his inherent good nature, Charlie pulled a half crown from his trouser pocket and slipped it to the old man. 'Thanks, Mr O'Connor, it was very good of you.' He was a little surprised that his generosity was not more clearly acknowledged, but Mr O'Connor seemed preoccupied.

Charlie turned to Gordon. 'All good things . . .' he murmured. He shook his hand firmly and looked him in the eye, hesitating for a moment before he said, 'Thank you . . . you know . . . for everything.'

'It's been fun,' said Gordon, sincerely. 'Just don't let the buggers grind you down. That's all.'

'Your final quote, is it?'

Gordon mused for a few seconds and then said, 'No. I ought to do better than that, oughtn't I? How about: "Life is what happens to us while we're busy making other plans"?'

'Who said that?' asked Charlie.

'Allen Saunders in 1957 in *Reader's Digest*. Then Walter Ward in 1962 and Henry Cooke in 1963. Before long someone else will lay claim to it.'

'Probably you.'

'Me? Oh, no. I haven't an original thought in my head.'

'No; that's why you're going to Oxford and I'm going back to the land.'

Gordon gave a final shrug and said, 'Safe journey. I hope your new stepmother is safe at the wheel.'

'Me too.'

Taffy O'Connor was by now hopping from foot to foot. 'Mr Stuart, I shall have to hurry you; we don't want to keep the young lady waiting. She seemed very keen to get away.'

Charlie laughed and said, 'Mr O'Connor, I know that by the standards of some mothers whose children attend this school that my stepmother might be a spring chicken, but to call her a young lady really is laying it on a bit thick.'

'Then, Mr Stuart, I am very envious of your father. He has done exceptionally well for himself.'

'It's all a matter of taste,' muttered Charlie, half to himself.

It was not until he arrived at the top of the school drive, with Taffy O'Connor beetling on ahead of him as though he were afraid of missing his train, that Charlie saw why he had been so complimentary. It was not Charlotte Stuart, née Niven, who was waiting for him in the dark green and cream Austin 1100 Vanden Plas so accurately described by Taffy O'Connor. It was Eleanor Fitzallan.

9

Invergarry House

July 1968

'Sins become more subtle as you grow older. You commit sins of despair rather than lust.'

Piers Paul Read in the *Daily Telegraph*, 3 October 1990

The view from the window was one he knew well – the summer-green slopes of Creag Sodhail, albeit from a slightly different angle, a different corner of the loch.

And yet the familiarity of it, coupled with the unusual slant, made the whole experience totally unreal. He was looking at it sideways. He was lying down. She was lying in his arms. They were both naked.

He could not remember feeling so happy, so fulfilled. His elation was akin to shock, so unexpected was Eleanor's attitude towards him – an attitude that had prevailed since that day she had picked him up at the end of term.

He had got into that silly little car, expecting to find Charlotte at the wheel; instead, Eleanor had beamed at him and said, softly, 'Hello, stranger'. In that one moment his heart had melted. Pathetic as it seemed to admit it, there really was no other way of putting it. She looked different; more knowing, more relaxed, more at ease with herself. Her blonde hair curled upwards as it reached her shoulders, her lips were a warm shade of pink, her darkened eyelashes were long and her floral mini-dress unbelievably short. Where had those long legs come from?

He had waited, as she drove back to the castle, for the moment when the old Eleanor might reawaken and become snippy and teasing. But the old Eleanor did not put in an appearance. It was not as though she had lost her fire or her spark, simply that she seemed more comfortable with herself. And with him. The days of being chippy and petulant were apparently behind her – sentiments she seemed no longer to need. A breezy confidence emanated from her now – not that unattractive kind of self-awareness that he had always found such a turn-off in girls (and which was probably designed to keep him and other men at arm's length until they had jumped through the requisite hoops), but an acceptance of his company that he found empowering.

He worried at first that the moment would come when she realised that he was just the same person that she had grown up with, and that her earlier attitude would soon return. But it did not. Its absence, and its substitution with this new-found tenderness, made him anxious to live up to the expectations he imagined she might have of him now: that he had become a man, rather than a callow, moody, mercurial youth. The relaxed attitude that she had in his company began to rub off. Over the next few weeks their closeness intensified.

The first time they held hands, as they walked along the edge of the loch, he felt a churning sensation in the pit of his stomach. When he kissed her properly for the first time, he was convinced that she would feel his heart pounding in his chest, not to mention stirrings of a more embarrassing kind.

It was some weeks before they slept together. Her parents had gone away for the weekend and she invited him round for supper.

She would cook, she said. He laughed. When she asked why, he said it sounded very grown up. She looked at him with her head on one side: 'But we are grown up,' she said. 'In September I go to St Andrews and you go to Ayr. We have to be grown up.'

She was right, of course. He had just not expected quite such a transformation in such a relatively short time. That evening, getting dressed in his room at the castle before he drove the old estate Land Rover around the edge of the loch to be with her, he stood and looked at himself in the mirror, wondering when he had changed; wondering *if* he had changed. The figure that stared back seemed different somehow. The mop of fair hair was still there, but he was no longer the wiry schoolboy with skinny legs. His frame had filled out; he was quite muscular now, broad shouldered, manly even. Strange how his body had altered more speedily than his frame of mind. Oh, he knew that he was regarded as an adult, in law at least, and yet his lack of experience in so many areas reminded him that he had, as yet, much to learn – about almost everything.

The love of nature and the countryside had fostered in him a kind of independence – a conscious detachment from things he considered to be of little value. The continued importance of this frame of mind was fostered by memories of his mother – a countrywoman whose wisdom had been firmly rooted in her home soil. She was well read and well-informed, but comfortable in her own skin and her own part of the world. At least, that's the impression she created, and it was one which moulded and framed the attitude of her son. His own experiences of metropolitan life – if such could be claimed of Inverness, and very occasional trips to Edinburgh and Glasgow – while opening his eyes in some degree to the wider world, did little to encourage him to embrace its priorities. The one visit he had made to England's capital, as part of a sixth-form visit to Hampton Court and the Tower of London, he had enjoyed. But at the end of three days he had been equally happy to return to the Highlands. It *was* possible, he believed, to live here and be detached from the hurly-burly of city life and – more importantly – the increasingly introspective attitude of those who seemed to live there, and yet not be divorced from reality. What was more real than the problems faced at the hands of nature? They were every bit as complex and challenging as those of man's invention. He wondered if, in two or three years, he would still feel the same way. But right now – for a few weeks at least – those worries could be put on one side.

He felt nervous as he drove along the rough road at the edge of the loch. It was a perfect evening; still water and still air – warm enough for shirtsleeves, even though the midges were beginning to bite. A cloud of dust streamed out in his wake, and with the windows down he could hear the mewing of buzzards on the slopes of Creag Sodhail.

The five-minute drive ended as he entered the old iron gates of Invergarry House – gates of ferrous twists and curlicues which were slung from sturdy sentinels of stone, topped with orb finials, and which had long since rusted into place in their open position. They framed the view of a long, granite-grey manse that seemed to crouch at the foot of the crag, the better to shelter from foul weather. There was no need for such provision on this balmy summer's evening. He noticed a faint plume of silver-grey smoke spiralling up from one of the chimneys. As he turned off the engine the silence enveloped him; the kind of stillness and calm that only this part of the world seemed to offer – an age-old acceptance of the passing of time and the futility of haste.

He got out, slammed the door and heard with more clarity than usual the crunching of his feet on the gravel of the drive.

Eleanor greeted him at the door. She wore another floral mini-dress, her legs and feet were bare and her face clear of make-up. Her natural prettiness took his breath away for the umpteenth time. 'When did you grow up?' he asked, thinking out loud.

'When you weren't looking,' she replied.

She leaned up and kissed him on the cheek, then turned towards the house, but he caught her arm and pulled her towards him, enveloping her in his arms and kissing her hungrily on the lips. Her sweetness encouraged him to pull her even closer, and he could feel the contours of her body through the flimsy dress. She was no longer the slight girl he had once known; that much was clear.

After some moments, he relaxed his grip and she eased away from him.

'When did you learn to kiss like that?' she asked.

Charlie smiled. 'About a month ago, when you came to pick me up.'

'Fast learner,' she said, teasingly.

He grinned. 'Good teacher.'

Eleanor took his hand. 'Come on,' she said. 'I've a bottle of wine in the fridge.'

They sat for an hour under the trees at the bottom of the lawn that stretched out in front of the house, talking, kissing and generally enjoying each other's company. 'Are you hungry?' she asked at last.

'Starving,' he replied.

'Come on then. I've laid out some supper.' She led him by the hand to an old octagonal summerhouse perched on a broad plank jetty that jutted out over the pebbled shore of the loch. He was surprised to find candles lit, another bottle of wine on ice and two comfortable chairs set either side of a small table covered with a gingham cloth. She produced salmon and salad from under a glass dome, poured two glasses of wine and motioned him to sit opposite her. The light was beginning to fade now; the sky turning a pale shade of apricot behind the towering mountains.

'This is very . . .' he hesitated.

'Romantic?' she offered.

'Unexpected.'

'Oh.' She looked crestfallen.

He smiled. 'And romantic.'

'That's better.'

As they ate, the conversation turned to their respective parents' shortcomings, but in a good-natured way. Charlie had no intention of spending the evening talking about his stepmother, and banished all thoughts of her from his mind. For once, it was not difficult.

Then the subject of university came up. At first they both spoke eagerly of their aspirations and apprehensiveness – she of the course in fine art at St Andrews, he of agricultural studies at Auchincruive, but soon the realisation that they would be parted cast a shadow over the evening.

'But it's only a hundred miles,' said Charlie. 'Two-and-a-half-hours by car.'

'If we had a car.'

'If one of us had one it would be fine.'

'At weekends. But what if . . .' For the first time, Eleanor seemed troubled.

'What?'

'What if there's somebody else?'

Charlie put down his knife and fork gently and leaned back in the wicker chair. Swifts were swooping low over the loch and as he spoke he could hear their shrill cries. 'You mean . . . you don't want there to be?' he asked.

Eleanor shook her head. 'No,' she said softly, all the while looking down as though she dare not meet his eyes.

'Not even Gordon?'

She looked up. 'Gordon?'

'You went riding together.'

'Oh, that. That was ages ago.'

'About a year . . . and three months.'

There was a glint in Eleanor's eye. 'Were you counting?'

Charlie nodded. 'I saw the letters when they arrived, but I never said anything. Why did you keep writing to him?'

'Well, because he wrote to me, mainly.'

'But you replied?'

'Yes.'

'So . . . ?'

'So I wrote back. Surely you can work out why?'

'Because you fancied him, presumably?'

'Don't be silly. There's no way that Gordon . . . I mean, he's very sweet but . . .'

Charlie was genuinely puzzled. 'Why then? Why would you write to him if you didn't fancy him?'

'Honestly?'

'Honestly.'

'Because I wanted to make you jealous.'

Charlie stared at her, his mouth open.

'Didn't you realise?' she asked.

Charlie shook his head.

'Well, there you are. All that letter writing wasted.'

'But I . . . I mean . . . I never thought . . .'

'No. That's why I had to come and get you. Your stepmother's face was a picture when I asked to borrow her car. If she could have found the words I'm sure she'd have said no. But sometimes a girl just has to take things into her own hands. Talking of which . . .'

She got up from the table and walked towards the open door. 'Come on,' she said softly. Charlie did not speak. He did not have to. Silently and hand in hand they walked across the lawn as the swifts skimmed the water. She led him into the house and up the stairs to her room. For two hours they made love before falling asleep in each other's arms. When he awoke in the morning, that view that he knew so well suddenly looked quite different. It was partly due to the different angle, but also due to the fact that he didn't feel like a boy any more.

10

Oxford

Easter 1970

'Surprises are foolish things. The pleasure is not enhanced, and the inconvenience is often considerable.'

Jane Austen, *Emma*, 1816

The dreaming spires of Oxford were barely visible though the fine drizzle as Charlie walked purposefully down St Aldate's towards the tower of Christ Church where Gordon had suggested they meet. He was surprised to discover that he was nervous, apprehensive even, of meeting the boy – now man – that he had shared a room with for the better part of two years. But, as he reminded himself, even then there were things they did not tell each other about; feelings they did not share.

It was Gordon who had written and suggested that they meet. Now that his father had retired from North Sea Gas and moved with his wife to the Home Counties, he had little need to visit Scotland and had found a flat with three other Christ Church students just off the Woodstock Road.

Much had happened in the intervening two years, certainly as far as Charlie was concerned. There were various bits of news he had been storing up, unwilling to commit to paper in the erratic correspondence that flowed between the two students. Gordon, it seemed, was still on his own, without a regular girlfriend. Charlie had not mentioned Eleanor at all in their exchanges and had been relieved that Gordon, too, had fallen silent on the matter.

And then he saw him; leaning against the arch of Tom Tower; still the same, gawky angular Gordon, one leg bent up against the wall after the fashion of a heron, both hands thrust deep in his trouser pockets, his lips muttering words that were indecipherable over the steady flow of traffic.

'Hello!' said Charlie.

Gordon looked up, coming to, it seemed, after a long journey into his thoughts. 'Hello, old chap! How nice to see you!' They shook hands heartily, and Gordon clapped Charlie on the back by way of greeting. 'You've not changed a bit. Yes you have; your hair's longer.'

'Everybody's hair's longer,' retorted Charlie. 'Even yours.'

'Oh, nothing to do with style, just that I keep forgetting to have it cut. How have you been? How are things north of the border? How's your love life?'

'Do you want me to answer those questions separately or all at once?'

'As you please, Charlie, as you please. Gosh, it's good to see you. "Since man with that inconstancy was born, to love the absent, and the present scorn."'

'The same old Gordon. Who said that then?'

'Aphra Behn.'

'Aphra who?' asked Charlie, grinning.

'Surely you?' then, realising he was no longer among his current intimates, Gordon explained gently, 'No, of course you wouldn't . . . She was the first female in England to become a professional writer. Beat Miss Austen by a couple of centuries. Born in 1640.'

'You're taking your English Lit. seriously then?'

'Every bit as seriously as you are taking your Agriculture.'

'Estate Management.'

'I stand corrected. Anyway, we're getting wet. What say we

go for a jar in The Bear and grab a bite before you come back and dump your bag?'

Gordon's habit of talking as though he were the love child of Oscar Wilde and P.G. Wodehouse seemed more pronounced than ever now that the two former room-mates no longer saw each other on a daily basis.

'Sounds good to me,' replied Charlie.

It was a short walk to The Bear, which Gordon informed his former schoolmate, waving his hands in the general direction of its upper storey with a proprietorial sort of air, was the oldest pub in Oxford. Charlie liked the atmosphere, and the quality of the beer, but was mystified by the vast collection of ties that adorned the walls, each with a paper label.

'A tradition,' explained Gordon. 'One that started about fifteen years ago. Oxford's like that. There was the story of a don who said, "As of tomorrow it will be a college tradition that we do not walk on the grass in the quad." And it was; simple as that.'

'Sounds a bit posey to me,' murmured Charlie over his pint of bitter.

'Yes, but classy posey. Cheers!'

'Cheers!' Having slaked his thirst, Charlie leaned back and looked around him. 'So this is where you're at now?'

'This is my milieu. The city of dreaming spires and dreaming students.'

'You don't look any different.'

'Don't I?' asked Gordon, absently, scrutinising the bar menu propped up on the small round table.

'Well, a bit. Taller, if anything. Even more ramshackle.'

'That's a good farming word. "Ramshackle." You make me sound like a rusty combine harvester.'

'I told you; I'm not a farmer.'

Gordon held up his hands. 'No. I'm sorry. You're in management.'

'*Estate* management.'

'Now if you keep going on about it, Charlie, I shall assume that you have a chip on your shoulder.'

Charlie laughed. 'I haven't. I just don't want you to get the wrong end of the stick.'

'OK, OK – I promise not to call you a farmer any more. "*O fortunatos nimium, sua si bona norint, Agricolas!*"'

'What?!'

'"Oh farmers excessively fortunate if only they recognised their blessings!" Virgil. '

'You know, a fellow could get tired of this.'

'Oh, many have, Charlie, many have. But it doesn't stop me. It prevents me from sinking into a slough of despond.'

Charlie took another pull on his pint. 'You get fed up then? Here in Oxford? Your dream city?'

'"At night in my dreams –", but no; you'll only tell me off for not being original.' He took a gulp from his pint glass, replaced it on the table and muttered, 'Dreams are not all they are cracked up to be.'

'Oh dear. That doesn't sound very hopeful.'

'No. But, hey! We're not here to be miserable; we're here to share news, scandal and gossip. What's yours?'

Charlie filled Gordon in on the developments of the last two years; the ups and down of the college course and the real meaning of Estate Management. He was aware, at times, that Gordon's eyes became glazed, and when that happened he tried to spice up his narrative with nuggets that would make his old friend laugh. When Gordon laughed, the brief years that had elapsed fell away, and they were schoolboys once more. But as they talked over a large plate of beef and onion sandwiches, Charlie observed a more haunted look in Gordon's eye. One he could not remember noticing before.

At first he thought that he must be imagining things; that Gordon was just older, more mature and that he had the weight of Oxford and his parents' academic expectations upon his shoulders; it was not surprising that he looked tired, preoccupied, hunted. If anything, he was more flamboyant when he was in full flow. Not only did he sound like Oscar Wilde when he launched into one of his aphorisms or literary bon mots, but thanks to the length of his hair – due, he insisted, to having no time to visit the barbers – he even looked like him.

Eventually Charlie asked, 'So no woman on the horizon then?'

'No. Not even the far distant horizon. But there we are.'

Charlie realised he could put off the moment no longer. He eased into it gently. 'You don't write to Eleanor any more, then?'

'Good God, no! That petered out years ago. The letters stopped coming as quickly as they started and that was that.'

'All down to horse riding really, I suppose,' offered Charlie.

'Yes. That was a good ruse, wasn't it?'

'What do you mean?'

'Saying that I rode horses.'

'You mean . . . you didn't?'

'No. Well, not regularly. I'm afraid I told a bit of a fib there. I had an uncle who had – this'll make you laugh – a farm, and when I was a kid I'd go there in the summer holidays. I'd ride then, but I hadn't really been on a horse for . . . ooh . . . ten years.'

'But you said—'

'I know. I lied. Sorry. But it did get me out of the house and away from your . . . well . . . you know . . .'

Charlie was speechless for a few moments. Then he said softly, 'I had no idea.'

'No,' said Gordon, with a note of apology in his voice. 'I hated lying about it but it was quite tense – the atmosphere between you and your step-mum.'

'I feel dreadful. Inviting you there and putting you through all that.'

'Oh, it wasn't all bad; when we had the chance to be on our own, to talk on our own – which wasn't very often, I'll admit – I had a great time. But I do sympathise with you; Charlotte was hard work, to say the least.'

'Not past tense, for me,' muttered Charlie.

'No. Anyway, all that *is* in the past and I haven't seen or heard from Eleanor in ages, so there we are. What about you?'

Charlie was still recovering from the revelation and took several moments to marshal his thoughts. 'Well, Eleanor and I—'

Gordon butted in, 'Are together?'

Charlie looked surprised. 'How do you know? I mean . . .'

'It was obvious; to me at any rate. She didn't have eyes for anyone else, and neither, I suppose, did you.'

'But even *I* didn't know . . .'

Gordon studied him. 'No. You always were a bit slow on the uptake, where women were concerned at least. It was obvious to me.'

'Even when you were, you know, writing to one another?'

'Yes; I could see why she was doing it, but I tried to avoid you finding out – I didn't want to be part of the calculated approach.'

Charlie sought reassurance: 'So you knew she was writing to you to make me jealous?'

'Yes. It was as plain as the nose on your face. But I didn't really want to toe the line and play my part.'

'I see.'

'Oh, there was nothing malicious about it; just classic feminine wiles. It was rather sweet, really; Eleanor thinking that if I droned on to you about the fact that she and I wrote to one another you'd get all macho and threaten to punch my lights out or something. I didn't want it to get in the way of our friendship so I didn't mention it. Not until it was too late for you to do anything about it, anyway, and by then we'd come to the parting of the ways and I knew you'd be able to step into the breach.'

'I saw the letters in your drawer.'

Gordon looked shocked. 'You mean you went through my things?'

'You know me better than that. Effie wanted the key to your trunk to drop off some linen you'd asked her to launder and the only place I thought it could be was in your private drawer. I didn't find it, but I did see the bundle of letters and I recognised the writing. That's all. I didn't look at them. I didn't want to.'

'Well, that's a relief; I wouldn't like to think that after all these years my judgement of you had been at fault. Mind you, that does mean that you had your little secret, too. We were both hiding something.'

'Yes; but for all the right reasons – because we didn't want to upset one another.'

Gordon sighed. 'What a delightful pair we were.'

'*Are*, more like.'

'Quite. So you and Eleanor are still together "after all these years", in spite of being at opposite sides of God's own country?'

''Fraid so. We have our ups and downs, but they are usually due to irritation at not being together.'

Gordon looked at Charlie with his head on one side. 'So is this *it* then, do you think? Till death us do part and all that?'

'Yes. I think so. I hope so. She's just . . . well . . .' he laughed softly, 'wonderful. I mean, when I'm with her I feel whole, happy, content, all those things you're supposed to feel when you're . . .'

'In love?'

'Yes. In love. Go on, take the mickey; I don't care.'

Gordon leaned back in his chair and smiled. 'I'm not going to take the mickey. Good for you. If you're happy with your first love at the tender age of twenty, for God's sake make the most of it; there are plenty of us who are not.'

'Oh. You mean *you're* not?'

'Charles Angus Rory Stuart, I doubt if I will ever be really, truly, deeply in love. Not in the way you are, anyway. But I've come to terms with it. I've learnt to live with it, for better, for worse, though I know you'll never hear me saying those words. Not in a church at any rate.'

'You won't marry then?'

'No.'

'Never?'

'No. Not the marrying type, Charlie.' Gordon looked him directly in the eye and Charlie realised, at last, what his old school chum meant.

Eventually, and after what seemed like an age, Charlie said: 'You mean . . . ?'

'Yup.'

'Oh bloody hell. I never thought. I mean, we shared a room. You never . . .'

'No, of course I never. What do you think I am? I knew *you* weren't, so . . .'

'But you've asked me here for the weekend, to Oxford . . .'

'Yes, Charlie, I have.' Gordon lowered his voice to a whisper. 'But there's no need to panic. We'll have separate rooms and you'll be in no more danger than you were when we were at school.'

Gordon could see the colour draining from Charlie's cheeks. 'Oh dear; I shouldn't have told you. I should have kept you in the dark. You're clearly not ready for it.'

Charlie protested. 'Of course I am. I'm a man of the world. Well, a small part of that world but . . . it's just that it's come as a bit of a surprise, that's all.'

'Shock, more like,' said his companion.

'All right then, a shock. But that doesn't mean I can't get over it; that I *won't* get over it.'

'So we can have a good weekend, and not a repetition of that Easter in your castle with the Witch of Endor.'

Charlie found himself trying to suppress a laugh.

'That's better, Charlie. Cheer up, chicken. It's not the end of the world. I'm just the same old Gordon, except that now you know me rather better than you did. There's no danger of me trying to get your knickers off; I've seen you without them often enough and managed to control myself. No reason to change now.' He noticed Charlie colouring up. 'Good God! The man blushes. Now I've seen it all.'

Charlie groped for words and eventually said, sotto voce, 'Look, I know it's the same old you. Except that it's not. But this is rather a lot to take in over one beef sandwich and a pint, after knowing each other for goodness knows how many years.'

'Six.'

'And sharing a room together.'

Gordon spoke with a mocking tone. 'I know, you're now going over all the things that happened when we were under Effie's care and wondering if I ever did anything that you didn't notice or which you misinterpreted. Well, I can tell you that you won't find any, because they don't exist. I might be odd but I do have principles.'

'No; I didn't mean—'

'Hey! Shall we lighten up a little? Do you want another pint or . . .' he winked, 'would you rather go straight back to my place?'

Charlie's eyebrows shot up.

'Only kidding; only kidding! Same again?'

11

Oxford

Easter 1970

> 'Five and twenty ponies,
> Trotting through the dark –
> Brandy for the Parson,
> 'Baccy for the Clerk;
> Laces for a lady, letters for a spy,
> Watch the wall, my darling, while the Gentlemen go by!'
>
> Rudyard Kipling, 'A Smuggler's Song', 1906

There was no time to sit on his own and muse on the lunchtime revelations. The afternoon consisted of a whistle-stop tour of Oxford, courtesy of Gordon, whose loping gait left Charlie breathless. The cloying drizzle had abated, to be replaced by dazzling sunshine that glinted on gilded finials and bathed the statue-furnished niches in the golden glow of a late March afternoon. The athleticism of their progress, coupled with the new light in which he saw his erstwhile school chum, left him reeling. Images of the Bodleian Library and the Radcliffe Camera, the Sheldonian Institute and the Ashmolean Museum swirled around in his confused and overloaded brain, merging together, then separating again until he was unsure which was which. The names of the universities themselves were the stuff of legends: Christ Church and Magdalen, Balliol and Oriel, All Souls, Keble and Trinity. It was as if he was being given a guided tour of a film set – all so amazing, so surreal. That this fine architecture should be crammed so close together and intersected by narrow streets so choked with traffic that it seemed barely to move only added to the claustrophobic feel of the place; so lacking in room to breathe and yet brimming with import and urgency. Charlie found its unfamiliarity thrilling, if a little unnerving.

'Glad the sun's come out,' commented Gordon. 'We can take to the river this afternoon.'

Charlie was already exhausted. On the overnight sleeper to King's Cross he had barely slept a wink; then there was the journey to Oxford, and now he was being swept around this seemingly sacred city at the kind of feverish pace that would leave an Olympic athlete gasping for breath. He would not complain; Gordon was clearly out to give his old friend a good time and leave no stone unturned in his mission to share the glories of the glittering city.

They were at the river's edge now. 'Grab this,' instructed Gordon as he tossed a rope to Charlie. No sooner had the line been cast in the direction of his friend than he leapt into the punt, clutching at a long pole after the fashion of a tightrope walker anxious to maintain his balance. The pole cut an arc through the air that threatened to take out anyone within striking distance, and just as Charlie had convinced himself that his next task would be to haul a dripping Gordon from the waters of the Isis, his friend steadied himself and enjoined Charlie to cut a similar figure himself and come aboard.

Taking rather more care than the self-appointed skipper, and with his overnight bag slung from his shoulder, Charlie carefully picked his way over the row of punts until he reached the chosen vessel. Then, seated at the stern of the shallow craft, where Gordon had taken some trouble to place him, he leaned back on the damp cushions and, for the first time in many hours, began to relax.

With barely a sound, other than a satisfying 'gloop' as the pole left the water, the punt glided across the river. Charlie had no concept of whether they were travelling up or downstream as willows speckled with lime green curls of unfurling leaves swayed in the breeze on the riverbank, first hiding, and then revealing with a theatrical flourish, the turret and tower, the dome and the spire as the city of Oxford slid by, at first hiding like some shy Eastern maiden, and then revealing itself once more in the dance of the seven veils.

'So what do you think?' asked Gordon.

'Magical,' murmured Charlie.

'A bit different to Inverness?'

'Just a bit.'

'Do you like it?'

'Very much.' Charlie was touched by Gordon's apparent need for reassurance or, at the very least, his intention that Charlie should enjoy himself. But then that was typical of him. He had always been considerate; anxious that those around him should be happy, even if he did seem somewhat preoccupied himself. Charlie wondered, sometimes, if Gordon's strange way of walking was in some way due to the weight of the world that he seemed to carry on his bony shoulders.

After an hour or so, Gordon manoeuvred the punt back into the cluster of craft at the boarding station and offered Charlie his hand. Charlie took it to steady himself, and could not but wonder how many men's hands Gordon had held since they had parted two years ago. It was an unworthy thought, he told himself, and he relinquished it as swiftly as Gordon relinquished his grip.

'It's very good of you to come,' said Gordon, as they walked out of town along the Woodstock Road. 'Considering you can only stay for a night.'

'I promised Eleanor we'd spend most of the week together,' said Charlie, 'but she knew I hadn't seen you for ages, and I think she was as curious as I was to know how you were.'

'And how am I?' asked Gordon levelly.

'Just the same, really. Revelation aside.'

Gordon stopped walking. 'It doesn't affect anything, you know. Not as far as you're concerned. At least, it shouldn't. It's not something I talk about much. And I do even less about it. It's just that I thought . . . well . . . I didn't want you not knowing.'

'Thanks,' said Charlie. He couldn't really think of anything else that was appropriate to say, and for a few minutes the friends walked on down the Woodstock Road in silence. Eventually Charlie asked, 'What are we doing tonight?'

'Oh, I'm pushing the boat out. And I don't mean a punt. It's not every night you get a friend journeying from Scotland to see you, so we're having supper at the Randolph.'

'That big hotel?'

'Yes. They do a great roast, and I thought that after your long journey you could do with more than a beef sandwich and a plate of spag bol.'

'Just the two of us?' asked Charlie.

'No. There is somebody else.'

Charlie raised an eyebrow.

'No; not that sort of somebody else. A college friend. One that you know, actually. Alex Jesmond. Remember him?'

'The sex maniac from school?'

'The very same. He's reading PPE – Philosophy, Politics and Economics – at Brasenose. Not a bad chap really. Anyway, he asked to meet you.'

'Me?'

'No; the Dalai Lama. Yes, you!' said Gordon, with mock exasperation.

'What on earth for?'

'Old times' sake possibly. Maybe he had a soft spot for you. Or maybe he wants to discuss the political and economic implications of *Lady Chatterley's Lover*.'

'What's he like? I mean . . . is he just the same?'

'Well, I think he's got over his obsession with the opposite sex, if that's what you mean.'

As they dined at the Randolph Hotel on roast beef with all the trimmings, and a 1964 claret that Alex explained was particularly good, it became clear that Alex Jesmond, while still the stocky dark-haired individual that he had been at school, had changed considerably in his general demeanour. Where once he had been boastful and outgoing, he now seemed withdrawn and circumspect. While not exactly morose, having ordered the wine he contributed little to the evening's conversation, so much so that Charlie wondered why he had bothered to come. He certainly found it hard to believe that he had asked Gordon if he could meet Charlie again, for nothing that he said or did in the first hour of their meeting gave any indication of his eagerness to be a party to their reminiscences or exchanging of news. What he did do was listen, quite avidly, as Charlie talked about his future plans, explaining that his father had it in mind to move out of Castle Sodhail in the next five years to allow Charlie to take over the estate – hence the management course at Auchincruive.

'I thought your father was wedded to Sod-all for life?' muttered Gordon between mouthfuls of Aberdeen Angus.

'So did he,' confirmed Charlie. 'But Charlotte has had enough of the winters in the Highlands and wants to move out.'

'And he's given in?' asked Gordon.

'Yes. Surprisingly. I thought he'd want to stay there for ever, having sorted the estate out over all these years, but I don't really think his heart is in it any more. And his health isn't too good these days. He seems to get breathless a lot.'

'But he's not yet fifty.'

'Forty-six.'

'Spring chicken! So why has he decided to move out?'

'Charlotte gave him an ultimatum; it was either her or the castle.'

Alex Jesmond raised an eyebrow.

Gordon was more vocal. 'Bloody woman!'

'She got tired of playing the laird's wife,' explained Charlie. 'Found that her friends from the south were no longer keen to schlep all the way up to the Highlands for a weekend of fun and frolics, and my dad isn't exactly a social animal. In the end, fun in the south outweighed grandeur in the north – if you can call Castle Sodhail grand.'

Gordon shook his head. 'But if he gives in and moves away then what will he do? He'll be bored rigid. God! It must be love!'

Charlie winced. 'I think she's just ground him down. I've tried to talk to him about it but there's no way he will enter into a conversation. He just said: "That's what we're doing and that's that, so just be grateful that the castle will be yours sooner rather than later."'

'How soon is soon?' asked Alex Jesmond, making a rare entry into the conversation.

'Early next year. I'll have finished my course by then and I'll have to jump in at the deep end.'

'Scared?' asked Gordon.

'Funnily enough, no. Excited. I feel sorry for Dad, of course, but I'm ready for the challenge. It's strange really; history repeating itself. Dad took on the castle when he was young and now I'll have to do the same. And with any luck I won't be on my own.'

Gordon smiled and turned to Alex. 'You might have been first off the blocks at school where the fairer sex is concerned, Alex, but I think Charlie is going to breast the marriage tape ahead of you.'

Alex shrugged. 'Overrated, in my opinion.'

'It took you long enough to come to that conclusion,' said Gordon.

'Older and wiser,' murmured Alex, taking a sip of his claret. 'Good luck to you, Charlie. I hope you'll be very happy.'

Charlie noticed that the expression on Alex's face did not reflect the expressed sentiment. 'Well, don't congratulate me yet. I haven't even asked her. Not sure when I will but . . .'

'You're hopeful?' asked Gordon.

'Yes. Hopeful. I suppose that's all I can say, really.'

The conversation that followed, with a second bottle of 1964 claret going down at a steady pace, dwelt on everything from reports of the My Lai massacre in Vietnam to Dana winning the Eurovision Song Contest for Ireland. Alex was dismissive of Eurovision and muttered darkly about something called 'Heavy Metal' and a band called 'Black Sabbath'. Charlie thought that Alex's predilection for 'the dark side' obviously stretched further than the black suit and black poloneck sweater he was wearing. The head waiter at the Randolph seemed singularly unimpressed by Alex's wardrobe, and his interest in pop music stretched only as far as the keyboard talents of Russ Conway. But at least Alex was ordering a decent wine, and not a cheap one, either.

Charlie wondered if Alex was going to say anything at all of any note, when, over coffee in a corner of the Randolph's lounge, he turned to Gordon and asked, 'Have you said anything?'

Gordon's reply was brief. 'Not yet.'

'Well,' said Alex, 'I think you ought to.'

'I'd rather it was you,' replied Gordon nervously. 'I'll probably couch it badly.'

Charlie looked from one to the other with a quizzical expression. The claret had created a warm feeling inside his body and a cloudy feeling in his head.

Alex glanced around them to make sure they were not within earshot of other hotel patrons. Satisfied that he could not be overheard, he asked: 'Aside from running your family estate, is there any chance that you could join Gordon and me in another venture?'

Charlie smiled. 'What sort of venture?' he asked innocently.

'Something important, but also something that involves a degree of discretion. You wouldn't be able to tell anybody else about it.'

Charlie laughed. The claret was beginning to tell. 'This all sounds a bit cloak and dagger.'

Gordon and Alex glanced at one another and then back at Charlie.

'You see,' continued Alex, 'aside from our studies we like to do something for our country as well.' He smiled.

It was not a sincere smile; more like the kind of smile the foxy-whiskered gentleman gave Jemima Puddle-Duck, thought Charlie. He rubbed his forehead as if embarrassed at such a childish thought and blamed it on the claret.

'It's to do with accommodation,' continued Alex.

'Accommodation?'

'Yes. As you can guess, Oxford is pretty crowded when it

comes to catering for all its students. There is . . .' he hesitated, '. . . overspill.'

Charlie did his best to understand where the conversation was going. He failed.

'We have an increasing number of foreign students who take places here. They come from all over the world. Most of them can be accommodated during term time but in the holidays – when there's a demand on rooms for tourists – they simply can't find anywhere to stay.'

Charlie was aware that both Alex and Gordon were staring at him. 'I'm not sure what this has got to do with me.'

Gordon looked uncomfortable. Alex continued: 'It's important that they are accommodated somewhere they can feel safe. We just wondered if . . . well . . . you would be interested in putting a few of them up in your castle.'

'In Scotland?'

'Yes.'

'But that's miles away from Oxford.'

'Exactly. They'd feel safe there. I mean, they'd be out of harm's way.'

'But who's going to hurt them?' asked Charlie, his mind now completely befuddled by the direction of the conversation.

'Nobody's going to hurt them. They just need somewhere to—'

'Study,' cut in Gordon. 'Somewhere they can get on with their studies without being interrupted or distracted by—'

'Events,' added Alex.

'But it's such a long way away,' muttered Charlie, almost to himself.

'That's why we're asking,' said Alex.

'Who's we? Just you and Gordon?'

'And a few others.'

'But what's this got to do with "doing something for your country"?'

Gordon answered: 'Some of them are connected with the foreign office. Diplomats' children. They need to be kept an eye on. You know; foreign threats and that sort of thing.'

'But doesn't the government take care of them?'

'Well, in a manner of speaking. But not on a day-to-day basis. Finding lodgings is not really their bag.'

'So why is it yours?' asked Charlie pointedly. His mind was beginning to clear, the retreat of the grey haze being hastened by the apparent seriousness of the subject.

'Have you ever heard of safe houses?' asked Alex.

'You mean where people can go – special people – and disappear?'

'Just so,' said Alex softly.

'Only in films,' said Charlie, 'and James Bond novels.' He laughed, but noticed that his dinner companions did not. Quite the opposite. He could not remember when he had last seen Gordon look so serious.

12

Invergarry House
Easter Monday 1970

> 'Time is
> Too slow for those who wait,
> Too swift for those who fear,
> Too long for those who grieve,
> Too short for those who rejoice;
> But for those who love,
> Time is Eternity.'
>
> Henry Van Dyke (1852–1933)

The Fitzallans were an old Scottish family who could trace their line back to Robert the Bruce. Granted, to so do took several leaps of faith, and Sir Robert Fitzallan – Eleanor's father – made light of both the connection and the use of the prefix granted to his family nine generations ago on the grounds that it was a result of his forebear's efforts rather than his own. He was almost fifteen years older than Angus Stuart and the relationship between the two, though relatively amiable, was not close. They were both men who took their responsibilities seriously and while, between them, they were responsible for the employment of no more than a handful of the people who lived in the scattered houses that constituted the village of Sodhail, they knew that as older inhabitants – particularly in the case of the Fitzallans – it was accepted that they would set the tone of the area. (While seldom admitting to anything approaching snobbery, by the dawning of the

1970s the residents of Glen Sodhail regarded themselves as something of a cut above the glens to north and south, and the presence of a baronet, at least as far as the female population was concerned, gave their neck of the woods more than a hint of added kudos.)

Tall, with iron-grey hair and of suitably patrician bearing, Robert Fitzallan was an affable and easy-going man who had retired from the cut and thrust of banking in Edinburgh at the age of fifty. Having lost his sons to spirits of adventure in Africa and New Zealand, it was not surprising that his fatherly instincts were concentrated upon his daughter. He referred to her variously as 'Hen', 'Ellie' and 'Half Pint', depending on his mood. She objected to none of them, though as she grew older the latter appellation was less frequently applied. Eleanor had grown into a shapely young woman and to those outside the family such a reference might be construed as inappropriate. Robert Fitzallan would never want to be thought of as disrespectful to any woman, even his young daughter.

He sat, as he did most mornings, in the long low drawing room of Invergarry House decorated by his wife Davina, who was moving away from her signature country-house chintz à la Colefax and Fowler in the direction of someone called Laura Ashley. He hardly noticed. The tall windows looked out across the loch, and the generosity of their size meant that this was the perfect place to peruse the morning paper, regardless of the pattern on the wallpaper or the upholstery print upon which he sat. When asked about it he always said that it looked 'very nice; you know . . . comfortable.'

His morning paper was brought, by dint of some effort and a temperamental moped, all the way from Strath Carron by the local postmistress, Aileen Bell. Only deep snow would keep Aileen from her duties, and the delivery of Sir Robert's

Daily Telegraph became her avowed mission. That, and a steamy mug of builder's tea constituted a morning ritual that only Sir Robert's daughter dared to interrupt, and then rarely. There he sat, in his favourite armchair, wearing corduroys and a cardigan, harrumphing occasionally over the state of the country and 'that wretched man Wilson' who seemed to be clinging tenaciously to the sinking ship that was Britain. 'Not that Heath looks a much better prospect,' he confided to his wife in a rare moment of pessimism. 'I don't envy him if he gets in. The country's in a dreadful state. I doubt he's got what it takes. Confirmed bachelor by all accounts. Still, he does like sailing. Can't be all bad.'

There was little else to cheer him on this particular morning – the hi-jacking of a Japanese aeroplane by the Red Army, and the return to earth of a US satellite after twelve years in orbit. He felt, if anything, even more divorced from the outside world than usual, as a result of which, when Eleanor stuck her head round the corner of the room, he welcomed rather than scolded her for the interruption.

'Hello, Hen. How are you?' He tilted his cheek towards her for the peck he was accustomed to receiving. His daughter did not disappoint, but her response to his question lowered his spirits even further: 'All right; a bit lonely.'

'Where's your chap then? No sign of him? I thought he was coming straight back from the great metropolis.'

'I think he must have been delayed. He said he was hoping to come back on the sleeper last night. I think he only intended staying down there until yesterday evening.'

'It's a long way to go just for one night. Maybe he was too weary to make the journey back. Like you, I expect he's had a heavy term and he's just . . . you know . . . "chilling out" . . . Isn't that the phrase?'

Eleanor looked thoughtful. 'I suppose.'

'Maybe he couldn't get to a phone.' Her father made to console her; he liked Charlie and felt that his daughter and Angus Stuart's son were good for one another; had a similar set of values. It concerned him that Eleanor had never really had another boyfriend (at least, not to his knowledge), but then he consoled himself with the fact that he could do worse than Charlie for a son-in-law, should it ever come to that. But they were young. There was plenty of time. You could not interfere; he knew that from experience, having once congratulated his eldest son on getting rid of a flibbertigibbet of a girl that he had never liked. Three months later, the boy had taken up with her again and Robert was in the embarrassing situation of having to pretend that he had never expressed an opinion. For that much, at least, his son was grateful, but Robert vowed that never again would he pass judgement on one of his children's amours. He felt more protective of his daughter, but knew that the less he said about her affairs of the heart the better.

Eleanor perched on the arm of his chair and put her arm around his shoulder. Her hair was tied back in a ponytail and she wore no make-up; it did not detract from her beauty; certainly not as far as her father was concerned.

Breaking the rule he usually espoused, Robert asked, 'You're quite keen, aren't you? On Charlie Stuart?'

'Daddy! What sort of question is that?'

Her father rubbed her arm affectionately. 'One I shouldn't ask.'

Eleanor sighed. 'Well, the answer's yes, anyway.'

'Don't you think you should . . . I hesitate to use the phrase "play the field", since that's something that boys do, but . . . I mean . . . do you think you've . . . ?' His question petered out on the grounds of delicacy.

'I did think about . . . playing the field as you put it. But there didn't seem . . . doesn't seem . . . much point. I like Charlie; why look any further?'

'Like? Is that enough?'

Eleanor nudged her father's shoulder. 'All right then, I *love* Charlie. Is that enough?'

'As long as you're happy, Hen, then I'm happy. But just remember you're still very young. You might change your mind.'

'Do you want me to?'

'It's not up to me. I'm not going to tell you what to do. I just get concerned when you're not happy. That's what fathers do.'

'Robert? Are you there?' They were interrupted by a distant voice, calling from the far end of the hallway that ran the length of the house.

'Now we're for it,' muttered Robert to his daughter. He glanced at his watch. 'I promised I'd run your mother into Strath Carron. She'll be champing at the bit. You be good and I'll see you when we get back. And don't worry,' he added, 'I'm sure he'll telephone before too long and let you know what's happening.'

But Charlie did not telephone, and Eleanor, out riding later that morning, realised, for the umpteenth time in the last few years, how desolate one's feelings can be when the person you love more than anyone else in the world is out of touch.

13

The Overnight Sleeper

April 1970

'He felt the loyalty we all feel to unhappiness – the sense that that is where we really belong.'

Graham Greene, *The Heart of the Matter*, 1948

The train had not moved for three hours. They were a hundred miles short of Inverness. The guard had done his best to placate those businessmen with important-looking attaché cases, but students, and those in less impressive attire, warranted little more than a nod or a shrug. A points failure, Charlie overheard. Many people would miss their connections and the guard was sorry about that but there was nothing he could do.

Connections. The very thing that had left Charlie feeling confused and incredulous. He had read spy stories and enjoyed them – the works of John le Carré and Ian Fleming had been staple fare in the sixth-form at Egglestone – but he little imagined that they would ever be something that could translate into real life. Not his life, at any rate. Hunched up in a corner seat, he rubbed at the condensation on the window, the better to make out the view. Not that it contained anything surprising; after three hours it was almost as familiar as the view from his bedroom window at Sodhail – a view that seemed not a hundred miles distant but a hundred light years.

The events of the previous day played over and over in his mind; there were even moments where he thought that he might be dreaming. Or hallucinating. Or making too much of it. The word 'spy' had never been used. Nor had the word 'agent'. Or even 'espionage'. But then, if he thought about it, it was unlikely that those words were ever actually uttered. Not by the people involved. It was absurd! And yet the Cambridge Spy Ring was something that had given rise to all kinds of speculation over the years. Burgess, Maclean and Philby were now notorious enemies of the state with much talk of fourth and fifth men. But Oxford? He was unaware of anything going on there, but then why should he be? Here he was, innocently studying Estate Management at an obscure Scottish college. He had travelled to Oxford to see an old school friend who had invited him out to dinner and suggested that his Scottish castle could be used as a 'safe house' for 'foreign students'. Gordon had used the words 'safe house', hadn't he? But did he just mean somewhere that the offspring of foreign diplomats would feel safe? That was what he called them – not 'double agents' or 'spies' or anything quite so emotive. Charlie had seen *On Her Majesty's Secret Service* only a few months ago – the latest in the James Bond franchise. This could not be happening to him. He was not a diplomat or a politician. He was – he had to admit – nothing more than a glorified farmer.

Time and again, while he sat cooped up in the immovable train, he cast his mind back to the previous evening and the conversation at the Randolph. Before long, when they could see that he would take more than a little convincing, Alex Jesmond and Gordon Mackenzie had taken him back to their lodgings off the Woodstock Road. He had found himself in a typical student house that smelled of stale sheets and old carpet. There, sitting on the edge of a rickety bed, which in light of the day's revelations made him feel particularly uneasy, he had been able to ask innumerable questions, trying to see through the haze brought on by one glass of claret too many. Some of the answers seemed highly implausible. None of them offered any kind of precise detail. He was also aware that he had been told nothing that would in any way incriminate either of them. So much of what they said was of a general nature, and when he tried to pin down in his own mind just what they had asked of him, it remained vague and in the broadest of terms.

It appeared that throughout their first year, both Alex and Gordon had been befriended by one particular history tutor who, at the beginning of their second year, had begun entertaining them at his house in Olney. The 'entertainment' was innocent enough – musical evenings and poetry readings. Through the passage of time it became evident, they said, that the tutor was 'well connected in certain quarters'. That's how Alex put it. Charlie understood that the universities of Oxford and Cambridge were well-known recruiting grounds for MI5, and what Alex and Gordon were saying led him to believe that if neither of them had been 'recruited' (which they both denied) then they had certainly been sounded out. But for what?

Gordon was at pains to point out that neither he nor Alex was interested in working for any foreign power. Neither had they axes to grind in terms of political affiliations. Alex explained that since their days at Egglestone Academy they had both vowed to do whatever they could for their country and that things were 'moving on'. The Cold War could not last forever. Charlie began to piece together little nuggets from his school days – small things which, when added up, might have given a clue as to the political stance of both Alex and Gordon. They were both members of the debating society; they both ran as candidates in 'mock elections'. They were always talking about politics but even these facts, knowing what he now knew, would hardly have foreshadowed future events. They were not, as far as he knew, connected to any political party; that much they had both been silent about at school.

All they were asking of Charlie, they said, was whether or not he would be willing to allow Castle Sodhail – conveniently placed off the beaten track – to house certain 'foreign students' who needed between-term accommodation. These students would appear in twos and threes and would need to stay for just as long as the break lasted – usually just a week or two, though in summer, two to three months. If that was too long they could make other arrangements. It was important that nobody knew the students' backgrounds. If he were asked, the easiest thing, they suggested, would be to say that they were paying guests – that much would be true. These were tough times, nobody could argue with that, and Charlie was taking them in as a means of supplementing his income. 'Foreign exchange students', he could say.

When he asked what would be his involvement, apart from providing accommodation and a hearty Scottish breakfast, they confirmed that confidentiality would be the only requirement; it would not be necessary for him to know any details about his 'guests', but he would have Gordon and Alex's assurance that all was 'above board' and he would in no way be implicated, officially or otherwise. This would be a financial arrangement, as simple as that. He would be doing his country immeasurable service and he would be well recompensed for his trouble – especially in the longer holidays. The 'students' would be delivered to him and collected when they needed to return to college.

After a fitful night's sleep in Oxford, the whole scenario kept spinning round in his head. There were moments when he wondered if he should seriously consider it. His father was moving on and the estate would be in his own hands within a few months. A little extra income would always come in handy; in fact, Alex and Gordon gave him to understand that the income would be rather more than 'a little extra'.

And yet, whenever he thought that it really might be worth considering, some inner voice advised caution.

He had left the house the following morning in a state of supreme confusion. For Alex he felt little. He had known him only vaguely at school and so there was nothing about his behaviour that would cause Charlie to alter his judgement of him one way or the other. But Gordon had been a close friend – as close a friend as he had – and yet how much did he *really* know him? Within the past twenty-four hours he had had to come to terms with his friend's homosexuality, and the possibility that he was working for MI5. Were the two things linked? That had certainly been the case in the Burgess and Maclean scenario, hadn't it? Was Gordon cast in the same mould? He clearly did not know him at all. He gave an involuntary laugh. The woman sitting across the carriage from him looked up from her book. He coughed, partly in embarrassment and partly to mask the laugh. The woman returned to her book.

He was jolted out of his thoughts by the jolting of the train. They were moving at last. The guard came through the carriage apologising yet again and saying that they should be arriving in Inverness in a couple of hours. Charlie glanced at his watch. It was one o'clock. He should be home by late afternoon. It might still be daylight, but probably not. And then he remembered that Eleanor would be wondering where he was. In the confusion and the anxiety of it all he had lost all awareness of time. He hoped she would understand; that somehow she would work out that his train had been delayed. Yes, of course she would; she was not prone to hysteria or recriminations. She would be there, as usual, ready to welcome him. He could not remember when he had wanted or needed her close to him quite so much; to tell him that life was back to normal, that he really was not going mad and that he did not have to be a part of the world created and apparently relished by his school friends. But could he, or should he, tell her what had happened?

He had left Alex and Gordon the previous afternoon. At Gordon's suggestion they had all three gone off to the Head of the River for a pint. A riverside pub, he would normally have found it charming and admired the picturesque setting, but that day he barely noticed his surroundings. They asked him what he wanted to eat, but he found that he had no appetite. Blaming the heavy meal of the night before, he stuck with the beer, but after a couple of pints his head swam more than ever and seemed to be filled with a thick and impenetrable fog. At half past two, he got up to leave. Alex shook him more than usually firmly by the hand; Gordon gave him a hug and explained that he did not have to give an answer to their question immediately. Alex told him to think about it and let them know. If he spoke to them on the phone he was to say that 'There were rooms available in Scotland', that was all. It was not a good idea to enter into more fulsome conversation since they might be overheard, nor should he put anything down in writing; that would most definitely be a bad idea. They were quite confident about his security, but less trusting of their own. Charlie felt sick to the pit of his stomach. He was a countryman, not accustomed to the language of international espionage, if that was, indeed, what it was. Why on earth would they think that he would be interested?

The train from Oxford to London left on time, and he took the tube from Paddington to King's Cross where he killed time by drinking countless cups of coffee and reading copies of *Country Life* and *Farmer's Weekly* that he had bought at W.H. Smith. At eight o'clock he boarded the overnight sleeper to Inverness. Not that he had a berth. The entire journey would be undertaken in a seat by the window where he would have to get as comfortable as he could, using his anorak as a blanket.

The train was packed with folk returning from their Easter break. He had slept only fitfully and now, umpteen hours later, the events of the previous day seemed as far off as those of his childhood. He got up from his seat and stretched, then wandered off in search of the buffet car, but found it closed; the metal grill pulled down and bolted to the top of the counter. Leaning on the steel bar that ran the full length of the large window, he gazed out at the steeply undulating countryside. The train had finally reached the Highlands and at last the rugged terrain seemed more familiar, more welcoming. Strange how some people found the landscape up here forbidding and threatening. To him it was quite the reverse – a land of capricious moods when it came to the weather, but one that was as stolid and as reliable as the mountains themselves. This was where he belonged; this was where he felt comfortable. It seemed a million miles from Oxford and the milling throng, and for that he could not have been more deeply grateful.

14

Oxford

Easter Monday 1970

> 'It is better to suffer wrong than to do it, and happier to be sometimes cheated than not to trust.'
>
> Samuel Johnson, *The Rambler*, 1750

'Do you think he'll go for it?' asked Gordon.

'You know him better than I do,' snapped Alex Jesmond. 'But from where I was sitting I would have thought it extremely unlikely. He seemed shocked at the very prospect. Out of his depth.'

The two Oxford students were sitting on a bench outside the Head of the River, gazing at their empty glasses.

Gordon looked thoughtful, his usual ebullience muted. 'I don't think we should have asked him.'

'But it was your idea. You said you knew someone with a suitable property, and you got on with him at school. I always thought he was a bit wet.'

'That's because you didn't know him well. There's a difference between being wet and being cautious; Charlie falls into the latter camp. He can be tough when the need arises.'

Alex grunted. 'Well, he didn't look very tough this weekend.'

Gordon did his best to account for his friend's reactions. 'How would you have reacted? You live in the Highlands of Scotland and you're asked down to Oxford, where you've never been before, by a school friend you haven't seen for two years and he asks you if you're interested in being a spy. You're hardly likely to say, "Oh, yes please; when do I start?" are you?'

'We didn't ask him to be a spy, for God's sake. Far from it. Just to help us out with a little accommodation. We really shouldn't have used the words "safe house" – I should think that was what put him off. Far too Len Deighton. Anyway, I reckon that if we don't hear from him in a couple of weeks we should just let it go. He's clearly not the right material.'

'Because he's not Oxbridge?'

'No; because he doesn't have the mind-set.'

'And what sort of mind-set is that?' asked Gordon, beginning to be irritated.

'The mind-set that wants to do something; to make a difference.'

Gordon sighed. 'And do you think we really can? I wonder sometimes.'

'Don't you start, or I'll think that Charlie Macwimp has begun to change your mind.'

The further degeneration of the conversation into a trading of insults was curtailed by the arrival of a third party; an older man, in his forties, wearing horn-rimmed spectacles. His receding hair was cropped short and his wiry frame made only marginally more bulky by an ill-fitting donkey jacket. Tight jeans and black suede loafers completed the picture. He had a copy of *Melody Maker* tucked under his left arm.

'Afternoon,' he said, as he sat down, dropping the paper on to the table in front of them. 'You two look the picture of happiness. Fancy another drink?'

'Bar's closed,' muttered Alex, at which point the man took a bottle of beer out of each pocket.

'You're not allowed to do that,' said Gordon, as a reflex action.

The new arrival shot him a pitying look. 'I don't think I'm likely to be arrested, do you?' He took a bottle opener from his pocket, flipped off the bottle caps and poured them each half a glass, saving half the contents of one of the bottles for himself. 'Cheers!' He took a swig, then set down the bottle alongside his paper.

'Judging by your expressions you haven't had a very successful mission.'

'No,' confirmed Alex. 'Bloody hopeless.'

'Gordon?' The man looked enquiringly at him.

'My mistake. I thought he might be interested.' Gordon brightened. 'He still might; you never know. That's the one thing about Charlie Stuart; every now and then he can surprise you.'

'Not this time,' muttered Alex, before draining the contents of his glass in one.

The man looked unperturbed. 'Well, let's just let it go, shall we? If it's not his bag then it's not his bag.' He looked more serious. 'I'm presuming you told him nothing of any consequence? No details, no reasons?'

'None,' confirmed Alex. 'It's just a shame. The house is in the perfect spot.'

Gordon said nothing, but turned his glass around and around, seemingly unwilling to toast the moment.

The man put his empty bottle down on the table and picked up the paper. 'I suggest we do nothing for a few months. If we hear nothing from him then we'll know he's not interested. If you told him nothing—'

Gordon interrupted. 'Look; the one thing we can do is trust him. Charlie has never ratted on anyone about anything. He'll not breathe a word to a soul. I know that. We could just have asked him if he could put up a few students and said nothing more. I didn't want to do that. I felt we had to at least let him know that it wasn't . . . well . . . quite so straightforward. But he's as reliable as the tide. And loyal. I asked him not to say anything and I am absolutely certain he won't. Not to anyone.'

'In which case,' said the man, 'we have nothing to worry about. Except finding another house.' He got up from the table. 'And who knows, in a few months, maybe even a year or two, your friend Charlie might be in a position to change his mind. And there are various ways of convincing him to do so.'

'I'm not willing to—' interjected Gordon.

'Nothing heavy. Nothing like that at all. Just . . . well . . . temptations. Incentives. You know the sort of thing.'

The man tucked the magazine under his arm and made to leave. Then he turned for a moment and addressed them both. 'They are a useful way of helping us out in the long run you know; events and encounters that allow us to see things more . . . clearly.'

15

Castle Sodhail

April 1970

'Now hatred is by far the longest pleasure;
Men love in haste, but they detest at leisure.'
Lord Byron, *Don Juan*, 1819–24

It had taken several days for Charlie to recover his equilibrium after the visit to Oxford. He thought hard about whether or not to share his concerns, and Gordon's revelations, with Eleanor, but two things stopped him. First, he did not want to worry her or cloud the water and, second, he still felt some kind of loyalty towards his old school friend. He took the view that in a few weeks the whole thing would be forgotten about and that he could carry on his life – his new life – as normal.

The Oxford trip had taught him two things above all else: that he was at his happiest in the Highlands, and that he was at his most content in the company of Eleanor. It was on one of those days when he sat high upon Creag Sodhail, gazing out over the loch, as clear in his mind as the view before him.

He would not ask her without first thinking things through; working out his true feelings for her and considering the wisdom and constraints of a life to be spent in a place where most people would consider themselves isolated; cut off from the mainstream. They were both very young; at twenty, did either of them really know their mind? Were they grown-up enough to make such a decision? Neither did he assume that she would say 'yes'. She had expressed her love for him, true enough, but did that constitute a lifetime commitment? Did it imply that she would be happy in the long term at Sodhail? He knew that there was always a chance that she would laugh at him for suggesting they tie the knot so quickly.

What he also knew was that he had to tackle his father about his own plans for the immediate future; while he knew that he and Charlotte had been planning on moving out, it was by no means clear just when that would be, or where they would go. The meeting would be uncomfortable, of that there was no doubt, but he would have to bite the bullet. If he were man enough to take on the estate, he would have to be man enough to face his father.

He waited until Charlotte was out, and tapped tentatively on the door of Angus's study. For several days he had gone over in his mind just what he would say, and which questions needed to be asked and satisfactorily answered – from the point of view of both men. Now, at the moment of truth, these questions seemed no more than a jumble in his mind. At the sound of his father's 'Yes?' he opened the door and went in.

Angus Stuart had his back to the door and was staring out of the window. As his son entered, he turned round. Charlie saw a single tear running down his father's cheek. It was quickly brushed aside. 'Quite a draught from this window; you'll need to get it repaired.'

The shock of his father expressing emotion, at least in his son's presence and, at the same time, mentioning the impending hand-over of the castle took Charlie by surprise. Before he had a chance to get his thoughts in order his father said, 'Sit down; we need to talk things through.'

Charlie did as he was bid, lowering himself into the leather armchair that faced his father's large oak desk. It was like being back in the headmaster's study: the hairs on the back of his neck stood on end; there was a clamminess to his hands – feelings that, mercifully he had not experienced for two years. Angus sat in his desk chair and took out his pipe. Charlie prayed that it was already filled, or the wait – until he had filled and lit it to his satisfaction – would be interminable. Thankfully the pipe was full, and after a few draws, the Swan Vesta match was shaken until extinguished and deposited in an ashtray. Slowly his father reappeared through the blue-grey haze to which his inhalations and ministrations had given rise.

'You'll have been wondering, I suppose?'

'Sorry?' Charlie thought he knew where the conversation was going, but wanted to be sure before he committed himself.

'When Charlotte and I are moving out.'

Charlie shrugged; it seemed an easier option than offering words that might be misconstrued.

His father continued, 'You know that I don't want to?'

Charlie sat perfectly still, meeting his father's eye with a steady gaze; he did not want to admit to knowing anything, lest his motives be thought inappropriate, and yet he wanted his father to see that he had his full attention. He had never felt completely at ease with him, but there were some things they did have in common – the future of Castle Sodhail being one of them.

Angus sucked on his pipe, then took it from his mouth and cradled it in both hands as if he were trying to warm himself by the fire. Gazing at the smouldering tobacco, he spoke as though he was thinking out loud. 'I was sixteen when I inherited this place. Sixteen. Far too young; at least that's what the locals said, and not without good reason. But with help I managed to turn the place around – not straight away, and not without making a lot of mistakes. And a few enemies. I grew up fast. I had to. And with your mother at my side we managed to make a go of it.' He paused, as if reviewing the years that had gone by and appraising their worth.

'I didn't imagine that I would leave the place so soon.' There was an anguished look upon his face, and it was clear to Charlie that this was not a decision he was happy to be making. 'But life changes; circumstances change, and I have to think of someone else now, as well.'

Charlie had planned on remaining silent for as long as possible, but he found himself blurting out, 'Charlotte?'

His father nodded. 'I thought, when we married, that it might change her view of this place; that she might feel more proprietorial, but it seems that aside from entertaining her friends here at weekends, she finds the surroundings less than congenial.'

Charlie felt suddenly angry. 'But the fountain in the drive; the decorating . . . ?'

'Yes, I know. I thought that if she had some say in the way things were done – made changes of her own – that it might make her more attached to the place; give her a sense of belonging. It seems not. She's quite determined.'

Siding with his father for perhaps the first time in his life, Charlie said, 'But this place means everything to you. Isn't it worth fighting for?'

'Of course it is. That's what I've been doing for the last thirty years; it's why I didn't have to fight in the war – because I was working on the land. This land. My land. And now, your land.'

Angus Stuart was always a sturdy man, of robust constitution, but the man who sat before Charlie now seemed a crumpled shadow of his former self. Charlie felt angry that this woman could come in and reduce his father to an ineffectual cipher.

'So you're just going to leave?' asked Charlie.

'I'm going where I have to go. I have made my bed . . .' There was an uneasy silence that lasted several seconds. 'I prize one thing above all others, Charlie. Loyalty. There is loyalty to a place, and there is loyalty to a person. The loyalty to a person must always come first, even if . . .' His words petered out. He seemed unable, or unwilling, to finish the sentence.

'Dad; you don't have to. You can stay; we can work together.' Charlie knew that what he had just said was, at the very least, wishful thinking, and his father's expression confirmed the fact.

'Charlie! Two chiefs and not enough Indians? You know it wouldn't work.'

Charlie paused for a moment, marshalling his thoughts, then he asked, 'Where will you go?'

'Edinburgh.' Then, seeing the look of horror on his son's face, he added: 'I'd hoped Mallaig, or Oban, or Ullapool, but Charlotte has her sights set on the bright lights.'

'Do you know when?' The look of disbelief on Charlie's face did not lift.

'By Christmas. We'll move at the end of November or early December.'

'Have you found anywhere?'

'Charlotte's found a house near the centre of the city. It should suit her requirements.'

'And you? What about *your* requirements?'

His father shrugged. 'I'll get used to it. As long as you keep this place going, I'll reconcile myself to the fact that at least I achieved something. And I might drop in from time to time – when I'm invited.'

'But you're only forty-six. You can't just give up. I mean, how will you earn a living?'

'I'll try for a post as factor somewhere. I've plenty of experience at turning round estates. That must count for something. I'll find something in the Borders. I'm not that old.'

Charlie could not believe what he was hearing. Castle Sodhail belonged to his father, *was* his father. And yet here he was relinquishing it on the whim of a woman who . . . Charlie did not like to ask if his father still loved his second wife. It was not the sort of question a son asks his father, though it seemed clear that the spark which always used to be there, the light in his father's eye, had dimmed almost to the point at which it was extinguished. For a man who had always regarded loyalty and constancy as vital attributes in life – something Charlie did not need his father to articulate; it was implicit in his actions – this must be a bitter pill to swallow. He had clearly been blinded by love at first, and it had lasted for several years, but eventually he must have seen Charlotte for what she really was – a woman in love with a certain lifestyle rather than a certain man. In love with the romantic *thought* of living in a castle but not with the reality. By upholding his own principles, Angus Stuart was having to forgo the one thing in life into which he had poured more of himself than he believed possible; the one thing he loved more than any other.

His pipe had gone out; he seemed to have little inclination to re-light it. The two men sat silently for a few moments, and then Charlie asked, 'Would you be surprised if I said that I wanted to get married?'

For the first time during their conversation, a look of something approaching pleasure came into his father's face. 'Eleanor?'

Charlie nodded.

'Good.'

'You don't mind, then?'

'No. There will be some who will tell you you're too young, but there are always wise-acres.' Angus got up and walked to the window. As he gazed out over the loch – a view that was achingly familiar and soon to be denied him – he said: 'Mistakes are not just the province of the young. They say that with age comes wisdom. Well in my experience, as the old song goes, "It ain't necessarily so."' He turned from the window and faced his son. 'Good luck, Charlie. I hope you'll both be very happy.'

'Dad. I'm sorry. I mean, for the way things have turned out for you. I just . . . don't know what to say.'

'No need. Not your fault.' He looked Charlie in the eye. 'I've watched you grow over the last few years, and not just physically. You've changed; matured. Oh, you're still very young but you've got your head screwed on. Just make sure you're certain of your own mind where . . . you know . . . matters of the heart are concerned.'

Charlie was emphatic. 'I am. I've never been more sure of anything.'

His father nodded. 'Good. She's a nice girl, Eleanor. I hope the Fitzallans will be happy.'

'Yes. There's just one thing . . .' Charlie managed a weak smile. 'I haven't asked her yet.'

16

Invergarry House
September 1970

''Tis less to be wondered at that women may marry off in haste, for if they took time to consider and reflect upon it, they seldom would.'

Mary Astell, *Some Reflections Upon Marriage*, 1700

Her father had always said that she should not consider marriage until she was twenty-one, but when a pretty daughter sits upon the arm of her father's easy chair, drapes her arm around his shoulder and lays her head alongside his, only the hardest-hearted parent can remain implacable. When that daughter also informs her parent that she intends to give up university a year early, before attaining her degree, then the most likely result is a confrontation that will, in all likelihood, end in tears.

Robert Fitzallan was no stronger than the average father when it came to withstanding the persuasive powers of his daughter, and having ascertained that there was no possible chance of her waiting the extra six months, nor of her falling in love with anyone else, he finally acquiesced to her wishes and, with a sigh of resignation and a kiss to the top of her head, gave in gracefully and said that he hoped she would be very happy.

On Saturday 19th September, Charlie and Eleanor were married at Strath Carron Kirk. The reception was held in a flower-garlanded marquee in the garden at Invergarry House (to Charlotte Stuart's chagrin) and was attended by a hundred guests on whom the sun shone as if upon the righteous. Gordon was on the guest list, but Alex Jesmond, unsurprisingly, was not.

The midges had finally retreated, and Davina, Lady Fitzallan, expressed relief that her daughter had not opted for a July wedding, when they would all have been eaten alive. Charlotte wore an expression that indicated she was being eaten by something else. Angus did his best to ignore it. Murdo and Mrs Murdo looked happier than Charlie could ever recall having seen them – for a few years at any rate.

Charlie had asked Eleanor to marry him just before they went off in separate directions at the end of the Easter holidays. His anxiety over whether or not she would say 'yes' proved unnecessary. A few years previously, he mused, she would have teased him and kept him waiting. But he was relieved that in this instance she did nothing of the kind; instead she flung her arms around his neck and hugged him. Then she stepped back from him, held his hands tightly and explained that her father would not be happy, having made it clear on more than one occasion that he would prefer her to be twenty-one before she committed herself.

'So we'll have to wait?' he had asked.

'Hopefully not,' she replied, with a glint in her eye and the confidence of a daughter whose father was at least partially wound around her smallest finger.

The loch glistened in the late summer sunshine, as if showing off to the wedding guests, many of whom remarked on the delights of September weather in Scotland. Most were from Eleanor's side of the family, but regardless of their affinity, the atmosphere, except around Charlotte, for whom nothing seemed satisfactory, was buoyant and happy.

To Angus's embarrassment, the Stuarts senior left the wedding feast early. 'Charlotte's not feeling too well,' he confided to Davina Fitzallan, who had the grace to look suitably disappointed. Always the consummate hostess, Lady Fitzallan espoused the hope that Mrs Stuart senior would soon recover her spirits and her health and that they would all get together again before too long. She managed to convey this with both dignity and sincerity, helped by the fact that such a reunion was unlikely, bearing in mind the predisposition of her opposing number, and her imminent departure in the direction of Scotland's capital city.

Dabbing her forehead and leaning heavily on her husband's arm, Charlotte tottered off in the direction of the Austin 1100, but not before assuring the new wife that, once the honeymoon was over, she would be happy to offer her the benefit of her experience in interior design when it came to decorating the castle to suit their own particular tastes. 'Though you will,' she added, 'discover that it is so much more elegant than it was. I doubt you will want to make many changes, at least to the rooms that I've managed to get my hands on.'

Although she may have left university before her further education had been completed, Eleanor's grasp of manners and diplomacy was thorough, comprehensive and well practised. While her father might be indulgent and forgiving of the occasional solecism, her mother moulded her daughter's manners with a rigour worthy of a local justice of the peace. Eleanor thanked her stepmother-in-law politely and said that she would most certainly be in touch should the need arise.

Satisfied that she had done her duty, even if that did not stretch to enduring the evening's festivities to the full, Charlotte slid into the car, which was driven away by her husband. Charlie could see her in full flow, her wide-brimmed hat bobbing like a cork upon the water. He also noticed that his father's head was, as usual nowadays, cowed. He wondered if that was the way all marriages ended up, then banished the thought from his mind as being both unworthy and unbearable.

They honeymooned in Venice; somewhere Eleanor had always wanted to go. It was, she said, the beginning of a dream.

17

Hotel Danieli, Venice

September 1970

'I stood in Venice, on the Bridge of Sighs;
A palace and a prison on each hand.'
Lord Byron, *Childe Harold's Pilgrimage*, 1812–18

They could not have afforded to stay there had they paid the bill themselves. To Charlie's surprise his father had slipped an envelope under his bedroom door a week before they were due to be married. It contained a brief message, written on Castle Sodhail headed paper:

My dear Charlie,

While I applaud your sensible intention that your honeymoon should not cost so much that it becomes a worry, I think that bed and breakfast in a backwater is not the best place to begin a marriage. I hope you do not mind that I have booked for you a double room in the Hotel Danieli. I have heard that it is central, comfortable and, I hope, as good a place as any to start your married life together.

Good luck and my very best wishes.

Yours aye,

Dad

The containment of emotion and the thoughtful intentions on his father's part moved Charlie to tears. He knew that he and

Eleanor would have been happy wherever they had been accommodated, but the fact that his father wished them to enjoy a little luxury at the start of their married life he found unexpectedly touching. The sadness at his father's premature departure from Sodhail would not be assuaged, but it heartened Charlie that in spite of a bleak prospect ahead in his own life, Angus Stuart had, at this moment, turned his attention to the immediate comfort of his son.

Eleanor gasped as the bellboy opened the door to their room. The tall windows that looked out across the lagoon were open. They were framed by long brocade drapes of faded ivory, heavy with tassels and thickly lined. Through them the sound of vaporetti and gondolas plying their trade, the muffled voices of a thousand tourists and the clanging bells of churches and cathedrals resonated in their ears. Walking towards them and looking out across the water to her right, she could see the sun glinting on the gilded orb of what would come to be one of her favourite Italian names: 'Santa Maria Della Salute'. The sunlight was dazzling – bouncing off the water like a million stars, shimmering and sparkling under the fleet of little boats. The bellboy put down their suitcases and slipped out of the room – he knew that honeymoon couples invariably forgot to tip; their preoccupations were elsewhere.

As the door closed, Charlie crept up behind his wife and put his arms around her waist, gazing with her upon the scene in front of them, mesmerised by the bustle, the brightness of the light and the other-worldliness of it all.

'Is it real?' he murmured.

'Oh, I hope so,' she sighed. 'It's so beautiful.'

They did not dine in splendour that evening, but ordered, instead, a bottle of champagne and some strawberries for their room. It was a night that Charlie would never forget; for all the right reasons. He was here, in a dream-like city with a dream-like girl. His girl. The fact that she had turned, if not from an ugly duckling, then certainly from a girl of whom he had thought little into a woman of whom he thought the world, and had said 'yes' to his proposal, he still found hard to believe.

Over the next few days they did all the things that tourists do in Venice. They took the lift to the top of the Campanile and looked out across the many-peopled square towards St Mark's Basilica; they drank chocolate in Café Florian and were astonished at the price; sighed at the Bridge of Sighs, ambled down pathways beside shaded backwaters, peeping into bakeries and fruiterers, confident that the sign 'Per San Marco' would help them regain their bearings. They bought carnival masks on the Rialto Bridge and visited the glass factories at Murano, and Charlie watched Eleanor's face as she gazed with wonder upon the glass blowers, her pink cheeks seeming even pinker by the light of their furnaces.

They took a trip in a gondola, irritated only by the fact that the gondolier seemed to want them to disembark only forty minutes into their one-hour tour. They shook their heads and frowned in admonishment, as the oarsman shrugged and turned into another canal, murmuring '*viaggio di nozze*'.

By the end of the week Charlie had grown so used to the feeling of her hand in his that it felt odd when they were separated even for a few minutes.

He could not ever remember feeling so completely at ease in another person's company; so calm, serene even. Only when he thought about Sodhail did a nervous tension cloud his mind. But he put it to one side. As a couple they would have many unfamiliar bridges to cross on their return home, but that would come soon enough. Right here, right now, it was just the two of them and the cares of the Highlands seemed a world away.

On their last evening they dined on the roof terrace at the top of the Danieli. They had been ready to go out; to amble off in search of a small bistro, a glass of Soave and a plate of pasta, when the tall, elegant hotel manager had accosted them in reception and informed them that a table had been reserved for them on the terrazzo. Charlie explained that there must be some mistake, but the manager had been insistent: the table had been booked for them and the bill was settled.

Unable to extricate themselves, Eleanor and Charlie had thanked him very much and asked if they could go up straight away. The manager tilted his head on one side and smiled. 'But of course; just as you wish,' his accented English adding to his solicitude.

'How exciting,' murmured Eleanor as they climbed the stairs. 'A secret benefactor.'

'I thought Dad had done more than enough,' said Charlie. 'Still; good of him to provide us with a grand finale.'

The meal was all they could have expected. Chilled Pol Roger replaced the Soave; prawns and lobster the pasta. As the sun set over campanile and dome, over palazzo and piazza, the two of them gazed on the view and upon each other, wondering if life could ever get any better.

At ten o'clock, the waiter, depositing small cups of espresso in front of them, asked if there was anything else they would like – a Vin Santo, or a Verlit perhaps?

Shaking their heads in unison and smiling beatifically, they both declined.

'Ah!' said the head waiter. 'A note. I have a note for you.' He slid his hand into his waistcoat pocket and pulled out a small cream envelope bearing the crest of the hotel upon its sealed flap. '*Buona notte*,' he said, bowing gently. 'I hope you have had a wonderful evening.'

'We have,' replied Eleanor. 'Oh, we have.'

The waiter departed, leaving just the two of them in their corner of the terrazzo, the only other diners an elderly couple at the far end of the roof terrace.

'What is it?' asked Eleanor.

'The bill for the wine probably. Maybe that wasn't covered.' Charlie slid his finger under the flap and tore open the envelope, withdrawing the folded piece of paper it contained.

He read it and then murmured, 'Good God!'

Eleanor looked at him in questioning silence.

Charlie turned the piece of paper round so that she could read the message written upon it:

Felices ter et amplius
Quos irrupta tenet copula nec malis
Divolsus querimoniis
Suprema citius solvet amor die.

'What does it mean?'

'We were taught it at school. It's Horace. I was never very good at Latin, but I remember that one. Probably because it seemed unlikely ever to happen to me. '

'And?' Eleanor looked at Charlie questioningly.

'Thrice blessed (and more) are they whom an unbroken bond holds and whose love, never strained by nasty quarrels, will not slip until their dying day.'

'Oh! How lovely. I didn't know that your father knew any Latin.'

'No. Neither did I. But I know someone else who does.'

18

Castle Sodhail

December 1970

'In nature there are neither rewards nor punishments – there are consequences.'

Robert G. Ingersoll, *Some Reasons Why*, 1881

The sight of a removal lorry in the drive of the castle gave rise to mixed emotions in Charlie. The fact that anything should be taken away from Castle Sodhail seemed strangely alien – over the last half century the Stuart family had added to its contents rather than subtracted, and while Angus Stuart had been determined to leave behind his own father's desk and various goods and chattels that he felt belonged to the dwelling rather than to himself, there still seemed to be much to extract from the place that had been his home since birth.

Reflecting on his own feelings for the place, Charlie understood that his father must be possessed of even greater proprietorial instincts. Not that these were given more than short shrift by Charlotte who seemed to regard the wrapping and packing of a dozen David Hicks cushions as being of far greater importance than the safe passage of a large Joseph Farquharson scene of sheep in the snow, bathed in evening sunlight, that had hung in Angus's study for as long as Charlie could remember.

'Why you want to take that old thing to Edinburgh, I can't understand. It will look quite out of place in the drawing room.

Can't you leave it here? If you must have a Scottish artist on the wall, why don't you buy a Samuel Peploe?'

Charlie heard his father mutter under his breath, 'If I could afford one I would.'

Her hearing was as sharp as that of a bat. 'Or a Fergusson then. You can get some very nice prints. Not for the drawing room, I wouldn't want them there, but for your study.'

At this Angus's expression remained impassive. The Farquharson had been left to him by his father and forever reminded him of walks in the snow with Old Rory when he was a boy. But sentimentality – certainly about her husband's affairs and former life – was foreign to Charlotte Stuart. For her the prospect of finally moving into a Georgian townhouse, just behind Edinburgh's George Street, was the only thing that had kept her going these past few months. Finally the moment had arrived and a note of triumph crept into her voice.

Charlie could bear it no longer. He slipped out of the castle and down the track to the old lodge where he knew he would find Murdo, cleaning his guns or mending a pheasant pen – something that would take his mind off the exodus being enacted at the castle.

'I wondered when you'd turn up,' murmured Murdo, not taking his eyes off the landing net he was endeavouring to repair.

'That's not very welcoming.'

'I thought you'd be glad to see the back of her.'

'I am. I mean, well . . .'

'You'll miss your faither.'

'I know.'

The two kept silence for a few moments before Murdo looked up from his net and said, 'I'll bet you never thought it would come tae this. Not so soon, at any rate.'

'No. I know we've never really been close, but he's changed over the past year. I feel sorry for him.'

'Aye, well you'll nae be on your ain there. 'Tis a pretty pass when a woman can force a laird out of his ain hame.'

'Sad really. But all the fight seems to have gone out of him.'

'I'd noticed.' Murdo got up from the old chair on which he had been sitting and made to hang up the net on a nail protruding from the wall – a wall adorned with assorted antlers and foxes' heads that had once hung in the castle but which, on Charlotte's instructions, had been summarily evicted. 'Dreadful things,' she had said. 'Like living in an animal mausoleum.'

Charlie had felt some sympathy for his stepmother's feelings, but none for the unceremonious delivery of her verdict, neither for the speed with which she had banished them. Murdo, conscious of the past that they depicted, had rescued them from the gardener's wheelbarrows – four of them, bound for the bonfire – and transferred them to his own private retreat where Charlotte was unlikely to encounter them.

The net secured upon its peg, Murdo surveyed the menagerie that adorned the walls. 'Aye, well, these wee fellers can go back up to the castle now,' he muttered.

'Mmm. I'll wait and see what Eleanor says,' said Charlie.

'But these are your heritage; your birthright,' growled Murdo indignantly.

'I know but . . . I'm not sure that . . .' He was trying to avoid giving offence to the ghillie, aware that he was dealing with the fruits of his and his ancestors' labours, when he saw the twinkle in the older man's eye.

'Are you teasing me?' he asked.

'Jest a wee bit.' Murdo smiled. 'I've never been very fond o' dead heads mysel'; 'twas only the fact that she removed them so swiftly and that she has no feelings for your faither's inheritance – other than what it can get for her – that upset me. Ye can leave them here; I've got kind of used to them.'

'I've never heard you speak about her before,' said Charlie.

'Nay, she disnae warrant a lot of time spent thinking about her, though perhaps I should'na say that. 'Tis none of my business. Not any more. Not since your mother . . .' Murdo stopped and checked himself. Then he cleared his throat and asked, 'When will they be leaving?'

Charlie looked at his watch. 'In about half an hour. Are you coming to see them off?'

'I'd rather not, but I'll no neglect my duty to your faither. I'll keep out o' the way o' yon woman, but I'll bid your faither farewell. T'would be rude not to after all these years. He *is* my brother-in-law. There are those who say he *was* my brother-in-law, but Fortune would not want me to forget . . .' His voice trailed off again, and he turned to pick up another net, avoiding any further eye contact with Charlie. 'You get on up to the castle, I'll be there shortly to see him off.'

Charlie left the hunting lodge – the name they always gave to the Murdochs' glorified stone-built shed – and walked back up the track alongside the loch. A skein of greylag geese came honking across the water and disappeared over a clump of pines. It was almost as if they were giving his father a fly-past, albeit a perfunctory one.

He knew that in his heart he should be feeling joy at finally becoming laird – a title that Murdo and the other locals would now bestow upon him – but there was a deep-seated sadness in his heart at his father's departure. Had it been undertaken willingly, the feeling would have been quite different. As it was, he felt, as yet, more a sense of loss than of gain. It was something he hoped would not linger. There was, beneath the sadness, a faint degree of excitement and apprehension. It was a feeling he hoped would be allowed to grow, without being constrained by regrets. If he were to make a success of his tenure here it would have to.

As he rounded the corner at the end of the loch, the castle hove into view. The removal lorry had gone, and the granite towers were caught for a moment in a brief ray of sunshine on a day that had hitherto been as grey as his mood. His spirits lifted, and continued to rise as Eleanor drew into the apron of gravel in front of Sodhail in her battered Morris Minor – a present from her father on their return from honeymoon.

'You took your time,' he said. 'I thought you were only picking up a few things for supper.'

'I got delayed,' she said. 'Am I in time to say goodbye?'

'Just,' he said, kissing her gently on the top of her head. He would have continued the conversation, were it not for the increasing volume of another exchange echoing from the doorway of the castle.

Unsurprisingly, it was Charlotte who was in full flow. 'We said we'd be there in time for tea, but at this rate we'll be lucky to be there by nightfall.' She bustled out into the drive with a large mohair blanket under one arm and a newly purchased Yorkshire Terrier puppy in the other, opened the rear door of the Austin 1100 and deposited them both on the back seat before slamming the door and shooting a pained look at Angus, who was coming out of the front door with one arm clutching half a dozen horn-handled shepherd's crooks and the other cradling a large bottle of malt whisky. He looked, thought Charlie, like Adam being turned out of Eden.

Silently, Angus deposited the bottle and the sticks in the back of the car, taking care not to let the dog escape and closing the door as quietly and purposefully as Charlotte had slammed it. Her chatter did not subside as Angus walked over to where Charlie stood with his arm around his new wife.

Angus bent and kissed Eleanor on the cheek before holding out his hand to his son. 'There we are then,' he said. 'All ready for the off.' He turned and looked up at the grey turrets, stark against the watery sky, and murmured, 'Take care of it.'

He took a breath to continue, but something stopped him. Instead he shrugged, and Charlie noticed that his lips were contorted in an effort to avoid any further utterance. He had never, in his entire life, seen his father weep, but he knew that at this moment if either of them were to say anything more, the tears would flow.

'Come along, Angus!'

Angus did as he was instructed. He walked steadily towards the passenger door of the car, his head sunk into his shoulders. Without looking at his son or daughter-in-law, and without any further glance at the castle, he fastened his seat-belt and closed the door behind him.

Charlotte had already started the engine, and as she turned the car around and pointed it in the direction of their new home, she shouted through the open window. 'I'm sure we'll see you before long. Eleanor, do ring me if you need any advice.' Then, turning to her husband she snapped, 'Buck up, Angus; it's not the end of the world.' And with a cursory wave and a screaming clutch the vehicle departed in a peppering of gravel.

Charlie and Eleanor watched until it snaked out of sight and the sound of the engine died away. Now all they could hear was the distant cawing of a crow. How appropriate, thought Charlie.

He was distracted by the sight of a single figure walking up the track beside the loch. It was Murdo. As he drew closer to them he said, 'I'll have missed them then?'

'Just,' said Eleanor.

'Aye, well maybe it's just as well. I didna relish saying goodbye.'

'He won't be gone forever,' offered Charlie.

'No. And neither, I suspect, will yon woman.'

'All right, you two,' said Eleanor. 'There's no point in moping. Today is the start of a new chapter; there's no point in being miserable. Yes; we'll be sorry to see Angus go, but we've a castle and an estate to look after. We need to think about the future, not the past. Murdo, would you like to come in for some lunch? I've bought a pie and there's plenty to go round.'

Murdo touched his cap. 'That's very kind, miss – I mean, ma'am – but I've my work to attend to and you two should have your first meal together on your own.' With that he made to walk back down the track.

'There'll be changes, Murdo,' Eleanor shouted after him. 'We're not going to run the estate on feudal lines.'

Murdo turned and looked at her with a puzzled expression that betrayed a hint of alarm. Then he saw her smile.

'At least, I don't think that's what the laird has in mind.' She turned and looked up at Charlie. 'Isn't that right, sir?'

Charlie, surprised by the outburst, hesitated and then said, 'No; certainly not. I mean, no. Not feudal at all.'

Murdo smiled. 'Mmm,' he said, before turning and resuming his journey. Anyone close to him would have heard him muttering under his breath, 'Strong women. Aye, the world is full o' them . . .'

'That was a bit presumptuous,' said Charlie. 'He's only just got rid of Charlotte and now you start on him.'

'Only in a nice way,' said Eleanor as they walked towards the door of the castle. Once inside she slipped her hand from his, walked to the centre of the hall and looked about her. 'Oh yes, there'll be changes here.'

Charlie regarded her with a worried expression.

'Don't look so fearful. I mean, good changes.'

'What sort of changes?' he asked apprehensively.

Eleanor walked back to him and slipped her arms around his waist. 'Numbers.'

'What do you mean, "numbers"?'

Eleanor coloured up slightly. 'I'm sorry I was late getting back. I had to go to the doctor.'

There was a note of alarm in Charlie's voice as he asked, 'Why? What's wrong?'

'Well, nothing. It's just the effects of Venice.'

'What do you mean? Are you ill? Have you contracted something . . . from the water?'

'It's not the sort of thing you can contract from the water. I know you're an unsophisticated Highland boy but I thought you knew the ways of the world.'

It came like a bolt from the blue. 'Oh my goodness! You're not . . . ?'

'Yes. You'd better start saving, Mr Stuart. By June, your clan will have expanded to three.'

19

New Town, Edinburgh

May 1972

'Every generation revolts against its fathers and makes friends with its grandfathers.'

Lewis Mumford, *The Brown Decades*, 1931

Becoming a father at the tender age of twenty-one was not something that Charlie had ever foreseen. To be fair, neither was it something that Eleanor had envisaged. Nor her parents. While Sir Robert and Lady Fitzallan were taken aback, they consoled themselves that at least the child would not be born out of wedlock, and reconciled themselves to a greater than average quota of babysitting, not least because of their close proximity and the relative remoteness of Angus and Charlotte.

Ellie Fortune Stuart was born on 17th May 1971. The name was a compromise. Charlie had wanted to call the child after her mother, but Eleanor said that it would be too confusing to have two Eleanors in the same household.

The Fitzallans soon put aside their concerns relating to the overly rapid arrival of their first grandchild, having waited in vain for issue from either of their sons – both too busy with their careers on the other side of the world to think about starting a family.

Before too long it was clear that Robert Fitzallan's granddaughter would have him in equal thrall as his daughter – a fact not lost on his wife Davina, whose matter-of-factness when it came to child-rearing was tempered by her own feelings of grand-maternal pride.

But as far as Angus and Charlotte were concerned, no visit to see Charlie's firstborn was mooted. Angus offered his congratulations over the phone, with Charlotte shouting hers from a distance in the by now accepted fashion, but repeated entreaties by Charlie – Eleanor being too embarrassed to enter the fray – failed to yield any tangible results. As a consequence, in the month of Ellie's first birthday, the two of them grasped the nettle and proposed a visit to Edinburgh so that the grandfather and step-grandmother could become acquainted with the next generation of Stuarts.

Eleanor was dreading the encounter. She found Charlotte unpredictable at the best of times and knew that her reaction to Ellie would be either complete indifference or extreme effusion, with all the associated cooing and prodding that entailed. But she steeled herself; it had to be done, and she felt sorry for Angus. Not that she had ever known him well, but he had certainly commanded respect in Sodhail, and his late wife she remembered with great fondness. It was Fortune Stuart who had scooped her up one day when, at the age of eight or nine, she fell off her pony while out hacking. Lifting her from the long grass and popping her straight back in the saddle before leading her home – a walk that took a good half hour. Eleanor had never forgotten her smile, or the gentle lilting voice and the kind, encouraging words. The first Mrs Stuart had had about her an innate grace and contentment that was totally lacking in the second. Any man Fortune had chosen to marry must be worth something. With this always at the back of her mind, Eleanor had endeavoured to maintain good relations with Angus; a determination fostered by the apparent indifference of his new wife to his own feelings.

'What number?' asked Charlie, as the car crawled along the elegant street of Georgian terraced houses that ran parallel to Edinburgh's fashionable George Street. 'So much nicer than Princes Street', had become one of Charlotte's catchphrases, not that she noticed. It was Charlie who had alighted on the fact and would raise his eyes heavenward whenever it was mentioned.

From those early days, when Charlotte had bullied and picked at him – the days when Gordon had come to stay and to witness the uncomfortable dysfunction of the Stuart household – their relationship had developed into a kind of diplomatic stand-off. On his return from college, Charlotte realised that not only had her stepson grown in stature, but also in character. There was something about him that discouraged her from engaging with him closer than at arm's length. As a result, a kind of rapprochement was achieved, where each managed, for most of the time at any rate, to effect a kind of détente for the sake of those around them. It was a rare concession on Charlotte's part, probably fostered by a feeling that to get on the wrong side of Charlie now would not be advantageous to her future plans – whatever they might be. During those early years her ambitions were unclear. Only when they had married did she reveal what Charlie considered to be her true colours.

'Number thirteen,' answered Eleanor.

'Oh yes. How could I forget?' muttered Charlie. He pulled the Morris Minor in to the kerb some twenty yards distant – as close as he could get to the glossy black front door of the elegant four-storey house – and turned off the engine. 'Here we go then; brace yourself.'

As they disembarked with the one-year-old Ellie cradled in Eleanor's arms, fractious after the long journey, they could see, a few doors down, the figure of what appeared to be an old man standing on a doorstep. At first Charlie imagined that they must be looking at the wrong house, but as they drew closer, he saw that the figure was indeed his father. Seeing the shock on Charlie's face, and hoping to disguise her own feelings of horror at the appearance of her father-in-law, Eleanor said brightly, 'Hello Grandpa! Look who's come to see you!' She hoped that it was not disrespectful. She had always referred to Charlie's father as Mr Stuart, and he had never suggested she do otherwise, but some way of brightening up the moment had to be found.

From the expression on Angus Stuart's face it was clear that no offence had been taken. The grey, lined countenance broke into a smile. 'Well, well, well,' was all he could say, as he reached out a hand and stroked the cheek of his granddaughter. Ellie stopped her grizzling and looked directly at him.

'Goo,' she said. And 'Goo' he remained.

Their few moments of intimacy were fractured by the familiar voice. 'Don't stand out there on the pavement letting all the heat out; come inside.'

The three of them did as they were bid; Charlie carrying two large bags, his father a high chair, and Eleanor the baby as they climbed the few steps to the front door and entered the spacious hallway, painted that rich shade of chocolate brown so beloved of Charlotte. It was, thought Charlie, like drowning in a deep vat of Bourneville.

The fuss over the child was minimal on the part of Charlotte, though Angus could hardly take his eyes off her. Having been sent upstairs to divest themselves of their luggage, Charlie and Eleanor exchanged glances but few words. Neither wanted to admit how dreadful Angus looked, neither did this seem to be the moment to exchange opinions on Charlotte, the house, or anything other than the state of the baby's nappy, which was changed along with the clothes in which she had travelled. Ellie, blissfully unaware of the domestic atmosphere, gurgled happily now that the journey had come to an end, and gave voice, occasionally to 'door', 'bed', 'dink' and her new word, 'Goo', – an addition to her vocabulary that neither of her parents could attribute to any particular cause. As yet, the child had shown no reaction at all to the presence of Charlotte.

Downstairs in the drawing room, with the baby crawling around her grandfather's feet while her parents drank Earl Grey tea, Charlotte did her best to make polite enquiries as to Ellie's health and their future plans for her education, though they were clearly of little real concern to her. Aside from bobbing up to remove some precious knick-knack that looked perilously close to being within the child's reach, she kept glancing at her watch and finally announced: 'Well, I have to go out. I've arranged to go to the Usher Hall with a group of girlfriends to hear James Galway.'

Angus glanced at the carriage clock on the mantelpiece. 'So early?' he asked half-heartedly.

'We're meeting up for drinks first.' And with that, Charlotte rose from her seat and left the room, only to appear a few minutes later wearing a smart jacket and carrying a Chanel handbag. 'I'm sure you've got lots to talk about, but don't wait up; I'm not sure when I shall be back. I'll probably see you tomorrow morning before you go. Do mind the baby on the coffee table, won't you? It's got very sharp corners.' And with that she swept out of the room in a back draught of Madame Rochas.

Charlie offered a weak smile at his father, who did his best to offer one back, though he found it hard to meet his son's eye.

Ever ready to lighten the atmosphere, Eleanor said, 'Can we get Ellie some tea? I've brought her stuff.'

'Of course,' replied Angus, relieved at the chance to talk of other things. They made their way into the kitchen – an expensive hand-painted kind that seemed to have 'Smallbone' written all over it – Eleanor had seen the adverts for this smart new firm's handiwork in *Country Life* and was, to her embarrassment, envious of its appearance; a feeling she quickly dismissed as being unworthy, and anyway such a culinary arrangement would be far too expensive in a large and draughty old castle. She would stick with her scrubbed pine and the cupboards gloss-painted by less skilful hands and be content.

They chatted about inconsequential matters until Eleanor, aware that her husband and his father would not feel able to converse about weightier topics while she and Ellie were there, said, 'I'll take the baby out for a stroll and let you two catch up.'

Neither of the two men demurred, and with Eleanor and Charlotte out of the house, the conversation looked set to take a more serious turn.

Charlie was aware that 'man-to-man' conversations with his father had been thin on the ground, only being regarded as necessary in times of crisis or great change – going off to school, taking on responsibility for the castle and suchlike. Shamefully he could never recall ever saying to his father the words which came out now, instinctively and genuinely felt: 'How are you, Dad?'

Angus had, for too long, learnt to keep his feelings to himself, and a mixture of pride and embarrassment prevented him from opening up as many fathers would to their sons. 'Managing,' was all he offered by way of reply, his real feelings being betrayed by a deep sigh.

Realising that this might be an uncomfortable exchange, Charlie asked, 'Have you got a beer?'

This seemed to jolt Angus out of his introspection. 'Beer? At half past five?'

Charlie looked at him and smiled. 'Special occasion.'

The older man melted. 'Yes. Yes, of course. A *very* special occasion.' He pushed himself up from the chair, which was more of an effort than Charlie felt it ought to be, opened the fridge and took out a bottle of beer. Seated on either side of the bespoke hand-painted table, the two men raised their glasses – one of beer and the other of malt whisky.

'To Ellie,' said Angus, chinking his glass against that of his son.

'To Ellie Fortune,' responded Charlie.

Angus looked meaningfully at his son, and as he did so Charlie saw his eyes fill with tears. His father tried to repeat the names of his granddaughter but no words would come. Gently, the older man put his glass down upon the table, buried his face in his hands and wept.

20

Loch Side

May 1973

> 'It's no use telling me there are bad aunts and good aunts. At the core, they are all alike. Sooner or later, out pops the cloven hoof.'
>
> P.G. Wodehouse, *The Code of the Woosters*, 1938

She had always been known as Mrs Murdo and never as Aunt Letty. She was one of the Crosbie girls – a trio of crofter's daughters – and she had married Murdo relatively late in life, barely a year before Charlie was born. Nobody thought that Murdo was the marrying type – wedded to his rod and his net was what the locals said; it came as a surprise to them that Murdo had, himself, finally been landed. But it soon became apparent that the two were of like mind – seldom offering an opinion unless counselled to do so, and even then, considered in their approach to life. Not that they were a dull pair; the stubborn streak that ran though both of them could give rise, on occasion, to fireworks, though usually in the secluded confines of Loch Side, the long, low, granite-built cottage some half a mile from Castle Sodhail that was their home.

It was part of the estate and had, previous to Murdo's marriage, been nothing more than a roofless old crofter's cottage, long since left to ruin. Angus had had no intention of making it habitable, it being too far gone to make such a project financially viable. It was Murdo who approached him and asked if he could turn the cottage into a home for himself and his new missus. At first Angus had demurred; the prospect of renovation being both expensive and time consuming. But Murdo had put a proposal to him – that he, Murdo, should undertake the work and even pay for it himself. He had some money put by and could turn his hand to most things. It would not be a speedy job, but if Angus would let him and Letty live in it rent-free once the work was complete, he would be willing to spend all his spare time doing it up.

Under such pressure, Angus had given in to the proposal, insisting, however, that it should all be legally drawn up and that when Murdo relinquished his position as ghillie the cottage would revert to the estate. With this proposal Murdo had had no quarrel. Ghillies seldom retired. Who would willingly give up fishing until life gave up on them?

It was the one thing over which Murdo and Mrs Murdo had a difference of opinion – she scathing of the fact that her husband had not had the foresight to take care of their retirement. And then Charlie had taken over and Letty Murdoch had felt slightly more assured that their future would be safe. The boy was a gentler soul than his father, less likely to ask them to leave when Murdo's time came to retire. She was fond of him, not that her fondness manifested itself outwardly in any form of effusion. Many thought her a stern woman, not readily given to praise or enthusiasm. In Letty's case, inscrutability was a way of life – she had learnt from her two sisters the folly of wearing your heart on your sleeve and letting others take advantage. The brightest of the three girls, a place at university had been offered to her, but she had declined to take it up. Her life, she said, was in the Highlands, and nothing could persuade her to desert her home territory. No one would ever have accused Letty Crosbie of being unkind, and yet her reserve – and her evident intelligence – made folk wary of attempting over-familiarity. In respect of their propensity to keep themselves to themselves, she and Murdo were like peas in a pod, but on this particular day, the pod seemed rather too small to accommodate them both.

'I'm away to Strath Carron,' she declared, dropping a neatly folded copy of the *Scotsman* on the kitchen table. Murdo could see that the crossword was all but complete, as his wife reached up to the peg for her tweed coat.

'Suit yersel,' muttered Murdo, washing his hands at the sink and staring through the window in the direction of the castle. 'You'll be missing their return then?'

Pushing the large bone buttons through their holes on her coat, Letty offered, 'I think they'll manage without me in attendance. They'll not be expecting us to line the drive and tug our forelocks, will they?'

Murdo did not dignify the remark with any reply, knowing that his wife would not have meant any slight on Charlie and Eleanor for whom, in spite of her reticence, she clearly had considerable regard.

He let the rhetorical question hang and waited for her to go out of the door. But Letty did not. Instead she came and joined her husband at the window, realising that, on this occasion, her remark had been of unwarranted asperity.

'It was a short visit then?' she enquired.

'Aye. Just the night. T'would be enough for any man with that woman there,' confirmed Murdo, drying his hands.

'She's lucky they went at all. Fancy not coming here to see the bairn; putting the youngsters to all that trouble, what with baby things to take – pushchairs and carrycots and the like.'

'I should think the laird – I mean the old laird – would have come . . .'

'Aye; had he not been brow-beaten by yon woman. Pitiful, I call it. You would'nae have caught him being so hen-pecked by—' Letty paused, knowing that she was entering uncomfortable territory. 'Well; it's a shame, that's all.'

Murdo cut in. 'Here they are, then.' He could see, through the small window, the curl at the end of the drive where it ran up to the castle, and the small car that had made its way back home from the city.

He hung the towel on its hook and reached for his jacket. 'I'll be off to see if they need a hand.'

'Aye, you do that,' said Letty, offering reassurance after her hasty remark earlier in the conversation. 'Will I give you a lift to the end of the drive?'

Murdo demurred. 'Nay, I'll walk. It's a fine morning and I've a couple of pheasant pens to check on the way.'

'Well, if you're sure.' Letty made to leave. 'Tell them if they're short of a meal tonight I've a pie and some apple crumble they can have. I've only to take them out of the freezer.'

'Aye, I'll tell them.' Murdo opened the door and began to walk up the road. His wife was left with an uneasy feeling of regret; regret at having been sharp with her husband, and regret that he might have thought her disapproving of the young couple who had, for the last year and a half been their new landlords. She had nothing but admiration for them, and sympathy, too. To take on an estate like this, at such a young age, was a daunting prospect for anyone. His father had done it, she knew, but there was still a kind of innocence about Charlie that worried her. And Eleanor, how would she cope with the responsibility of a castle, a young child, and an estate? Letty banished such thoughts from her mind and glanced down at the paper and its irritating crossword. There were a handful of clues unsolved, but she tutted as her eye lighted on one in particular which now seemed to be staring her in the face: five across, nine letters, 'Young, in the case of Charlie'.

Picking up the discarded pencil she filled in the letters: PRETENDER. Then she left the house, bound for Strath Carron in the battered old Austin van that offered what she considered to be the most practical form of transport for the wife of a ghillie.

21

Castle Sodhail

June 1973

'I do not believe that friends are necessarily the people you like best, they are merely the people who got there first.'

Peter Ustinov, *Dear Me*, 1977

The clarity of the air on top of the crag was remarkable, and the view of the apparently miniature castle several hundred feet below him was as crisp and well-defined as Charlie could ever remember. His routine work done – that of checking over the half-dozen cottages that constituted Castle Sodhail's holiday lets and the daily meeting with Murdo to talk through the day's fishing trips on the loch – he could treat himself to a spot of practical work, something he regarded as a kind of therapy. Repairing a length of dry stone wall or replacing a broken fence rail or two was something which Charlie never tired of undertaking himself – the physical work helping him to feel that he was at least in some way responsible for the upkeep of the estate, rather than just the man who managed others who attended to the nitty-gritty of its daily requirements.

Careless hikers or wayward livestock had demolished a section of one of the shooting butts on the slopes at the foot of the crag. He had spent the last hour piecing together the scattered heap of stones, his hands abraded and cut by the sharp-edged granite, until, once more, the lumpy yet strangely elegant arc of granite regained its former integrity. The job completed, he scaled the peak of the crag and sat on a rock

– as he had done many times before – to catch his breath and to admire the view on this clearest of days.

The novelty of being responsible for this patch of the Highlands – small though it was – had never left him, and the joy of being the custodian and steward of its future filled him with joy and apprehension in equal measure. He never took his tenure for granted; familiarity with this segment of the landscape never bred in him the merest hint of contempt; never gave rise in him to the kind of feelings which led him to assume it was his by right.

He glanced at his watch. It was almost noon. Time to be setting off down the hillside – Eleanor would have his lunch ready for half past the hour and he enjoyed catching up on the morning's news and spending an hour with Ellie before going off, again, to clear a pathway of overgrown vegetation or renew the wire netting on a pheasant pen.

As he slid down from the rock he saw a car pull in to the front of the castle. Way below him though it was, he could see that it was not a vehicle he recognised as being local or familiar. Perhaps it was a holidaymaker who'd come to take one of the cottages. But it was Tuesday today, and the cottages were let from Saturday to Saturday. He thought no more about it, but continued the downward journey, walking briskly, zigzagging across the lower slopes of the hillside and finally approaching the castle along the drive that ran beside the loch.

As he strode across the apron of gravel towards the castle he could see that the car was a battered Volkswagen Beetle in a pale shade of green. It had seen better days, and on the back seat were piles of luggage, not placed in an orderly fashion, but higgledy-piggledy, after the fashion of a stall at a jumble sale rather than being neatly packed for long-distance travel.

Bags spewed out an assortment of clothing, and there were odd shoes scattered among the garments, which were barely hidden by an old tartan car-rug that had, at some point, been loosely arranged to cover them. The car itself was mud-spattered and weary looking. In spite of the fact that the engine was no longer running, there emanated from it a prolonged sighing sound, as if some part of it were still trying to catch up and found itself out of breath; a low sizzling, akin to that made by sausages frying in a pan.

Charlie was musing on the good fortune of the owner – managing to arrive here, clearly from some miles distant, in a car that looked as though it would have trouble travelling from one end of a street to the other.

The back window bore a sticker: PAX OPTIMA RERUM, and at the precise moment that Charlie realised to whom the car belonged, Eleanor stepped out of the door of the castle and said, 'Guess who's here?' She was followed by the familiar gangling figure of Gordon Mackenzie, whose long flowing hair was now accompanied by a beard.

'Hello, dear boy!'

Standing staring at his old school friend, Charlie felt apprehension and pleasure in equal measure. The pleasure was born of old memories, the apprehension as a result of their last encounter, of whose details Eleanor had remained ignorant since Charlie had chosen, after some deliberation, not to share them with her.

'Isn't this nice?' she asked innocently. 'After all this time?'

'Yes. Wonderful,' stammered Charlie, doing his best not to look either shocked or fearful and failing miserably on the former count, slightly on the latter.

Realising that he needed to find some way of taking charge of the situation and, in front of his wife, looking pleased to see his oldest friend, he asked, 'What brings you here? You didn't say you were coming.'

Eleanor looked bemused at Charlie's less than effusive greeting and Charlie realised that he would have to do better. 'I mean, it's great to see you. You're just in time for lunch.' He glanced at Eleanor who nodded and looked more concerned about her husband's strange demeanour than the difficulty of finding lunch for an unexpected guest.

Charlie followed up the invitation for refreshment with, 'Can you stay long? Are you on your way somewhere or have you come especially?'

'On my way to John O'Groats. Want to see if the car can make it.'

It was an answer that offered some relief. Charlie relaxed a little, hoping that the subject that had troubled him on his visit to Oxford would not be raised again.

Charlie regarded the VW Beetle with some foreboding. 'You mean that's managed to get you all the way from Oxford to here?'

'You bet. We needed one or two stops along the way for minor adjustments – well, pretty major, actually – but we've made it this far and that's the hardest part of the journey.'

Charlie felt some of his old feelings towards his schoolfriend returning. He remembered the Gordon of old, their years sharing a room and the battles fought together. He smiled ruefully. 'You think you've done the hardest part? Have you seen what you've got to go through to get to the north coast? The size of the mountains?'

'German car. Very efficient. Very . . . capable.'

Charlie laughed a hollow laugh and went across to where Gordon stood. He shook him warmly by the hand. 'Welcome back; it's good to see you again.'

* * *

The afternoon was spent walking alongside the loch in the early summer sunshine, Eleanor alternating between pushing Ellie in her pushchair and letting her get out and walk, and all three of them remembering the early days when Eleanor and Gordon had been horse riding and Charlie had felt those pangs of jealousy that had pushed him into making sure that he did not lose her.

'So, did you guess?' Gordon asked Eleanor.

'That you weren't really interested in me? Oh yes.'

Gordon looked hurt. 'How soon?'

'Oh, straight away. But I could see why you were doing it, and I thought it was rather sweet actually.'

'I see.' He looked introspective. 'I thought I might have covered it rather better than that.'

'Mmm,' murmured Eleanor. 'But I saw other letters that girls in my school were getting from boys who were keen on them and yours were so . . . well, different. I decided pretty early on what you were up to.'

'And it didn't upset you?'

'Not really. You see, there was only one person I really fancied.'

Gordon tilted his head in the direction of Charlie and raised his eyebrows.

'Yes,' confirmed Eleanor. 'Pathetic really. You'd think I'd have set my sights a bit higher, wouldn't you?'

Charlie was stung to reply. 'Do you mind? I'm not that bad a catch.' He gestured around him. 'I gave you all this.'

Eleanor laughed, and nodded at the buggy. 'And this!' she added.

Charlie winced. 'Yes. That was a bit unexpected.'

Gordon asked, 'You mean you weren't paying attention in those talks your dad had with you?'

Charlie thumped him playfully on the arm. 'Cheeky bugger!'

'Well, you've only yourselves to blame. Good honeymoon then?'

'How do you know she was a honeymoon baby?' asked Charlie.

'I can do the maths you know, begging her ladyship's pardon.' He smiled apologetically at Eleanor and she shook her head and grinned.

'Same old Gordon,' she murmured.

'As long as you enjoyed the meal.'

Charlie stopped in his tracks. 'Of course! The meal. And the Latin. At first I thought that Dad had paid for it but then it dawned on me that it might be you.'

'You mean you weren't certain?' asked Gordon, the note of disappointment plain in his voice.

'Well, I did have other things to think about.'

'Mmm. I rather hoped that the Latin would have given it away. I mean, there's no point in giving someone a secret present if they don't realise who it's really from, is there?'

'What did it say? Remind me,' asked Eleanor.

Charlie remained silent, his eyes on the ground in front of him.

Gordon cleared his throat and intoned: '*Felices ter at amplius, quos irrupta tenet copula nec malis, divulsus querimoniis, suprema citius solvet amor die.*'

'Which means?' asked Eleanor.

Gordon turned to Charlie. 'Which means?'

Charlie looked distracted. 'I forget,' he murmured.

'I don't,' said Gordon. He looked directly at Charlie and said: 'Thrice blessed (and more) are they whom an unbroken bond holds and whose love, never strained by nasty quarrels, will not slip until their dying day.'

'How lovely,' said Eleanor. 'I remember now. Charlie translated it for me when he read out the note. Strange that he's forgotten, but then Latin's never been your strong point, has it, Charlie?'

While Eleanor was bathing Ellie that evening, the two men found themselves alone in front of a log fire in the sitting room of the castle. Although it was June, the evening air was still cool and the cheering flames took the edge off the chill that would otherwise have pervaded the atmosphere within the old stone walls.

It was an atmosphere whose tension was added to on this particular evening by things hitherto left unsaid.

It would not be long before Eleanor returned and the three of them would have supper at the round table positioned in the corner of the room just across from where they sat. Charlie knew that once Eleanor returned, Gordon would be unlikely to broach the subject of foreign students, of safe houses and paying guests. He almost wondered – all these months later – if he had dreamt the whole thing up.

'I'll just go and see if they're all right,' said Charlie, making to get up.

Gordon had a glass of whisky in one hand, but with the one that remained free he reached out and held Charlie's arm as he attempted to rise from his chair.

'You've not forgotten, have you?' he asked softly.

Charlie feigned ignorance. 'Forgotten what?'

'The thing that we talked about. In Oxford, nearly two years ago. The offer still stands. There really is nothing to worry about and we still need . . . accommodation.'

'Are you expecting me to risk the safety of my wife and daughter for some hare-brained scheme involving foreign students?'

'There is no risk involved. It's not hare-brained. The workings of it don't involve you at all. You really *are* just providing accommodation; it's virtually risk free – and you'd really be helping me out of a spot.'

Charlie noticed the look of fear in Gordon's eyes. It was not a look that he had ever seen before. Gordon Mackenzie seemed almost to be pleading with him.

'Look, it would really help me out if you could say "yes". The powers that be are not very impressed with me lately, and I thought that you, as a friend . . . well . . . that I could rely on you to get me out of a spot.'

Charlie felt a sinking feeling in the pit of his stomach. Gordon had asked him for very little over the years that he had known him. Truth to tell, he could think of not one occasion when he had been called on to provide support; if anything it was Gordon who always seemed to be supporting him. Supposing it really was risk free; not as risky as his imagination had led him to believe back in Oxford? But the feelings he had felt then resurfaced. He looked Gordon in the eye. 'I'm sorry, but I told you; I'm not interested.'

'Not interested in what?' Eleanor asked. She was walking back into the room with a tea towel in her hands. Neither of the two men spoke as she strode towards the fire, picked up the poker and prodded at one of the logs, causing a shower of orange sparks to shoot up the chimney in a brisk spiral. She turned to face them. 'Not interested in what, Charlie?'

22

Creag Sodhail
June 1973

'Sir, I have found you an argument, but I am not obliged to find you an understanding.'

James Boswell, *Life of Samuel Johnson*, 1791

'But why not? It seems to me such an obvious thing to do. We have the accommodation and you said yourself that it's not always as full as it could be. By taking more paying guests in the holidays we could guarantee our income.'

They were walking on the lower slopes of Creag Sodhail, blowing the cobwebs away, with the baby strapped in a papoose on Charlie's back. He tried to sound reasonable in his argument as Eleanor did her best to bring him round to her way of thinking.

'But we would also have to turn away those who come for a holiday,' countered Charlie.

'Only if the guests were staying in the cottages.'

'Where else would they stay?' he asked.

'In the house. It's not as though we're short of rooms.'

'But the baby . . . and our privacy?'

Eleanor shot him a pitying look. 'She's not really a baby any more, Charlie, and there's more than enough room. We've twelve bedrooms and at least eight of them are far enough away from our wing to avoid sleepless nights on account of a toddler crying. They'd never even see us, never mind hear us; not with walls two feet thick.'

'And the catering . . . Haven't you got enough on with Ellie?'

'There's plenty of help in the village. I can put a card in the window of the post office in Strath Carron.'

'And have every Tom, Dick and Harry coming for a look?'

'Well, we can ask around then. I'm sure Mrs Murdo will know of somebody. She might even be prepared to help out herself.'

Charlie was beginning to find himself on the back foot. He would have to come up with better arguments than these if he were to avoid the can of worms that now presented itself.

On interrupting their conversation of the night before, Eleanor had winkled out of Gordon exactly what it was that he was proposing. Gordon, it seemed, was only too glad to take Eleanor into his confidence, though Charlie noted the distinct absence of any details regarding the provenance of the guests, either their nationalities or their diplomatic associations. 'Well-behaved students' was his full and final description of them, the 'well-behaved' epithet clearly added when Gordon saw the decorative state of the castle, which had changed somewhat since his previous visit. The chocolate brown and deep moss-green walls so beloved of Charlotte had been replaced by cream and pale yellow, white and duck-egg blue. And then he remembered that Eleanor had studied art at university – it should not have come as a surprise to him that she would have very definite ideas on her surroundings.

Charlie stopped walking and turned to face her. 'It's just that life is so good at the moment – just you, me and Ellie. I don't really want to spoil it all. I know the holiday lets are a bit thin on the ground at the moment, but we'll manage. All the guns are taken for the grouse shooting in August and that will help a lot. We'll manage.'

Eleanor gave him a kiss on the cheek and looked deep into his eyes. 'Is there something you're not telling me? Some other reason why you don't want to take in the students?'

For a moment Charlie hesitated. Then Ellie let out a cry: 'Tag! Tag!'

They turned to see the magnificent stag leaping into the distance, kicking its heels high into the air in rapid bounding movements, and then it was gone, beyond a heather knoll that hid it from view.

'I just don't want to rock the boat, that's all,' said Charlie, convincing himself that he had not lied to Eleanor, even if he had been somewhat economical with the truth. 'Let me think about it.'

They walked on in silence, for the best part, remarking briefly now and then on the health of the moorland, the state of the grouse and the brightness of the day. It would not last; by mid-afternoon the heavens had opened and the rain was beating down on the turrets of the castle until the lead water-butts were overflowing.

Gordon's car was packed and ready to leave – or what passed for packing in the world of Gordon. Everything he had brought with him had been rounded up and deposited in the vehicle, but the state in which it was arranged left a lot to be desired. What had looked like a stall at a jumble sale on his arrival, now had the appearance of a skip on wheels. He seemed not remotely bothered. By late afternoon the torrential downpour had abated, and only some of Gordon's extensive wardrobe had been dampened by the deluge, he refusing all offers of an umbrella as he loaded up the VW.

True to his word he had only stayed the night and, in spite of Eleanor's entreaties to prolong his visit by a few days, insisted on setting off at half past five en route for Strathpeffer.

'It might have been a good idea to have planned your trip a little better,' teased Eleanor. 'Suppose you can't find a bed in . . . where are you heading for?'

'Strathpeffer. Funny name. I only hope the residents have a sense of humour to match.'

'And a spare room,' added Eleanor.

Charlie said little. Gordon noticed his reticence and did his best to make light of it. 'Cheer up, Charlie. Parting is such sweet sorrow and I'll drop in on my way back, if that's OK? Just to let you know I survived. And to see if you've made any decision about my offer. It really would help us out.'

Without waiting for a reply, Gordon eased his angular frame into the VW Beetle and fired her up. With a roar typical of the marque, the engine sprang into life. Gordon slammed shut the driver's door and the orange trafficator that had been stuck out at an angle of ninety degrees dropped back into the slot intended for it.

Through the open window he shouted his final greeting: '*Haec olim meminisse iuvabit!*', and the car, in a series of kangaroo-like leaps and bounds, made its way down the drive and out of sight, the backfiring engine scattering crows like black confetti from the branches of the Scots pines.

'What did he say?' asked Eleanor.

'Oh, another of his Latin phrases.'

'Have you forgotten what that one means as well?'

'No. But I'm not sure I agree with his sentiment.'

'Which is?'

Charlie sighed and looked at his wife. 'One day we'll look back on this and smile.'

23

Oxford

July 1973

> 'In preparing for battle I have always found that plans are useless, but planning is indispensable.'
>
> Richard Nixon, *Six Crises*, 1962

Alex Jesmond was sitting opposite Gordon Mackenzie in a quiet corner of the bar at the Randolph Hotel. He looked, for Alex Jesmond, relatively happy. The merest hint of a smile crossed his face as he murmured, 'So you did it then?'

'Apparently so.' Gordon himself looked far from happy. 'I felt dreadful. I knew he didn't want to.'

'And you went for the softer target, the wife; very wise.'

'It's not wise. It's deceitful. I don't know that I'll ever forgive myself.'

'You will, Oscar, you will.'

Gordon took a large gulp of the whisky that sat before him.

'You'd better go steady on that stuff at this time of day,' warned Alex. 'Are you off your beer?'

'I need a bit of a stiffener, that's all.'

'Very Wodehouseian.' Alex finished off his pint.

'I only wish it were half as amusing,' muttered Gordon.

Alex lowered the empty glass to the table and said flatly, 'You'll get over it. Anyway, you'll have other things to concentrate on. Another week and we can start shipping them out. How many are the Stuarts taking?'

'Four, to start with.'

'Any high-risk ones?'

'No. They're all quite reliable. I didn't want to raise suspicions. Or make more trouble than we needed. I thought if we sent the low-riskers to start with then their hosts might be more cooperative in the long term.'

'Good move.'

Gordon drained his glass. 'You know, I'm really not comfortable with all this cloak and dagger stuff. I think I'm going to pack it in after this year.'

Alex regarded him with suspicion. 'Are you losing your bottle?'

'No. I'm regaining my self-respect; or trying to.'

'I thought you needed the money?'

'Not that much. I thought when we started that I was doing something for my country.'

'You are doing something for your country: arranging "Cultural Visits" for foreign students. So what's changed?'

'I'm not comfortable with persuading other people to take part in this whole thing when they don't know the full story.'

'Aren't you making mountains out of molehills? The truth of the matter is that they don't *need* to know the full story. We're just using them as safe houses for diplomatic families; all the concerned parties know that. If they come after anybody it will be us, not the landlords and landladies of assorted bed and breakfasts.'

Gordon looked irritated. 'The phrase that concerns me is "using them". And that's what we're doing. Taking advantage of relationships – friendships even – and putting lives at risk.'

'That's a bit dramatic.' Alex got up to go.

'But it's true. We came very close to disaster with that couple in Bicester. We only just got the girl out in time.'

'That was Bicester. Far too close to home. I was against it from the start. I mean, who goes on a "Cultural Visit" to Bicester? There's no danger of that happening in the wilds of Scotland – a bit thin on culture but riddled with history.'

'Yes: most of it bloody. Have you forgotten the Battle of Culloden?'

'Of course not. My ancestors fought in it. But there's no danger of history repeating itself. All the Jacobites have long since given up and gone home.'

'Yes. Now we face a different enemy.'

'Not in the wilds of Bonnie Scotland.'

'Isn't that a bit naïve? Your native land is attached to England, you know; it might seem remote, but if I can reach it in a clapped out VW Beetle, then it doesn't exactly take a lot of working out for anyone else.'

Alex sighed. 'The trail will be cold. We'll be switching them round all the time, with several stop-offs on the way. There's no chance that we'll be followed. Their families will know they are in Scotland and they know that Scotland is large and wild. For all they know, electricity still hasn't reached the place. Of all the places we could put them up, Charlie Stuart's castle has to be one of the safest. No one will suspect a thing.'

Gordon got up and walked with Alex through the door of the bar and into the street. 'There's always a chance,' he said. 'You know that.'

'A very slim one. And, anyway, as you said, we're not sending any high- risk ones there to start with, so there will be no reason to worry. Nobody's going to be that interested in following them, and there's no reason why they shouldn't have the low-riskers for a few years before we step them up.'

'Years?' asked Gordon, his voice betraying his dismay.

Alex looked him in the eye. 'You don't imagine this whole thing is going to be over in a matter of weeks or months, do you? It's ongoing. It needs commitment. And if you're not sure you can give that then you really should get out; though, to be honest, I don't envy you telling the boss right now. He won't be at all pleased.'

Seeing the look of despondency on Gordon's face, Alex made to pacify him. 'Look; you've done a really good job in setting up the Scottish connection. Lots of Brownie points. Don't spoil everything now. Let's just get it bedded in and move forward slowly. It'll be fine. You'll see.'

'Brownie points. Good God! It wouldn't be so bad if we weren't playing with people's lives.' He paused, and then murmured as an afterthought, 'And loves.'

'What?' asked Alex.

'Nothing. Just thinking out loud.'

The two men strode off into the crowd of shoppers and disappeared in opposite directions.

Later that day, Alex Jesmond met up with the man that he and Gordon encountered on a monthly basis, their meeting place this time, a bench outside the Radcliffe Camera. He seemed pleased with 'The Scottish Connection', as Alex referred to it.

'Tell Gordon he's done well,' instructed the man. 'Anyway, why isn't he here?'

'He had some business to attend to. He sends his apologies.'

'A shame. I should have liked to have congratulated him. We've been trying for . . . what is it . . . two years to get a base north of the border. I mean, well north – and this place fits the bill perfectly. It's isolated, you say?'

'Yes.'

'But accessible?'

'There is access by water – the loch is connected by river to the sea – and there is room to land a helicopter right by the castle if we need to extract anybody very quickly.'

'With any luck we won't need to, but it's good to know that things are in place for any eventuality. Gordon has clearly done his homework. ' He tucked his copy of *Melody Maker* under his arm and rose from the bench. 'So the "students" go out next week then. Good luck, Mr Jesmond. Though I'm sure you won't need it.'

24

Castle Sodhail
December 1973

'And girls in slacks remember Dad,
And oafish louts remember Mum . . .'
John Betjeman, 'Christmas', 1954

The first summer of having 'paying guests' had, to Charlie's relief, passed without incident. One of the four students, a Yugoslav by the name of Florin, had been rather withdrawn and kept himself to himself, but the others – two Americans and a Russian – had been quite friendly. To have the four of them under one roof, fitting in as best they could around the family, had, on occasions, tried his patience – not to say his nerves. He reproached himself continually for not telling Eleanor the full story, for putting his wife and family at risk – a prospect that caused him to wake up in the middle of the night in a cold sweat. There were moments when he came close to putting her in the picture. But she was so happy right now, with the child doing well and Charlotte at a respectable distance, and at their last meeting Gordon had reassured him – told him that there really was no risk. He could only console himself with the belief that if he trusted his friend then there was nothing to worry about, and yet the look of fear he had seen on Gordon's face continued to haunt him.

As far as domestic arrangements were concerned, Eleanor had taken the extra housekeeping in her stride, and Mrs Murdo, refusing to let anyone else encroach upon Stuart territory, had taken it upon herself to be in charge of catering. Murdo had kept a characteristically low profile and, anyway, the grouse shooting had occupied him pretty much full time with all the cottages full of guests who, mercifully, either catered for themselves or had hired one of the capable ladies of Strath Carron to do the job for them.

Charlie, too, had had his mind occupied by juggling the various shoots and, on the Glorious Twelfth, acquitting himself pretty well. 'To see the laird shooting well is good for business,' offered Murdo, 'provided he disnae shoot *too* well.'

Charlie hoped that he had got the balance about right. The gun was put away with some relief; he felt more comfortable with a shepherd's crook in his hand than a 12-bore shotgun.

With the passing of the summer holidays, the shoots had decreased in number – just one or two a week – and then, on the 10th December, the last day of the grouse-shooting season, they had a fair bag of birds and a clutch of satisfied clients. Murdo was a happy man. He wished the assembled guns well – mainly locals this late in the season – and enjoyed more than usual the final lunch held in the hall of the castle. The menu was, as it always had been, grouse with all the trimmings, plus some 1961 St Julien that Charlie had found in the cellar. 'Is this good?' he had asked Murdo, only to be met with a predictable response: 'If it was malt, I could tell ye.' The colour of Murdo's cheeks after the meal provided the answer, and it was clear that he was pleased Charlie had hosted the occasion himself, a tradition begun by his father, now regrettably absent for the second year running.

'A good year,' he murmured to Charlie as the guns drove off from the castle. 'As good as we've had for a long time. Yer faither would have enjoyed that.'

'I know. I want to make sure he comes next year. I know he doesn't want to get in our hair but I don't think it's right that he never comes here, especially for the shoot.'

'Aye, well we know why that is . . .' muttered Murdo.

Charlie barely heard the remark. 'Do you think he'd come for Christmas?'

Murdo shrugged. 'How should I know?'

'He refused last year, but I want Ellie to get to know him better. I'll ask Eleanor if she'd mind.'

'What about yon student?'

For a moment the situation had slipped Charlie's mind. The summer had passed so uneventfully that the prospect of another student influx for the Christmas holidays seemed not to have quite the same import as it had had all those months ago. The first four had come and gone with little fuss. They had been brought in separate cars and left in the same way, all within a few days of each other. They came, they walked, they ate and slept, then they went away. Simple as that. The money Charlie had been promised was paid in advance without fuss – and in cash. It had come by post in a registered parcel. Charlie had been convinced, on the way to the bank with a cheap carrier bag underneath his arm, that at any moment, a hired assassin would leap out of the shadows and overpower him. It had not happened. He had deposited the money in an account that he had opened especially and was, if anything, rather disappointed that the bank clerk made no remark as she counted the used notes and handed him a slip to sign.

All the way back to the castle he could not resist glancing in the rear-view mirror at frequent intervals to see if he was being followed. It was a something of an anticlimax to see nothing more than an empty road. A relief, but an anticlimax all the same. By the end of the summer he had begun to treat the students as just what they were – paying guests. He was polite, cordial even, but kept his distance. Eleanor, with Mrs Murdo at her elbow, seemed to relish the prospect of providing for four hungry mouths, though even she expressed relief that they were absent at lunchtimes, being provided with just bed, breakfast and evening meals. After supper, the guests would retire to their rooms and not be seen again until the morning. Eleanor worried at first that they would be bored and starved of entertainment, but they all seemed to have plenty of reading matter and gave voice to not one word of complaint. Only the Russian, Oleg, was of a surly disposition, but Eleanor wasted little time worrying. There was, as her Yorkshire schoolfriend used to remind her, 'nowt so queer as folk'.

The four who had been with them during the summer would not be returning, they were told. Communication came sparingly and, when it did, it came by post. They were offered no surnames for their guests, just first or given names: Florin, the Yugoslav, Oleg, the Russian, and Mark and Randy the Americans, had been the first quartet. Eleanor had to suppress a smile every time she addressed Randy, on account of the fact that at their first meeting, when the boy had said he was reading fine art she had replied, 'Are you really, Randy?'

She had turned a bright shade of pink and subsequently endeavoured to avoid calling him anything at all.

They would be sent just one student over the Christmas holidays and, as yet, had not been told his name. He would be arriving in five days' time, on the day after Boxing Day. It struck Charlie that perhaps having his father around might not be a good idea – there would be too many questions asked. But matters were taken out of his hands on Christmas Eve when a taxi deposited Angus Stuart on the drive outside the castle. It was lunchtime and, having wished Mrs Murdo a merry Christmas over a glass of sherry and toasted Murdo with a wee dram, Charlie came out of the front door to greet the unexpected guest.

He saw immediately that his father was alone. 'No Charlotte?' he asked, greeting the older man with a formal handshake and a pat on the shoulder.

'No.'

He saw at once that his father was troubled; the look of anguish on his face betrayed an inner turmoil.

'What on earth's the matter?' asked Charlie. Before his father could answer, Eleanor came out of the front door.

'Mr Stuart!' she cried. 'How wonderful to see you.' And then she, too, noticed the absence of Mrs Stuart, senior.

In his usual fashion, Angus Stuart came straight to the point: 'I wonder if I could stay with you for Christmas?' In his voice there was the merest trace of a tremor, as though he were trying to rein in his emotions.

'Of course,' said Eleanor, before Charlie could answer. 'On your own?'

'Yes.' He saw the look of curiosity on his son and daughter-in-law's faces.

'I'm afraid I've left Charlotte. I did my best but . . .'

Instinctively, Charlie put his arm around his father's shoulder, but he was politely rebuffed.

'Please, no. It is entirely my own fault. I can't blame anyone else. I won't stay for long, but if you wouldn't mind putting me up just for a few days until I work out what's best to do . . .'

'I'm so sorry, Dad,' offered Charlie.

His father nodded. 'Yes,' he said. And then: 'Would someone mind paying the taxi? I'm not sure where I've put my wallet. It's somewhere in one of these bags.'

There were just two bags on the drive – soft hold-alls – which, judging by their bulging contents, Angus Stuart had clearly packed in haste.

Charlie reached into his pocket for some notes and, having established with the taxi driver that the bill was considerably larger than the norm, went inside to write a cheque. The driver, on seeing the size of the castle, decided that the fiscal reliability of the owners was beyond question and that payment by cheque – normally refused – would, in this case, be unlikely to give rise to problems.

While Charlie busied himself with chequebook and pen, Eleanor kissed her father-in-law on the cheek and whispered, 'It will be lovely to have you here. Ellie will be thrilled to see "Goo" again.'

At this, Angus managed a weak smile, and the pinched look relaxed a little, though it pained Eleanor to see how much he had aged yet again in the few months since they had left him in Edinburgh. He had also developed a stoop, and it was Eleanor who insisted on carrying his two bags into the castle; fearing that the weight of them would be sufficient to cause him to crumple to the ground.

After lunch around the kitchen table – Angus having made some positive remarks on the state of the redecoration – he opened up about the reasons for his return.

'I was prepared,' he said, 'to try and make a go of it in Edinburgh, though leaving the castle was a tremendous wrench. I felt that if that was what Charlotte wanted, then I had to go along with it. Too many people give up too easily on marriage. I'm not one of them.'

Charlie butted in. 'But she knew how much you love this place; how much you are – were – tied to it. Surely she understood that when you got married?'

Angus continued patiently and almost without emotion: 'So I thought. But as time went by, it became clear that I had been labouring under a misapprehension. I tried not to believe it at first – probably because I felt such a fool and that it showed poor judgement of character – but then I had to admit to myself that it seems the only reason Charlotte married me was for my money.'

He paused. 'I still find it hard to believe.' Then he sat quietly for a few moments, seemingly spent of emotion and energy, before adding, 'It really is as simple as that.'

Eleanor felt unable to say anything at all. Charlie asked, 'So where is she now?'

'In Edinburgh. At the house.'

Charlie hesitated before asking, 'And did you buy the house?'

Angus nodded. 'Yes.'

'I see.' Charlie thought carefully before asking the next question, wondering if it was any of his business. Then he convinced himself that it was one which would need answering: 'And is the house in your name?'

'I'm afraid not. It was a present to Charlotte; the deeds are in her name.'

'So you have . . . ?'

'Nothing, I'm afraid. I'm just relieved I made over the estate to you, otherwise heaven knows what would have happened to Sodhail.'

'How did she take your leaving?'

'She doesn't know. I'm afraid I couldn't face a showdown. I left a note.' Angus managed a smile. 'Feeble, isn't it? It's usually wives who leave a note saying they've left their other half. Not the husband.'

25

Castle Sodhail

Christmas Day 1973

'And Christmas morning bells say "Come!"
Even to shining ones who dwell
Safe in the Dorchester Hotel.'
John Betjeman, 'Christmas', 1954

They had risen early, partly by force of necessity – Ellie was not one to sleep late – but also because both of them wanted to be up and about when Angus appeared.

'Did we get him a Christmas present?' asked Charlie, gazing out of the bedroom window and pulling on his jeans.

'Of course we got him a Christmas present. We got Charlotte one, too, if you remember. Though what we'll do now with a fondue set I can't imagine.'

'What on earth did we buy her a fondue set for?'

'Because when I bravely rang up to ask her what they would both like – since you kept putting it off, if you remember – that's what she said she wanted.'

Charlie heaved on a sweatshirt and muttered 'Bloody woman,' under his breath.

'Charlie!' admonished Eleanor. 'Not in front of Ellie.'

'Sorry.'

'She's picking up words now and I don't want her copying your colourful vocabulary.'

'She'll learn them all sooner or later . . .'

'Well, later would be preferable to sooner.'

He came and sat on the bed beside Eleanor, who had her arm around her daughter. 'And a Happy Christmas to both my girls,' he said, kissing each of them on the top of the head. 'Even though it's not going to be quite what we expected.'

'No. Your poor dad.'

'Yes. I think he's well shot of her. Though what happens now I don't know. I mean, do you think he'll want to come back here to live?'

'Well, if he does, there's plenty of room.'

'I know that. It's the running of the estate that concerns me. He's bound to want to have a hand in it, and I really don't want to fall out with him. Too many chiefs and all that.'

'Aren't you jumping the gun a bit? We don't know what he's got planned. He might not want to stay here.'

Charlie looked at her questioningly. 'Where else can he go?'

'Who knows? He might want to travel. He might fancy a quiet life in Ullapool. Until he's thought about it I don't expect he'll know, but I think it's important that he knows he has somewhere to stay.'

Charlie kissed his wife on the cheek. 'You're very kind.'

'Not kind. Just concerned. It probably hasn't hit home yet. I think we need to be ready with a bit of moral support.'

Charlie got up from the bed. 'And tea. A cup for you?'

'Please. I'll be down in a minute – I'll just change Ellie and then we'll be with you. Oh, and a Happy Christmas!'

Charlie turned at the doorway of the bedroom and smiled at her. 'Yes; a Happy Christmas – whatever it may bring.'

Angus was already sitting at the kitchen table when Charlie came down. He had been up for some time, he said. Charlie didn't push him as to what the future held. It seemed far too early to go there. They exchanged pleasantries, almost as though nothing had happened, and as though Angus being back at the castle on his own were the most natural thing in the world.

Stockings were opened by the fire in the hall – one for Charlie, one for Eleanor and one for Ellie, and the fact that Father Christmas had thought that a bottle of twenty-five-year-old Glenmorangie whisky would be preferable in Angus's case proved not to have been wide of the mark. He smiled and said softly, 'Thank you, Father Christmas,' and Charlie felt engulfed by a wave of sympathy.

At noon, Murdo and Mrs Murdo arrived and covered very well their surprise at seeing Angus. Something in the way that they were greeted by Charlie and Eleanor let them know that although the household complement was not as they would have expected, things would carry on as though everything was going exactly according to plan. The two of them – Murdo clad in his Christmas Day best of rough grey tweed suit with knee breeches, check shirt and tie, topped off with a larger than usual flat cap, Mrs Murdo in a rather constraining lavender-coloured tartan two-piece – made polite conversation about the chilly but bright weather and the likelihood of the snowfall that had been forecast. An hour later, red-cheeked and swaying just a little, they made their way back along the track to Loch Side for their own Christmas dinner, clutching their Christmas boxes of the obligatory bottle of single malt and a single row of pearls which had belonged to Charlie's mother and which made Letty Murdoch come over all unnecessary. Charlie could not remember seeing her so emotional and put it down to the sherry.

The table was laid and ready for Christmas lunch by 2pm, but the trio (Ellie having had her version served early and been put down for her nap) had barely started on the Royal Game soup when a car pulled into the drive in front of the castle. Charlie got up to investigate. He opened the heavy front door and bridled at the sight of the all-too-familiar Austin 1100 Vanden Plas. Charlotte stepped out of it, slammed the door and walked towards Charlie with a face like thunder.

'Where is he?'

Charlie barred her way, with one arm on the door and the other on the jamb. 'Where's who?'

'Your father. I presume he's here, since he would have had nowhere else to go.'

There were several things that Charlie could have done at this point. He could have let his stepmother in. He could have followed his basic instinct and sent her packing. He could have reasoned with her and hoped that she would see his father's point of view. But before he could decide upon a course of action, he was aware that his father was standing beside him.

Softly he said, 'Leave this to me, Charlie,' and before Charlotte could respond he added, 'You'd better come in. It's very cold out there. They say it's going to snow.' He turned to his son: 'Charlie, would you mind if we went into my . . . your . . . study?'

Charlie shook his head, unable at this precise moment to conjure up words of any significance. Angus said nothing to Charlotte but turned on his heel and walked across the hall to the door that had once been his study and which was now Charlie's domain. Charlotte followed him, so pent up with emotion that it seemed to both Charlie and Eleanor that she might, at any moment, burst a blood vessel and save them the trouble of making any further arrangements, let alone conversation. The door of the study closed behind them, and Charlie and Eleanor looked at one another. 'Main course?' asked Eleanor.

'Would you mind if I just had a drink?' asked Charlie.

Father and stepmother did not emerge from their conclave for over an hour. There were raised voices from time to time – though, in actual fact, it was just one raised voice, that of Charlotte – though thanks to the thickness of the walls and the solidity of the oak doors of the castle, the conversation itself was inaudible.

'We need to eat,' said Eleanor. 'If you keep on drinking that claret you'll be sloshed by five o'clock.'

'I just don't feel like eating,' said Charlie. He was looking out of the window at the changing scene. Snow was falling heavily now. The mountains were all but invisible, and the woods and rough pasture that surrounded the castle were disappearing under a white mantle.

Eleanor came and stood by him. She laid her head on his shoulder.

'If this continues we'll be cut off,' she said.

'Oh God! That's all we need,' said Charlie. 'Being stuck here with her.'

At that moment, the door of the study opened and Charlotte stormed out, alone. Her face like thunder, she strode across to the front door, heaved it open with some difficulty, walked out into the cold and slammed it behind her. Moments later, Angus emerged.

Seeing the questioning looks on both Charlie and Eleanor's faces he said, calmly and levelly, 'I'm driving Charlotte back to Edinburgh.'

'In this? You can't!' exclaimed Charlie. 'The roads will be dreadful.'

Angus took his coat from the hatstand in the hall and, as he put it on, said, 'The alternative is that Charlotte stays here with us for Christmas, and that's something I wouldn't wish on anybody.' He smiled wanly. There was an air of resignation about him, quite different from the overwhelming sense of gloom that had enveloped him since his arrival the previous day. The fact that he had faced up to her, thought Charlie, must have somehow lifted his spirits; given him a shot in the arm, albeit a slight one.

'Have you got what you need for the journey?' asked Eleanor, ever practical. 'I mean water and something to eat?'

'Apparently,' said Angus. 'Charlotte brought things with her.' He was buttoning up his coat now and took down his flat tweed cap before coming over and kissing Eleanor on the cheek. He turned to Charlie. 'Take care,' he said.

'Never mind me; what about you?'

Angus opened the front door and scanned the ever-whitening landscape. 'I'll manage somehow.'

At this point the little loud speaker beside the fire in the hall crackled into life. It resonated with the sound of a baby's voice.

'You'd better go and see to Ellie,' said Angus. 'I'm sorry I've rather messed up your Christmas.'

'What about your things?' asked Eleanor.

'Don't worry about them. I'll manage for now.'

As Angus stepped out of the front door, Charlie said, 'Keep in touch, Dad. Let us know what you want us to do. Ring us when you get there.'

'Stop and call us on your way if you can, just to let us know you're safe,' added Eleanor.

The older man did not reply. He was crunching his way across the gravel now, towards the car, whose engine was already running and whose headlights were illuminating the ever-worsening blizzard. They could just make out the figure of Charlotte in the passenger seat; they could sense that she was glowering.

'We should stop him,' said Eleanor. Her voice was weighted with concern. 'He really shouldn't be setting off in this.'

Charlie shook his head. 'There's no way you'll put him off. You know Dad. Once he's determined to do something, that's it, and the quicker they set off the better. I can't see this snow slackening off any time soon.'

As they spoke, the car, now covered in half an inch of snow, turned in a slow arc before disappearing down the drive. As the sound of the engine died away, Charlie and Eleanor retreated into the hall and shut the door.

'I'll go and get Ellie,' said Eleanor. 'We might as well try and salvage something from this Christmas, though I don't see either of us enjoying ourselves until we know that they're safely back in Edinburgh.'

'No,' said Charlie softly. And then: 'I think I'd better have some of that turkey now; my head's beginning to spin.'

The telephone did not ring for the next three hours. When it did, the voice at the other end was one that Charlie did not recognise. 'Mr Stuart?'

'Yes?'

'Mr Charles Stuart?'

'Yes? Who's that?'

'This is the Lothian and Borders Constabulary, sir.'

Charlie's heart beat so loudly he could hear it.

'I'm afraid there's been an accident, sir.'

'Oh God! I knew it!' exclaimed Charlie.

'It involves your father and your mother, I'm afraid.'

'My stepmother.' Charlie instinctively corrected the misapprehension.

'Yes, sir.'

'We told them not to go. Are they badly hurt?'

'Sir, we'd normally come to see you rather than speak over the phone, but I'm afraid the weather is such that on this occasion—'

'Yes; yes, I understand. What's happened?'

'I'm really sorry to have to tell you this over the telephone, sir, especially on Christmas Day, but I'm afraid it appears as though your father has taken his own life.'

26

Loch Sodhail

New Year's Day 1974

'Better be killed than frightened to death.'
R.S. Surtees, *Mr Facey Romford's Hounds*, 1865

Christmas was effectively abandoned. The decorations were taken down and the cards put away. Only the nativity scene in the hall of the castle was left in place, Eleanor having set it up with Ellie on Christmas Eve and feeling in greater need of divine intervention than at any time previously in her life.

The snow stopped after falling for two days, but then the freeze set in and the inhabitants of Sodhail were effectively cut off from the rest of the world. The drifts at the sides of the drive were waist deep and on the drive itself a foot of snow denied the castle residents access to anywhere, including the Murdochs' cottage, Loch Side. Eleanor would have dearly loved to have visited her parents and poured out her feelings, but the road to Invergarry House was as impassable as that to Castle Sodhail. She had to content herself with frequent telephone calls, during which she tried – and failed – to avoid letting her emotions overtake her. 'Ellie knows there's something wrong,' she confided in her mother, 'but I'm doing my best to make things as normal as possible.'

'Keep to her routine dear,' her mother had advised, 'that's always a good idea – meals, sleeping, that sort of thing. If she still has that pattern, it will help.'

Charlie had taxed the policeman who telephoned with news of his father's death for further details, but the officer was reluctant to commit himself more than saying that it appeared Angus had taken his own life with a shotgun; more than that he could not say until a post-mortem had been undertaken, and the likelihood of that happening within the next few days was slight. It was Christmas and the extreme weather conditions had affected Edinburgh and its environs as well as the Highlands, though perhaps not to the same extent.

When Charlie enquired as to the whereabouts of his stepmother, he had been told that she had been sedated and was staying with friends. As to where the tragedy had taken place, and any further details, the policeman was apologetic but unforthcoming, though he did confirm that there was no suggestion of foul play, or any other party being involved.

Charlie's thoughts remained confused and debilitating during the days following the event. He alternated between blaming himself for not stopping his father from leaving, and blaming Charlotte for driving his father to despair. He hoped that she was suffering as much as he was, and then reproached himself for such callous thoughts. But how could he be charitable when his father lay dead at – it appeared – his own hand, and Charlotte was 'staying with friends'? How could such a woman have anybody that she could call a friend – a woman who had behaved so abominably towards his father and who had clearly driven him to his death?

Eleanor did her best to reassure Charlie that it was not his fault, but found him distant and hard to reach. She could understand his utter despair, but found it hard to cope with his sorrow, his introspection and his apparent unwillingness to be comforted.

She took to calling her mother twice a day, to ask for advice and to find for herself some crumb of comfort, but her mother – although sympathetic and helpful when it came to the well-being of her granddaughter – was at a loss when it came to pacifying her own child. It was a series of events beyond her compass. Grief she could advise upon first hand, but she had no personal experience of suicide, let alone of such a close relation. Davina Fitzallan did her best, but felt, to her own chagrin, that on this occasion, when she would have dearly loved to have put her arms around her daughter and convince her that all would be well in the end, she could only recite platitudes at the end of a telephone.

The atmosphere within the walls of Castle Sodhail was understandably tense, not least because of matters unresolved. Anxious in some way to work through the confusion and mixed emotions that spun around in his head, and finding no other possible physical outlet thanks to the blanket of snow, Charlie set about digging a pathway to Loch Side. He told himself that it was to make sure that Murdo and Mrs Murdo were all right, but he knew, too, that the physical exertion might work some kind of magic upon him and at least clarify his thoughts, if not assuage his grief.

Loch Side was around a quarter of a mile from the castle. He did not care. He worked feverishly, sweat pouring from his brow, discarding his windcheater and then his sweater as he threw the powdered snow into towering piles at either side of the path, the fine peppering of crystals frequently blowing back and temporarily blinding him in a freezing shower. The snow had stopped, but a biting wind lacerated his face and, when he paused, stung at the perspiration on his back and his brow.

He had dug just over half way to the Murdochs' house when he heard another shovel scraping at the frozen earth. He cried out and, from around the corner, masked by a snow-laden stand of pine trees, he heard the familiar and welcome voice of Murdo.

Within fifteen minutes their combined labours had resulted in an open pathway between the two dwellings and the two men stood face to face on the ribbon of frozen earth that linked them.

For a few moments neither of them said anything. It was Murdo who spoke first. ''Tis a sad business,' he said. 'The missus and I wanted tae offer our condolences tae you and Eleanor and the babby.'

Charlie could only nod and look along the pathway they had cleared together.

Murdo continued: 'It was good of you tae telephone.'

Charlie shrugged. 'There was nothing else I could do. No one else I could call.' It reminded him once more how dependent he was upon those closest to him.

Murdo nodded. 'I know. But a man disnae need many good friends. A handful he can call on is worth a heap o' acquaintances.' He patted Charlie on the shoulder. It was not something that Murdo was given to doing, and the unexpectedness of it caught Charlie unawares. He found himself sobbing into his hands.

'Oh, Murdo!' he said. 'It was all my fault! I shouldn't have let him go out – it was already starting to snow and I told him it was dangerous.'

'But you said it wis nothing tae do with the snow,' said Murdo. 'How could it have been your fault?'

Charlie impatiently wiped away the tears that stung his cheeks. He was beginning to feel the cold now, and he started to shiver. It caused his voice to come out in uncontrolled bursts: 'Because I let him leave . . . with that bloody woman!

He'd come to us to escape her. He was going to leave her – *had* left her – and I let him go off into the night with her in her own bloody car.'

Murdo walked away from him, down the track towards the castle. Charlie wondered if he had offended the ghillie. Then he saw him bend to pick up Charlie's windcheater and sweater. Having retrieved them, Murdo returned with them, motioning Charlie to put them on. 'When did your faither ever do anything you asked him tae do?' asked Murdo. 'I mean, something he didn't want tae do hisself? When did you ever manage tae change your faither's mind?'

Charlie shook his head. 'Never.'

'Well, there ye are then; you just answered your ane question. Nothing you could have said or done would have altered yer faither's resolve. If he intended tae drive back tae Edinburgh, nothing you could have done – short of tampering with his car – would have stopped him. And you certainly couldnae have said anything tae dissuade him. His mind was made up.'

'But to . . . you know . . . take his own life.'

Murdo took a deep breath. 'We dinnae ken how that happened. Not yet. 'Twill be as well tae wait until yon postmortem before we start speculatin' about that.'

'I suppose so.'

'How's Eleanor taken it?'

'As well as she could. I've not been very easy to live with these past few days. I think it's all getting her down. She can't even go and see her mum and dad.'

'Aye, 'tis a bugger, this weather. They say it'll be a few days before the thaw comes an' all. Anyway, you'd best be gettin' hame afore Eleanor starts worryin'. The missus and me will be there in a wee while.'

'What do you mean?'

'There's nae point in you bein' cooped up in yon castle all on your ane. You'll only mither. We'll be there shortly. Letty will do the cooking and I can make mysel' useful in other ways.'

Charlie made to interrupt, but Murdo cut him short.

'We'll like as not get in the way, but that'll give ye somethin' else tae think aboot at least. Take yer mind off them things that worryin' willnae solve. Off ye go.' With that, he motioned Charlie to walk back towards the castle, and he himself set off for Loch Side to gather up his wife and a few necessaries.

Charlie did as Murdo suggested; his head a confused mixture of grief and gratitude, his feet numb and his hands blistered from the feverish exertions of snow clearing. The day was beginning to die. The sun, watery, was setting behind the pines. It was beyond the shadow of any doubt the saddest New Year he had ever witnessed. He hoped that in the days to come, some form of solace would be his, though he knew that the years ahead would offer little but remorse whenever he remembered his father: the man he had never really known, the man who had left him the castle and all that he owned, the man whom he suspected he resembled more than he was prepared to admit to himself. The man who had made one final error of judgement that had cost him his life, and all because he fell in love with the wrong woman. It would be some time before Charlie could ever understand how that could possibly happen.

27

Edinburgh

January 1974

'Winter is come and gone,
But grief returns with the revolving year.'
Percy Bysshe Shelley, *Adonais*, 1821

The Lothian and Borders police were kinder and more considerate than Charlie had expected. The two officers who sat with him in the police station explained carefully and sensitively what seemed to have happened, though, of course, there would have to be an inquest to establish the cause of death without doubt. But it was as clear to them as it could be that Angus Stuart had taken his own life 'while the balance of his mind was temporarily disturbed'. It seemed to Charlie such a nebulous phrase. If it had only been disturbed 'temporarily', why did it have to lead to death?

But such questions were futile. He realised that. His father had been found in a copse in a patch of woodland on the outskirts of the city. He had left the car at the side of the main road which had been cleared of snow, and walked into the woodland where he knew he would be alone. No foul play was suspected. There had been just one cartridge in the gun; the other barrel was empty. Thoughtful, they said, without a trace of irony. Had the children who discovered the body found another cartridge in the barrel it could have resulted in a nasty accident.

The gun would be returned to Charlie once the necessary forensic procedures had been undertaken. The officers explained that it would not be necessary for him to identify the body; the deceased man's wife had already done that. Charlie still found it difficult to think of Charlotte as his father's wife. But then, she no longer was. Now she was his widow.

He wanted to avoid going to see her. Every fibre of his being rebelled against it, but some lone quiet voice within his head told him that it had to be done. Whatever she had caused to happen, whatever dreadful deed had transpired as a result of her marrying his father, she had, indeed, married him and he – as her stepson – had a duty to see her. He would do so just the once. His duty done, he could then carry on with his life as best he could. His father had provided her with a house; Charlie, as the stepson, would have no further obligations concerning her welfare.

He parked the Morris Minor where he had parked it before, in such different circumstances, and walked up to the front door of Charlotte's townhouse. It was some time before it was answered, and when it was, it was not Charlotte who greeted him, but a man whom, Charlie guessed, was in his early thirties. He was handsome and smartly dressed in chinos and a pale yellow cashmere sweater. Had it not been for the incongruous vibrancy of the knitwear, Charlie doubted, subsequently, that he would have remembered him.

'You must be Charlie,' said the man. 'I'm Sebastian.'

He saw the vacant look on Charlie's face and added: 'Sebastian Brodie. I'm a friend of Charlotte's. Come in. She's in the drawing room.'

How very like Charlotte, thought Charlie. She had a 'drawing room', not a 'sitting room'. A kind of numbness overtook him as he was shown into the large room to the right of the hallway. The drabness of the atmosphere matched the drabness of the day; Charlotte's dark green colour scheme did little to help. She was perched on a chair that faced a bureau, her body encased in a grey wool dress; Hermès scarf at her neck. She looked up from writing a letter, her face the picture of grief. It left Charlie quite unmoved. She held out a hand towards him, no doubt, thought Charlie, expecting him to clasp it and hold her to him in their joint grief. Charlie found himself unable to oblige. Instead he just said, 'I'm sorry.' He realised the inadequacy of his remark, but knew that if she expected more of him she would be disappointed.

Charlotte lowered her hand and then her head. Charlie could see that she had been crying – her eyes were red and her cheeks flushed.

Sebastian cut in, his voice rather brighter than suited the occasion: 'Would you like a cup of coffee? I've just made some.'

'No. No, thank you. I can't stop; I'm on my way home. I just wanted to call in . . .'

He could offer no more. He wanted to say that he had called in to say he was sorry, and indeed he was. But not for Charlotte. He was sorry for his father. And, if he were honest, for himself.

Charlotte cleared her throat and dabbed at her eyes with a tissue plucked from a frilly-covered box that sat to one side of the elegant bureau. 'I'm just writing a few letters. To tell people. I don't know what they'll think.'

Of you? thought Charlie. *Or of my father?* But he simply said, 'Yes.'

Charlotte looked up at him. 'I'll let you know when the funeral will be,' she said. This took Charlie by surprise. He had somehow thought that he would take charge of the funeral arrangements but, clearly, these were in the hands of the widow. He found himself wrong-footed by this unexpected disclosure. It was as though not only had his father's life been taken from him but so, too, had his mortal remains.

'When do you think . . . ?' he asked.

'I'm not sure. A couple of weeks at least, they say. When the police have released—' She stopped short of saying 'the body', for which Charlie was grateful.

'Yes. I see.'

Charlotte got up. 'Well, if you're sure you won't stay?'

'Quite sure.' He nodded at Charlotte, unable and unwilling to kiss her goodbye. He turned to leave.

'Before you go,' she said, reaching into the bureau. 'There is a letter for you. From your father.'

Charlie was taken aback. 'For me?'

'Yes. I found it on the kitchen table when I came back. I was out, you see, when he . . . when he left.'

She handed Charlie a small white envelope on which was written his name.

'It's been opened.'

'Yes. I'm afraid I opened it. You see, there was nothing else. Nothing for me. Just that.'

Charlie turned over the envelope in his hands. The front bore his name in capital letters: Charles Stuart. He slid out the folded piece of paper that it contained. There was no explanation of anything; nothing on the note to indicate that it was specifically for him from his father. But the handwriting was unmistakable and the message itself was simple. It consisted of just three words: 'Bring me home.'

28

Castle Sodhail

January 1974

'That a lie which is all a lie may be met and fought with outright,
But a lie which is part a truth is a harder matter to fight.'
Alfred, Lord Tennyson, 'The Grandmother', 1859

As instructed, they brought Angus Stuart home, and laid him to rest in a grave dug by Murdo and Charlie on a grassy promontory overlooking the loch. The two men had worked in silence; no words were necessary to convey their sorrow or their pride in laying the former laird to rest in the ground that had been so important to him.

The ceremony had been brief but moving, the grave surrounded by the immediate family, those few souls who worked on the estate, a handful of villagers from Strath Carron, the Fitzallans, plus Murdo and Mrs Murdo – the latter with her arm through that of her husband the entire time, and a look on her face that mingled disdain with disbelief. Charlotte stood to one side with her own arm through that of Sebastian Brodie, she clad in a black woollen cape and translucent veil, he in a long Black Watch tartan coat with a muffler at his neck.

Charlie barely noticed them. His eyes never left the Scots pine coffin, which was lowered into a grave lined with heather cut from the moor.

Respectful of his father's love of Sir Walter Scott, a passion that his son had not shared, Charlie read out some words from the pen of the wizard of the north, as the chill north-easterly wind whistled through the stunted trees on the shores of the loch:

> 'One hour of life, crowded to the full with glorious action, and filled with noble risks, is worth whole years of those mean observances of paltry decorum, in which men steal through existence, like sluggish waters through a marsh, without either honour or observation.'

It seemed fitting, if a little generous, since his father, while steady, could not really claim to have witnessed much in the way of 'glorious action'. For Charlie, though, it was enough that Angus had rescued the Sodhail estate from stagnation and possible disintegration and handed it on to his son in better order than it had, in turn, been bequeathed to him.

Murdo nodded his approval as more heather was tumbled onto the top of the coffin. It was Mrs Murdo who recalled, as the party walked back to the castle for a warming glass of hot toddy, the more familiar words of Sir Walter Scott. Glancing across at Charlotte, every inch the grieving widow, with the black veil now blowing into her face and threatening to take off and fly over the mountaintops, she murmured to her husband, rather more loudly than was polite: 'Oh, what a tangled web we weave, when first we practise to deceive.'

That night, Charlie and Eleanor lay side by side in their bed as the wind whistled and buffeted the windows of the castle.

'Well done,' offered Eleanor. 'It can't have been easy.'

'No,' confirmed Charlie. 'But at least Dad's where he wanted to be now. And that bloody—'

'Let's not mention her,' cut in Eleanor. 'Not any more. Not unless we have to.'

'No.' After a pause he said, 'What did you make of . . . you know . . . him?'

'Sebastian?'

'Yes.'

Eleanor snuggled up to Charlie and put her arm across his chest. 'I don't know. I can't make out whether he's her bit on the side or . . . well, just a friend.'

'He's very handsome,' conceded Charlie. 'Surely she wouldn't . . . I mean, not so soon?'

'Who knows? I wouldn't put anything past her.'

'You said we wouldn't talk about her.'

'No. Anyway, we've a guest arriving tomorrow.'

Charlie started: 'Oh God! I'd forgotten about that.'

'Don't worry. Everything's sorted. And it's only the one student this time. For a couple of weeks, Gordon said.'

'When did you speak to him?' asked Charlie, uneasy but doing his best to appear calm.

'Yesterday. He rang while you and Murdo were . . . getting things ready.'

'Just the one?'

'Yes. Florin. You remember? The Yugoslav. The one who didn't say much.'

'The one you fancied,' said Charlie.

'I didn't fancy him!'

'I saw the way you looked at him,' teased Charlie. The novelty of such light-hearted conversation found him relaxing more than he had felt able to do over the preceding weeks. He continued: 'Every time he came into the room – brooding – you looked up and smiled at him.'

'I was just being pleasant, that's all!'

'Mmm. You were never that pleasant with me.'

Eleanor squeezed his arm and then rolled on top of him. 'What are you saying?' she asked. But before he could answer, she was kissing him tenderly, and for the first time in many weeks they made gentle love before falling asleep in each other's arms.

The wild weather outside steadily abated, and by morning the fiercely turbulent water of the loch had subsided into gentle ripples.

The following day dawned bright and clear, the tops of the mountains, coated in crisp snow, stood out against the pale blue sky like sharp teeth, and the Land Rover carrying their 'paying guest' deposited him at the front door of the castle.

Florin Adzic walked forward with his bag in his hand, dropped it on the gravel and kissed Eleanor on both cheeks, before offering his outstretched hand to Charlie who, glancing at Eleanor, noticed that she avoided his gaze and was suppressing a smile.

'Good to be back,' said Florin, with rather more enthusiasm than Charlie could remember him expressing on his previous visit. He turned back to Eleanor: 'I like coming here. It feel like home.' Then, waving his arms about him: 'Big mountains; big lake. I like bigness!'

The Land Rover growled away down the drive, and Eleanor gestured their guest towards the front door. 'You know where you are,' she said. 'The same room as last time – in the north tower.'

Florin nodded, and then flicked back the dark floppy fringe. He was, as Charlie had noted, a good-looking youth, with a chiselled profile, a sensitive-looking mouth and a wild look in his eyes; a matinee idol if ever there was one. No wonder Eleanor was smiling.

* * *

Over supper in the kitchen, Eleanor and Charlie spoke softly of their return visitor, though their lowered voices were quite unnecessary since the north tower was at the other end of the castle and well out of earshot. The thick walls of one room alone would have been enough to prevent eavesdropping, notwithstanding the distance between them.

'He seems more relaxed,' offered Eleanor.

'Probably because we're more familiar to him now,' said Charlie, taking a sip of wine between mouthfuls of lasagne. He looked at Eleanor. 'That's *to* him; not *with* him,' he teased.

She ignored the intended slight. 'I hope he'll be happier than he was last time.'

Charlie sighed. 'We're not here to make him happy; just to put him up for . . . how long is he going to be here?'

'Just a couple of weeks, Gordon said.'

'And how did he sound? Gordon, I mean.'

'Odd.'

Charlie stopped eating. 'What do you mean by "odd"?'

Eleanor thought for a moment. 'A bit under the influence. Maybe he'd just had a glass or two.' She continued eating.

'What time did he call?'

'I told you; in the morning, when you and Murdo were . . . getting things ready.' She still could not bring herself to say 'digging the grave'.

Charlie looked directly at her. 'He sounded under the influence in the morning? That's not a good sign.'

'No. I hope he's all right. Maybe we should get him up here – for a break or something.'

Charlie, foreseeing complications, attempted to make light of it. 'Maybe he was just hung over. That would be what it was – he'd had a heavy night and was nursing a hangover.'

'Maybe.' Eleanor took a sip of her own wine. 'What does he do now?' she asked. 'Now that his course is finished. I mean, I know he helps students find accommodation in the holidays, but that's not a full-time job, is it? And it's certainly not the sort of job that someone as bright as Gordon would do. So what does he occupy his days with?'

Charlie summoned up his powers of ingenuity and hoped that his wife would not notice if he sounded unconvincing. 'He's part of the faculty or whatever they call it. On the university staff. Helping out dons or something.'

'That sounds a bit vague.'

'Well I don't know, do I? He was a school friend, that's all. I'm not his keeper.'

Eleanor was surprised at his sudden irritability. But she let the moment pass and put down her husband's ill temper to the events of the last few weeks. It had not been an easy time for either of them.

29

Castle Sodhail

August 1974

'Guests can be, and often are, delightful, but they should never be allowed to get the upper hand.'
Elizabeth, Countess von Arnim, *All the Dogs in My Life*, 1936

Florin's New Year stay had come and gone without event, though Charlie was convinced that there was certainly some kind of chemistry between his wife and 'Two Bob' as he rather rudely referred to the Yugloslav lodger, even if she herself was unaware of it. The relief of seeing him leave had been only partly due to Florin's increasing familiarity with Eleanor. That he should have come and gone without any kind of diplomatic incident was an even greater consolation, and Charlie had come to appreciate the additional funds that such a commitment gave rise to – far and away greater than the rate paid by any other guests.

But there were other things to think about now. Ellie had turned three years old, and another baby was due in a month's time. Eleanor was easily tired in the summer heat, in spite of the relative cool of the Highlands, and in between organising the grouse shoots and the cottage lets, the fishing trips and the general land management, Charlie did his best to lighten her load, along with Mrs Murdo's help.

As the mountain burns had thawed the previous winter and the snow receded on the high peaks, there followed a soggy spring, which slid imperceptibly into the Highland summer.

Florin returned for the longer break, and this time Gordon came with him – intending to stay for just a few days, he said. That 'few days' had already turned into a fortnight, and having the two of them there at the same time made Charlie more tense than usual, a fact exacerbated by the presence of three new students – one Greek and two Russians. There were times when the hall of the castle felt to Charlie more like an airport departure lounge than a baronial reception room.

In the same way that his father's demeanour had shocked him when he and Eleanor had visited Edinburgh, so he was alarmed by Gordon's general appearance. His old schoolfriend had always been less than particular about his mode of dress, but now there was something altogether more disquieting about his general turnout. His clothes were not just un-ironed, but frequently unwashed. There were occasions when Eleanor had jokingly told him to take off his clothes where he stood in the kitchen, throwing him an apron to hide his embarrassment, while she piled the whole lot into the washing machine, laundered and ironed it while he waited and then handed him back his habiliments and turned away while he dressed. All this he endured resignedly, with a wan smile.

While the students dined in a room in the north wing, waited on by Mrs Murdo, Eleanor, Ellie, Charlie and Gordon dined in the castle kitchen or, on special occasions, at a table in the hall by the log fire – rarely lit now that it was high summer, but still enjoyed on those occasional Highland evenings when there was a nip in the air.

Ellie would be put to bed early, and then the three of them could talk. Although Gordon made a pretence of being his usual sparkling literary self, there was something missing; a kind of hollowness to his mood that led both Charlie and Eleanor to worry about him.

On one particular evening, Charlie, keen to stir Gordon out of his apparent torpor said, 'I remember when you used to go out riding.'

'Good God!' said Gordon. 'I haven't done that for a while.'

'Did you ever shoot?' asked Charlie mischievously. 'Or should I not ask you in case you lie again and I risk letting you loose with one of my guns?'

'Purdey or Holland and Holland?' asked Gordon, with a rare smile.

'Ha! I might live in a castle but I don't own a pair of Purdeys!'

'Shame. I'd have settled for just the one – provided I could have a loader.'

Charlie looked at him suspiciously. 'Are you having me on? Is this another of your cock-and-bull stories like the old horse riding one?'

'That wasn't a cock-and-bull story. It was true; I had ridden when I was younger.'

'Yes, but not much. And I bet the horse had a brass rod like a stick of barley sugar running through its body and that it only galloped when the fairground owner turned on the merry-go-round. That horse of ours you went out on could have broken your neck.'

'Oh ye of little faith. I never came off, did I?'

'Nearly,' murmured Eleanor, smiling.

Gordon turned to her in mock indignation. '*Quam bene vivas referre, non quam diu.*'

'And what does that mean in Scots?' asked Charlie.

'It is how well you live that matters; not how long.'

There was an uncomfortable silence following his remark.

'Oh, I'm sorry,' he offered.

'No. Don't be. It's good to hear you back on form,' said Charlie. 'Anyway, if you really can shoot – and I want to know seriously now, no joking – then you can come out with the guns tomorrow. One peg has cried off due to illness and we could share it.'

Gordon looked brighter in the eye than the two of them had seen for some time. 'Yes please. And I really can; cub's honour. I had an uncle . . .'

'Please!' said Charlie. 'Spare me the history. I believe you. And I'll be able to tell if you're having me on from the way you shoot first thing. I'll put some clays up and if you're crap you can stay at home.'

But Gordon was not 'crap' the following morning. He turned out to be a fine shot, and as the day wore on the old Gordon seemed to reappear – Jeevesian asides and all – and the two friends found in one another that ease which had been sorely missing for the past few years.

Over lunch in one of the three timbered lodges on the estate, they fell in to talking at one end of the table while the other guns put away cottage pie and Bordeaux with a decibel level that assured them of privacy.

'You look better than you did when you arrived,' said Charlie.

'I feel better. Nothing like a bit of fresh air in the old lungs to perk a fellow up.'

'You even sound like your old self.'

'Mmm,' muttered Gordon, topping up his glass. 'I'm not sure I know who he is.'

'Your old self?'

'Yes. I left him behind some time ago. At around about the same time that I sold my soul.'

'That sounds serious.'

'It's meant to.' He took a long drink from his glass and his eyes looked rheumy. Introspection began to take hold. And the old Gordon expression slipped from view, to be replaced with a hunted look that caused Charlie genuine concern.

'Is it this business? The student thing?'

Gordon nodded. 'In its broadest sense, yes. This is not what I had planned. I was destined for literary greatness. Well, maybe not greatness, but a more fulfilling role. Something original; groundbreaking. Not being a bloody dogsbody for others with vested interests.'

'You mean you don't have vested interests?'

'I mean I don't have any interests at all – financial, intellectual or emotional – and certainly not vested.'

'So why did you get involved?'

'Do you really want to know? Honestly?'

Charlie nodded.

Gordon lowered his voice to a whisper and leaned forward. 'I fell in love.'

He could see the look of surprise on Charlie's face. 'And that's not all. I fell in love with the wrong person.'

'You mean . . . ?'

Gordon looked him in the eye. 'Alex Jesmond.'

'Bloody hell.'

'I know. Waste of time. Bloody stupid. I'm not his type at all. It dawned on me eventually, of course, but by then it was too bloody late; I was in it up to my eyeballs.'

'In what?'

'This business. National security.'

At this point, chairs were being pushed away from the table and the guns were getting up, red-faced and good humoured, ready to make their unsteady way back home, or else to the cottages they had rented.

Having heard the start of the general move to depart, Murdo came into the lodge and said in his best stentorian voice: 'The Land Rover's outside, gentlemen, hop in and I'll ferry ye back tae yer beds.'

'At three o'clock,' came the cry from one of the party. 'We should be so lucky!'

'Aye, yer luck's in today,' confirmed Murdo, winking at Charlie. 'We dinnae want the local constabulary on our backs so your chauffeur is ready.' And with that he slipped out and started up the Land Rover. The guns helped each other into the back of the vehicle, with ribald comments helping them on their way, and Charlie and Gordon stood and watched as the party was driven off with Murdo at the wheel.

'Redoubtable,' muttered Gordon.

'Murdo?'

'The same. Where would you be without him?'

'Up the creek without a paddle,' confirmed Charlie.

'A bit like yours truly.'

'Is that what it feels like?'

Gordon nodded.

'Then why don't you opt out?'

'Easier said than done. I'm looking for a way, but I'm not sure I've found it yet. One or two of the . . . sources of intelligence . . . are getting restless. I reckon it's going to come to a head soon. And I don't want to be here when it does.'

Charlie looked alarmed. 'Where does that leave us?'

'Oh, don't worry. I wouldn't do anything that would harm you. I'm more worried about you and Eleanor and the child – children – than I am about myself. I wouldn't do anything to risk . . . well . . . I wouldn't, don't you fear.'

'What do you know about Two Bob – this Florin chap?'

'Adzic? Funny you should mention him. He's likely to be one of the disaffected ones.' Gordon hesitated. 'Bright boy. Thoughtful. Sensitive. Look, the less you know the better. I don't want to tell you things that might cause problems in the future or cause you to lose sleep. None of this is anything to do with you, and as the owner of a bed-and-breakfast, anyone who comes looking for them will know that you are absolutely nothing to do with it.'

'I know that. At least I hope I do,' said Charlie evenly. 'But I'm also your friend, and if it helps you . . .'

Gordon hesitated. 'Florin is a Yugoslav. Not all Yugloslavs are happy. Tito's human rights record is, to put it politely, suspect. He maintained stability post-war but there were many national uprisings that were suppressed as well as ethnic cleansing – particularly of Germans. Things there have been very tense and students, in particular, have been rebellious. You know what students are like – and Florin in particular is quite a tempestuous character – hormones a go-go, full of righteous indignation, determined to create a better world and do what they can to assist those who can make it happen.'

'Like the British?'

'Like the British. They come over here, we give them a great education in our universities and they decide that they will help us to help them – with information, intelligence. Little bits here and there. Not full-blown espionage but little things that, when pieced together, give us a clearer picture of those countries with whom we have what Harold Macmillan used to call "little local difficulties". What may seem to some like relatively unimportant information can actually be very useful. Sometimes without even knowing it they give us a clearer picture of just what is going on in their own country – who is in favour and who is not; which way the pendulum is swinging, how we can make it swing further in a direction that suits us.'

'And they do agree to help?'

'Up to a point. We choose them carefully; handle them with care. Make sure that in their holidays they have somewhere safe to go – not just physically safe but somewhere they won't be burdened by responsibilities. But patriotism is a funny thing. For several years they assist us, and then it is as if they remember who they are and where they are from, and that instinctive national pride – whatever got in its way previously – comes to the fore and they decide that home is best after all.'

'And they turn on you?'

'Yes. Sometimes suddenly and quite unpredictably.'

'And Florin?'

'I'm not sure. I'm getting to know him better, but I'm still keeping an eye on him – that's why I'm here. But don't worry. I'll make sure that he doesn't do anything silly. Anyway, you're not to worry. You're my best mate and I won't let you down. By the way, is there any more of that Bordeaux left? It was rather delicious; not the sort of wine I'd expect to find on a second-rate shoot in Scotland.'

Charlie refrained from disabusing his old friend. He had rather too much on his mind.

30

Castle Sodhail

December 1974

> 'Every animal of the forest is mine, and the cattle upon a thousand hills.'
>
> Psalm 50:10

They were lying in bed, watching the slow breaking of dawn; a rare moment of peaceful togetherness now that they were in possession of a three-year-old and a three-month-old. Lucy Letitia Stuart (the middle name a note of gratitude expressed to Mrs Murdo) was born in the hospital in Fort William, Eleanor having been airlifted there in spectacular fashion, with Charlie at her side. The delivery was not an easy one; Eleanor lost a lot of blood and Charlie agonised over both mother and baby for what seemed like an eternity. But Eleanor slowly recovered her strength, and within a week they were all three back at the castle where Mrs Murdo, having looked after Ellie, could now ensure that her namesake, too, would thrive, thanks to her proprietorial ministrations.

Life had, once more, assumed a pattern, albeit a different one augmented by a fourth member of the family.

'I'm not sure what to do this Christmas,' Eleanor confided in her husband.

'What do you mean?'

'Well, should we invite Gordon?'

Charlie, remembering his and Gordon's summer conversations, said, 'Good idea. He could do with being taken out of himself at Christmas. It's a rotten time to be on your own.'

'Is he on his own? '

'Oh, I think so. Unrequited love and all that.'

Eleanor stroked Charlie's cheek. 'You've never said what you and he discussed in summer.'

'Oh, just the usual man stuff. Nothing important.'

'And you expect me to believe that?'

Charlie pushed himself up on his pillow and drew her close. 'You've enough on your plate with two small children and a house to run without worrying about Gordon.'

'I do have a brain, you know. And a heart. I can cope with more than one thing at a time – emotionally and physically. I'm a woman, not a one-track-minded man.' She thumped him playfully.

Charlie grinned. 'I know. Anyway, last Christmas was so bloody I just hope we can have a more relaxing time this year.'

'So do you want to invite him?'

'If he'll come. He may not want to be stuck in a Scottish castle with two screaming kids.'

As if on cue, at that precise moment the smaller of the screaming kids lived up to her name and rent the air with her own special version of the dawn chorus.

'Thank God for baby alarms,' said Eleanor.

'Or not,' muttered Charlie. 'Why do you think they built castle walls so thick, if it wasn't to muffle the sound of babies crying and give hard-working parents a lie-in?'

Eleanor slid out of bed and he watched as she walked over to the door where her dressing gown hung on a hook. Her naked figure was dappled by the early morning sun slanting through the window.

'You know, you're still worth looking at naked.'

'Really? I thought it was all getting a bit wobbly.' She reached up and took down the dressing gown.

'Not where it matters. Come here.'

Eleanor walked back over to the bed, her arms in the dressing gown but the front wide open so that her nakedness was in full view. Charlie reached up and stroked her left breast before she pulled away, fastened the dressing gown and said, 'Sorry; must go. Little girls needing me more than you do.' With that she opened the bedroom door and disappeared in the direction of the crying child.

Charlie flopped back on the pillow. So that was that. Third place on Eleanor's list of priorities. He sighed deeply. He didn't really think that such was the case, though there were moments when it certainly seemed so.

Around the breakfast table, mayhem reigned, as usual. Ellie was at the stage where no food seemed to please her, and Lucy was always hungry. Finishing his bowl of porridge, Charlie got up from the table and made to leave. Taking his coat from the back of the chair, he moved to kiss his wife goodbye and remarked casually, 'See you at lunchtime then.'

'Oh, I won't be here at lunchtime. I'm taking the children into Strath Carron. Do you think you can fend for yourself?'

'Of course. When will you be back?'

'Around mid-afternoon. Mrs Murdo's coming with me. You and Murdo can help yourselves to whatever's in the fridge – there's a pork pie and some coleslaw, and a carton of soup if you want something hot.'

'Thank you,' he said absently, trying not to feel that he was being fobbed off. Then he kissed her on the top of the head, said a loud and pointed 'Bye-bye' to the two girls, who were by now smothered in a mixture of Weetabix and jam, and left through the kitchen door.

Murdo was repairing a stretch of post and rail fencing around a patch of pasture just above the castle, the better to restrain a trio of Highland cattle that he had managed to persuade Charlie to invest in. 'A prize at the local show would be a good thing for Sodhail,' was his excuse. Charlie had been happy to go along with the idea, for although he could see no real financial benefit in these hairy long-horned beasts, they did brighten the landscape with their rufous long-haired coats, and would certainly keep those who rented the cottages amused, provided they did not escape.

Charlie greeted him brightly. 'They look happy,' he said, nodding in the direction of the three cattle who regarded him with curiosity as they stood staring at him beneath their foxy fringes while systematically chewing the cud.

'Aye. Yon big feller will do well for us next year. I'm just making sure they're secure.' He hammered away at a rail and then stood up and walked over to where Charlie stood.

'Aren't they supposed to be a bit bad tempered?' asked Charlie.

'Depends on the individual,' remarked Murdo. 'A bit like us. Some are trickier than others.' He winked.

'Yes. Well, I just hope we've got three even-tempered souls, that's all.'

Murdo gathered up his tools and tucked a roll of stock fencing under his arm. 'There we are. All secure. And they've plenty of hay tae be goin' on with.'

'Have you given them names?'

'Aye. Yon's Hamish – he's the big one; the one with the white blaze is Fergus and the smaller one is Jimmy.'

'You can't call a Highland cow Jimmy!'

'Och, it's the name he came with. I didnae bother tae change it.'

'Hamish, Angus and Jimmy,' muttered Charlie. 'What an unlikely trio. Ah well, as long as you can keep them under control.'

'Like babies,' Murdo reassured him. 'As long as they're left alone and nae bothered. Up here they're out of harm's way and I've put a sign on the gate: BEWARE OF THE BULLOCKS.'

Charlie laughed. 'Yes. Always beware of the bullocks,' he said; and with that he walked off towards the loch to repair yet another broken section of dry stone wall.

31

Castle Sodhail
January 1975

'We pray for peace,
But not the easy peace
Built on complacency
And not the truth of God.'
Alan Gaunt, 'New Hymns
for Worship', 1973

One thing became clear over that Christmas: Gordon had an alcohol problem. It had, if anything, got worse since his visit during the previous summer, and by nine o'clock each evening he was pretty much incoherent.

The situation worried Eleanor rather more than it appeared to worry Charlie, who consoled her by saying, 'But he's very good with the kids. He loves being with them, and he doesn't drink until the evening.'

Eleanor raised her eyebrows. 'Have you seen the sherry decanter?'

'I don't drink sherry.'

'Neither do I. But the level keeps going down, and it's not Mrs Murdo. She only drinks at Christmas, and you can see the effect it has on her.'

'Oh.' There was little he could do to defend his old friend in the face of such damning evidence. 'I'll talk to him.'

'You'd better do it before six o'clock then.' Eleanor flashed him a rueful smile. 'I just worry about him, Charlie, that's all.'

'I know. But at least we can take care of him here, rather than leaving him at the mercy of Oxford and . . .' his words tailed off; he was unsure of the collective noun for what, for want of a better word, he considered to be a bunch of shits.

He had never liked Alex Jesmond. Never trusted him. The fact that Gordon had been 'in love' with him made him shudder, not at Gordon's sexual preferences – he could come to terms with those – but at the chosen object of his passion. Some men, it seemed, just like some women, were bad pickers. Was he being unfair? Unreasonable? No; he just wanted his friend to have a happier life. Like his own. And he was happy now, wasn't he? Over the last year he had steadily regained his equilibrium. The shock of his father's suicide (though he never so much as articulated the word) had left him at an all-time low. The inquest, four months after the event, had been almost as harrowing as the discovery itself. Hearing the words 'took his own life' and 'the balance of his mind was temporarily disturbed' awoke in Charlie such feelings of guilt and remorse that he wondered whether he would ever recover. But he had recovered – very slowly at first, and then steadily – with the assistance of Eleanor and the children, Murdo and Mrs Murdo, all of whom helped to give his life some kind of purpose. And he had a real purpose now – that of father as well as husband.

The castle and the landscape had healing qualities, too. His father had recognised them – his last written words proved that. Almost every day Charlie would sit on the rock above the castle, looking down on the grassy promontory where his father lay, lifting his eyes to gaze out across the chilly waters of the loch to the far distant hills and mountains, feeling, as he did so, some kind of empowerment that only nature could provide. How he pitied those folk who knew only town and city, pavement and highway; whose life was bound up in bustle and rush, whose daily lives condemned them to crowded streets and traffic-clogged motorways. Where, for them, was the ultimate solace? Where for them was real life? He realised his good fortune in being made custodian of this piece of Scottish landscape; it was not something he ever assumed was his by right, but at the same time, he knew that this was what he was born to do – the toil and the stewardship did indeed, confer upon him some kind of possessive quality, but it was a reciprocal arrangement – the landscape possessed him every bit as much as he possessed the landscape.

He hoped that he would always feel like this; that the freshness and vitality of the Highlands would never pall – even on those days when the mists came down and you could not see the moorland track six feet in front of you. The days of dreariness were more than compensated for by the bright flashes of spring and summer sunshine; of snow-capped peaks in winter silhouetted against an azure sky. They filled him with hope, and with fear sometimes; fear that one day it would all vanish. But he did not dwell on that; tried to learn the wisdom of living each day as it came, to keep marvelling at the run of the salmon through the loch, at the bark of the stag, the call of the grouse and, now, the excited cries of Ellie as she waded through a field of buttercups, and the gurgling of Lucy as she lay in her crib. In spite of the tragedies of life, he recognised his good fortune, and every day took comfort from the presence of the blonde-haired girl who had agreed, for some unaccountable reason, to marry him.

★ ★ ★

'She's concerned about you, you know.' Charlie and Gordon were walking above the castle, Charlie anxious to get his friend out of the way to reduce the chances of their being interrupted.

'Why?'

'Oh, you know. The booze.'

'Ah. Yes. I wondered if that would crop up. Look, I'm sorry. I'll go out and get some to replace what I've had.'

'It's not that, you daft bugger. We're happy to have you here. It's just . . . well . . . by bedtime you're pretty far gone.'

Gordon leaned on the fence above the Highland cattle. 'I know.'

Charlie leaned beside him, and the two looked out over the glittering waters of the loch. 'I know it's none of my business, and I know you need to unwind but . . .'

'Oh, don't worry. It's just my way of relaxing. It's nothing serious . . .'

Their conversation was interrupted by the arrival of a car. It was not one that Charlie recognised. 'Is this anything to do with you?' he asked Gordon.

'Not as far as I know. Two Bob, as you call him, isn't coming here this holiday. He's gone back home for a spell, which is worrying. I managed to persuade the powers that be to let you have a break on your own, what with the new baby and everything. Beats me who it is.'

The two men walked down towards the castle. Charlie quickly recognised the figure who got out of the BMW on the driver's side. It was Sebastian Brodie, who walked around and held open the passenger door, through which Charlie's stepmother disembarked with all the pomp of Her Majesty the Queen on a royal visit.

'Bloody hell,' muttered Charlie. 'What's she doing here?'

Gordon was torn between keeping up and remaining at a safe distance to avoid any unpleasantness that might ensue. The two of them strode purposefully down the hillside, with Gordon holding back a little as they reached the apron of gravel at the front of the castle.

'Hello,' said Charlotte, flatly.

'What are you doing here?' asked Charlie.

'I've come to see you. To talk about the future.'

'What do you mean?'

'There are things to be sorted out.'

'I thought we'd done all that,' said Charlie, standing his ground.

'Not quite. There are – how shall I put it? – complications.'

'What sort of complications?'

'Housing complications.'

'But you've got a house – in Edinburgh. Dad saw to that.'

'So he did. But he didn't allow for running costs.'

Charlie could see where the conversation was going. 'Oh, come on, Charlotte; you've been very well provided for in the will. All you need to do is live within your means.'

'Ah yes; the will. We need to talk about that.'

'Why? Everything is settled.'

'Oh no,' said Charlotte, with a barely restrained smile. 'I've had a meeting with my solicitor. Everything is far from settled. Now then, do you want to have this conversation out here where it is rather chilly, or shall we go inside and do things in a more civilised manner?'

32

Castle Sodhail

January 1975

'I loved you, so I drew these tides of men into my hands and wrote my will across the sky in stars.'

T.E. Lawrence, *The Seven Pillars of Wisdom*, 1926

The atmosphere in the hall of the castle was icy, in spite of the logs blazing in the grate. Charlie had contemplated escorting Charlotte into his study, but had decided that the nearer to the front door he could keep her, the better.

Gordon slipped away into the kitchen and Eleanor made to do the same, but Charlie asked her to stay. Having entrusted Ellie and Lucy into Gordon's care, with just slight misgivings, she stood with her husband, their backs to the fire, though the warmth it gave out could barely counteract Charlotte's basilisk glare.

'I know you thought that this was all sorted out,' began Charlotte, 'but there is a problem with the will.'

'What sort of problem?' asked Charlie.

'There are concerns regarding your father's state of mind at the time he made it.'

'But you've never raised these concerns before. Why have you waited until now before questioning its validity?'

'It's obvious, isn't it? I was grieving. I had no idea that there was anything untoward about it. I took it as read that everything was in order and that I had been taken care of.'

'But you have been taken care of, Charlotte. You have your house in Edinburgh – the house that my father bought for you and registered in your name – and you have the contents of the house and your joint bank account. As far as I'm aware, you agreed these things with my father. Why should you want to change them now?'

'Because circumstances change,' sniffed Charlotte, glancing at Sebastian who was standing slightly behind her and closer to the door.

'Of course they change.' Charlie raised his voice and his cheeks took on a ruddiness that had nothing to do with the blazing fire behind him. 'My father is no longer with us, that's how they've changed, but he was good enough to make provision for you in his will in spite of—'

'In spite of what?'

'Don't make me say it, Charlotte. In spite of . . . events and changes in relationships.'

'What do you mean?'

Charlie took a deep breath, and Eleanor squeezed his arm with the intention of reining him in. The move had no effect. 'It was quite clear to me that in the latter part of his life, my father wasn't happy, and that unhappiness can't be put down to anything other than . . . his marital relationship.'

'Nonsense.'

'It's not nonsense; it's fact. My father left this castle because you wanted him to. He'd devoted his life to this place – he was born here and after his death he asked to be brought back here. He took it on from his father and I've taken it on from him. This is where we are meant to be; this is where *he* was meant to be until you asked him to move away.'

Charlotte bridled. 'I did not ask him – he offered. He could see I wasn't happy here.'

'He was a man of honour, Charlotte. He might have been reluctant to show emotion on occasions, but he was a fair man, a loyal man – loyal to his friends and loyal to this estate. When you married him he knew that meant he had to be loyal to you, even if it meant giving up all that he held dear. When you said that you were no longer happy living at Sodhail he agreed to move to Edinburgh, and you let that happen without a single thought for him.'

'Because I knew that you would take over. I *helped* you take over – I could see that you were as devoted to this place as your father, though heaven knows why.'

Charlie spoke quietly now. 'Don't insult his memory, Charlotte, or my family home. It might be a lump of cold Scottish granite to you, but along with the people who work and live here it's rather more than that to me.'

She cut in. 'Oh, I can see that. I've always known that. I saw the hold it had over your father and I can see the power it exerts over you. Buildings and land are more important to you than people, whatever you might claim to the contrary. Well, thank God that wasn't the case with your father.'

'And look where it led him. He was forty-nine when he died, Charlotte, though he looked seventy. Why was that, do you suppose? Because he was so happy living in Edinburgh? Living with you?'

Eleanor tugged at his arm and said, 'Charlie!'

'No. I'm sorry. It was all too plain why you married my father. We didn't want to believe it, but in the end we were forced to.'

'What are you suggesting? That I didn't love him? Why do you think I devoted myself to him after your mother died? Because I cared for him, that's why. I cared for you, too, though you've clearly chosen to forget that.'

Another tug at Charlie's arm from Eleanor had some effect. 'I don't want to prolong this argument, Charlotte. Tell me why you've come here and we'll try to sort it out, then you can be on your way. It will be dark soon and I'm sure you'll want to be home before the night closes in.'

'I've been talking to my solicitor. He tells me that there are grounds for challenging the will – based on your father's state of mind when he made it.'

'But my father made his will some time before he took his life.'

'That's as maybe. But it doesn't detract from the fact that he did take his own life and that proves he was unbalanced. That his mind was not nearly so level as we all assumed.'

'Unbalanced! He was the most balanced man I knew.'

'Nevertheless, I plan to challenge the will.'

'To what end?'

'I understand that your father would have wanted to make provision for you and for his grandchildren. That's only fair and reasonable. But as his wife I should be entitled to half the value of the estate.'

'To *what*?'

'Half the value. You have two options, as I see it. You can either buy me out, or else sell the estate and give me half the proceeds. The choice is yours.'

'But that's ridiculous! And completely unfair. You haven't a cat in hell's chance of succeeding with such a ridiculous claim.'

Charlotte looked frostier than ever. 'My solicitor thinks otherwise.'

'And who is your solicitor?'

Charlotte raised her hand and indicated the man standing behind her. 'Sebastian is my solicitor. You will be hearing from him.' And with that, she turned to go.

Charlie and Eleanor stared silently as Charlotte pulled on the large iron ring of the castle's front door and walked out.

Sebastian studiously avoided their eyes and followed his client through the door, closing it behind him silently.

Neither of them said anything for a while. The hum of the car gradually faded away and the only sound remaining was that of the occasional spark from the log fire.

'I should have seen this coming,' murmured Charlie. 'I should have seen it coming.'

'What will you do?' asked Eleanor.

'Challenge her. I mean, she hasn't a leg to stand on, surely.' He went to bolt the door, by way of putting a full stop on the interview. As he did so he noticed a small white card on the hallstand. He picked it up and read the seven words printed upon it:

SEBASTIAN BRODIE
SOLICITOR ADVOCATE
CASTLE TERRACE, EDINBURGH

'Bloody hell!' muttered Charlie. 'I can't see him giving up without a fight. And there was me thinking he was her fancy man. It just goes to show.'

'What?'

'That you can't judge a book by its cover. Or a solicitor advocate by his yellow cashmere sweater.'

33

Edinburgh

March 1975

> '"If the law supposes that," said Mr Bumble . . . "the law is a ass – a idiot."'
>
> Charles Dickens, *Oliver Twist*, 1838

For the next three months, Charlie and Eleanor, with occasional telephonic advice from Gordon, who had returned to Oxford, busied themselves in endeavouring to discover the validity or otherwise – and the likely outcome – of Charlotte's claim against the Sodhail estate. Their own solicitor, Henry Dundas – a grey-haired and grizzled partner in an age-old family firm, his grey suit and grey face an indication of his life-long absence from fresh air and daily closeting with bundles of paper tied with pink ribbon – was cagey about the likelihood of them succeeding in contesting Charlotte's assertion that she was entitled to half of all they owned – or thought they owned.

'I have consulted with the late Mr Stuart's . . . er . . . physician as to the likelihood of his mental state being . . . er . . . suspect and I have to tell you that Doctor Crawford feels that towards the . . . er . . . end, if I may call it that, there were signs that Mr Stuart was . . . er . . . how shall I put it? . . . not at ease with himself. The will is dated during this period of . . . er . . . unease.'

The news came as a blow, though as Charlie explained to Eleanor, there is a great difference between not being 'at ease' with yourself and being unbalanced. They would surely have grounds to contest the claim?

Henry Dundas shrugged. 'Grounds certainly, but this is by no means . . . er . . . straightforward. It could also prove considerably . . . er . . . costly.'

The moment had come when Charlie had been summoned to Sebastian Brodie's offices in Edinburgh – a call he had been expecting for some weeks – and as he walked beneath the ramparts of that city's towering castle the irony of its permanence – since the twelfth century – compared with the impending uncertainty surrounding Castle Sodhail, was not lost on him. Looking up at its lofty battlements filled him with apprehension. The castle was built on the site of an extinct volcano. It seemed that his own volcano was about to erupt.

The front door of the imposing building in Castle Terrace was shiny black; the hallway lit with brass lamps, and the office of Sebastian Brodie was pure white. The man himself sat behind a polished ebony desk, which, Charlie noted, was pathologically tidy. A blotter, a calendar, a fountain pen, and intercom-cum-telephone and a single slim file were all that sullied its mirror-like surface.

Gone was the pale yellow cashmere sweater. Sebastian Brodie was in work mode now – his dark suit the model of expensive Edinburgh tailoring, his Windsor-knotted tie perfectly symmetrical and his hair smartly styled. It surprised Charlie that he was greeted with a smile, but then he remembered that most James Bond villains were fond of smiling.

The soft-toned voice that he remembered so well from their first meeting welcomed him. 'It was good of you to come, Mr Stuart.' Charlie had half expected, 'Good morning, Mr Bond.'

Charlie made a sterling effort to be civil, though

friendliness was clearly out of the question. 'I don't think I had an option, Mr Brodie,' was his considered reply.

Sebastian Brodie smiled. 'Tricky times, I understand, but you have had ample time – three months, I think – to consider my client's wishes and I have to ask what steps you plan to take?'

'We have considered them, yes. But I'm afraid we intend to dispute them.'

'Coffee, Mr Stuart?'

The anodyne nature of the question, coming after the initial confrontation, surprised Charlie. 'Er . . . yes. Thank you. Milk, no sugar.'

The solicitor advocate pressed a button on the intercom. 'Two coffees please, Emma; one with milk but no sugar, and one black.'

He leaned back in his chair. 'Mrs Stuart – that is, Mrs Stuart Senior – is determined to proceed, so I must advise you that the likely outcome is either the sale of Castle Sodhail or the provision of funds that will satisfy her needs.'

Charlie was determined to meet steel with steel and to remain as calm as possible. He and Eleanor had discussed this and decided that it would not help their case if he became overheated or hysterical. That way, it seemed, he would play into Brodie's – and ultimately Charlotte's - hands. 'And what sort of funds are we talking about?'

Brodie flipped open the file in front of him. 'An independent valuation of the castle estimates its value – and that of the estate and its cottages – at around seventy-five thousand pounds. My client does not want to be greedy. She understands that you have a wife and family to support and that the estate provides work for a small local community. With this in mind she would be happy to settle for thirty thousand pounds

– rather than take the matter to court which would no doubt cost you dearly.'

'But that's ridiculous!' Charlie knew that he was meant to be being calm about the whole thing, but Charlotte's unreasonable demands found him losing control. 'It's an acknowledged fact that property prices in Scotland are depressed at the moment. Last year the country endured a three-day working week. A London estate agent says that at the moment half of Scotland is for sale.'

At this moment, Brodie's assistant brought in two cups of coffee on a smart tray. She placed one in front of her boss and one in front of Charlie, without looking at him. Then she quietly slipped out of the door.

Brodie took a sip of his black coffee. 'So what would you consider to be a reasonable sum, Mr Stuart?'

'I would consider a house in a very good part of Edinburgh and the contents of a joint bank account to be ample recompense for a marriage which lasted little more than ten years.'

'Twelve. My client was married to your father for twelve years.'

Charlie shook his head. 'What difference does it make? Ten years, twelve years, a house and a lump sum is a fair remuneration. There is simply no way that I can lay my hands on thirty thousand pounds, however reasonable Charlotte thinks she is being, and I most certainly do not intend to sell Castle Sodhail. It's been in my family for three generations and I'm not the one who's going to let it go – I owe its continued existence to my family and to the locals who depend on it for their livelihoods.'

Brodie drained his coffee cup and replaced it precisely on its saucer. 'Let's try and sort this out amicably, Mr Stuart. I realise that to sell Castle Sodhail would place you in a very difficult position. I also realise that you do not have sufficient liquidity to provide Mrs Stuart Senior with a lump sum of thirty thousand pounds. I could, however, explain this to her and suggest annual payments of, say, five thousand pounds a year over the next ten years. How would that sit with you?'

'But that's fifty thousand pounds, not thirty thousand!'

'Ah, but my client would not have the benefit of a lump sum, and that has to be compensated for by a larger overall figure. Above all, Mrs Stuart senior is keen to avoid the matter going to court and would far rather that the two of you came to some arrangement. It would be in the interest of both parties to do so – she is quite insistent upon that point. Do you see what I'm driving at?'

Charlie's composure disappeared. 'Oh, I see what you're driving at, all right. You're attempting to bankrupt me; to force the castle on to the market and to leave me and my family without a home – without *our* home.' He got to his feet, his coffee untouched and his self-control in tatters. 'Much as I dislike Charlotte, I never imagined she'd go this far to get her own way. She chose to marry my father and clearly the only reason for that choice was to feather her own nest. She's a gold-digger, Mr Brodie, nothing more, and that much is being proved by her actions now.'

'We'll get nowhere by trading insults, Mr Stuart.'

'And Charlotte will get nowhere with this case, Mr Brodie.'

'Oh, I'm afraid she stands a very good chance indeed. Dr Crawford—'

'You've been speaking to Dr Crawford?'

'I have had no need to speak with him. He has been good enough to provide a written affidavit. Everything is in order. It would have been very remiss of me not to have done my homework, Mr Stuart.' Sebastian Brodie stood up and walked across to the door of his office. He opened it, making it clear to Charlie that the interview, having failed to reach a satisfactory conclusion, had come to an end.

Charlie fought for a suitably crushing reply, but none was forthcoming. Instead, tight-lipped and shaking with anger he strode from Sebastian Brodie's office and out into the windswept Edinburgh street.

The solicitor advocate closed the door behind him and pressed a button on his intercom. 'Would you get me Mrs Stuart please, Emma? Mrs Stuart Senior.' There was silence for a few minutes before the conversation resumed.

'Charlotte? I've met with your stepson and we have had a conversation. No. Not pleased at all. Oh yes; I think he is all too well aware of the likely consequences. No; I suspect that the annual payment is out of the question – the least favoured of his options. Oh, yes, I think so. The doctor's report was the deciding factor. Now? Oh, I think we just let them stew for a while. Sit back quietly and wait. It may be a few weeks but I feel quite sure they will come round in the end. They really have no option but to do so.'

34

Invergarry House

Easter 1975

'Diplomacy is to do and say
The nastiest thing in the nicest way.'
Isaac Goldberg, *The Reflex*, 1927

'Patience; that's what you need. Don't rush things. The longer it goes on the greater your chance of coming through in the end.' These were the words of advice offered to Eleanor by her father. But then Sir Robert Fitzallan had lived long enough and dealt with enough nasty bits of work in his life as a banker to know the wisdom of proceeding with caution.

'But Charlie's convinced that if he doesn't act quickly then someone is going to turn up on the doorstep and force us out,' complained Eleanor.

'The omens aren't good, I admit, but I think there's more to this than meets the eye, and the longer that you can keep her dangling the more likely you are to find a way out. If she thinks she'll get her own way in the end she'll have been advised to proceed at a steady pace – making sure that everything is in place before delivering the final *coup de grâce*.'

'I rather feel she's done that already, but I suppose you know what you're taking about, Pops.'

'Dreadful woman,' confirmed Davina Fitzallan. 'I never took to her. Such a contrast to poor Fortune. Different kettle of fish altogether. What on earth Angus Stuart saw in her I shall never know.'

'Yes, Mummy, but don't go on about it to Charlie. He's doing his best to keep everything going – the cottages and the fishing at the moment, and he's had good bookings for the shooting and stalking come the summer – I just don't want him to start losing heart and thinking that there's no point in it all.'

'And are you still taking in lodgers?'

'They're not lodgers, they're paying guests, and the answer is yes. We need the income more than ever now, with this thing brewing.'

'A bit of a funny carry-on, isn't it?' asked her father.

'What do you mean?'

'Well, the same students – give or take the odd one or two – coming up here every holiday. All foreign. It's not as if you know them.'

'It was Gordon Mackenzie's idea. You remember Gordon? And I suppose we do know one of them now. Not terribly well, but he's become that thing in between a friend and an acquaintance. He's Yugoslavian.'

'Oh?'

'Florin, his name is. He's a bit of a loose cannon; sort of impetuous – excitable. He was very quiet when we first had him. Kept himself very much to himself. But he's opened up over the past couple of visits. To me, at any rate.'

Her father raised an eyebrow.

'Oh, don't you start, Daddy!'

'What do you mean?'

'Charlie tells me that Florin fancies me.'

'And does he?'

'It really doesn't matter. I'm just glad of the company sometimes, when Charlie's out with Murdo or up on the moors mending walls. It makes a change from the company of the girls and Mrs Murdo.'

'Just you be careful not to give him the wrong idea.'

'Oh, Daddy! He's perfectly harmless.'

'Henry Higgins,' muttered Sir Robert.

'Who?'

'Henry Higgins in *My Fair Lady*.'

'What's he got to do with anything?'

'He asked Colonel Pickering, very appositely in my view, whether he had ever met a man of good character where women are concerned.'

'And what was the answer?'

'I forget. But just you be careful. The Yugoslavs are a hot-blooded race. It seems as though you've had an inkling of that already. Just you make sure you're not alone with him in a room at any time.'

Eleanor laughed.

'You may laugh, but I'm just advising a little circumspection. And if Charlie thinks there's a spark there . . .'

'Oh now, really!'

'Well, just don't give him any more to worry about.'

Eleanor sat on the arm of her father's easy chair, leaned over and gave him a hug. 'I won't. And you're very sweet to worry. I'm glad someone's on our side, anyway.'

'Who isn't?'

'Well, that wretched woman for a start, and Dr Crawford it appears.'

'Crawford? What's he got to do with it?'

'He's told our solicitor that Charlie's dad had been in an "uneasy frame of mind" when he had last seen him.'

'What?' exclaimed Sir Robert. 'That old fool Crawford? Time he retired; he's about as much use as knickers on a kipper.'

'Robert!' admonished his wife.

'He is! The last time you went there with chest pains what did he say?'

Davina Fitzallan looked uncomfortable. 'I don't think we need to go there.'

'Angina! That's what he said: angina. And what happened? You came home and found that one of your corset bones had come out and was sticking into you. The man's a fool, and if they take notice of anything he says they need their heads examined.'

'Yes, Daddy, but it's in their interests to believe what he says, isn't it?'

Her father harrumphed a little and said, 'We'll have to see about that. You just bide your time and keep them guessing for a while. One solicitor's letter can go a long way – it needn't cost a fortune, but a prolonged court case would.'

Eleanor's mother asked, 'Does Murdo know about all this?'

'No. Charlie doesn't want to worry him. It's not just that his job is here, but his house is, too.'

'And it goes with the job?'

'It's Murdo's for as long as he works here, then it reverts to the estate. If the estate is sold then he'll have to negotiate with the new owner.'

'What rent does he pay?'

'Nothing. He did it up himself and Charlie's dad allowed him to live there rent-free because of the work he'd put into restoring it.'

Sir Robert cut in. 'So Murdo will be in a very tricky position if madam gets her way.'

'Yes.'

'Bad news all round then?'

'You can say that again,' said Eleanor.

35

Oxford

August 1975

'His flight was madness: when our actions do not,
Our fears do make us traitors.'
William Shakespeare, *Macbeth*, 1606

It was a hot day – too hot to do anything but laze on a punt on the Isis. That was where Gordon Mackenzie found himself at the beginning of the summer break. Tomorrow he would be heading off to Scotland, making sure that three foreign students were safely ensconced with the Stuarts. For Florin it would be the last time he stayed there, and Gordon had high hopes that this would be the last time he, himself, would play any part in the sequestration of foreign nationals at the behest of he knew not who. It was time for a change; time to get his own life back; time to be less reliant on the restorative properties of anything that came out of a bottle – anything containing alcohol, at any rate.

He had been on the wagon for a month now. It had been hard at first; it was still hard, but the clarity of mind and the increased interest in his old loves of literature and Latin convinced him of the need to clean up his act. He knew the Stuarts would be pleased. He smiled at the thought of the probable look on Eleanor's face when he arrived. He would turn up freshly laundered and sweet smelling, and she was sure to remark on the change – the improvement. She and Charlie had helped him so much over the past couple of years;

he was determined to repay the favour. But how? How to help when it seemed as though their world was not only about to crumble but to vanish altogether? There must be some way of resolving the situation.

The bells of Magdalen College clock tower chimed the hour – three o'clock – and the punt glided beneath a willow tree, resplendent now in its high summer livery, the veils of branches drifting across his face as he poled his way gently downstream. As he came to the bridge he spotted an oncoming skiff careering through the water beneath the arches. It was almost on top of him. Smartly he dug in his pole and propelled the punt to the right, and as he did so he was startled by a large splash to the port side of his craft. Instinctively ducking, he then looked out across the water, trying to identify the source of the disturbance. But he saw nothing; only the widening circles of ripples and a few bubbles rising to the surface. He looked up at the bridge and, partially dazzled by the bright sunlight, could just make out the shape of a figure retreating. 'Little buggers!' he muttered to himself. 'Should know better. Bloody students.'

He poled on towards the row of punts tied up at the riverside jetty, unaware that there might have been more to the disturbed water than a bit of harmless student mischief. He would go and get ready for the trip up north. For the first time in a long while, he was excited at the prospect.

Alex Jesmond had been closeted in the corner of the beer garden at the Turf Tavern with the man in black for half an hour. He was not happy. For a start, it had been suggested that it was all Alex's fault when, in reality, Alex knew that it was Gordon taking his eye off the ball. And Gordon had been very strange of late. Difficult to talk to. Alex had called for him that morning to take him on to the meeting with the man in black and he had not been at his digs. He knew he was due to check that the students were safe in Scotland but that was not until tomorrow. Where was he?

It was a question the man in black asked, too. But his main concern was Florin Adzic. His time at Oxford had come to an end. They had agreed that he should go back to Yugoslavia – they were hardly in a position to stop him – but managed to get him to agree to a final debriefing session.

'He's been noticeably reluctant of late,' said the man in black. 'When he came to us three years ago he was keen to help. He's reverted, like a lot of them do, but he doesn't seem willing to go quietly.' He mopped his perspiring brow with a black handkerchief. It was not the weather for dark clothing.

'Evangelical fervour,' suggested Alex.

'Yes. It used to work in our favour, now it seems to be working against us. However much he dislikes Tito and his regime he now seems to dislike us, and what we're trying to do, more.'

'Perhaps we should have let him have more trips home. He would have been in a position to have given us more accurate information then.'

'And more at risk from being repatriated. It's always a swings and roundabouts situation. And now he's done a bunk.'

'What do you want me to do?' asked Alex.

'Nothing. With any luck Mackenzie will call in with news. I expect he's on his tail and just keeping quiet. Probably making sure he gets to Scotland safely.'

'Right,' said Alex, getting up to go, and knowing that he had no idea where Gordon was or what he was doing. It would be better for both his sake and Gordon's not to share such intelligence with the man in black. If he were to discover that Gordon were becoming disaffected then not only could things become unpleasant, but that would land a whole heap more work on his own shoulders.

'At least I hope he is,' said the man. 'And if what you say is true – that Florin blames Gordon as much as anybody for keeping him here – I hope he doesn't do anything stupid.'

Gordon waited for Florin Adzic for two hours the following morning at the agreed rendezvous on the Woodstock Road, but he did not show. There was nothing he could do except drive on up to Scotland in the battered old VW and hope that Florin would be there when he arrived. The student had been churlish of late, unwilling to be pressed into doing things that he did not want to do. Gordon sighed and set off on the long journey north, cursing the Yugoslav for delaying his journey. He felt an unwanted sense of foreboding and more than a little concern as to his charge's welfare.

36

Creag Sodhail

12 August 1975

'Life, to be sure, is nothing much to lose;
But young men think it is, and we were young.'
A.E. Housman, 'Here Dead We Lie', 1936

The mist was slow to lift that August day. It was the start of the grouse season; ten guns, a hearty lunch got ready in the hall of the castle and a fine shoot promised, once the mist had lifted. Charlie was apprehensive but excited at the prospect of a good beginning. He would not carry a gun himself, and neither would Gordon; both would act as beaters – that way Charlie could make sure everything ran smoothly, without reducing the revenue. Ten guns was the largest number that the Sodhail shoot ever fielded; Angus had always felt that eight was better, but ten made more economic sense in these straitened times. The guns tramped uphill to the butts above the castle – four locals and six visitors who paid more handsomely for the privilege of being there on the Glorious Twelfth than the locals who were given preferential rates.

The beaters, led by Charlie and Gordon, had followed, moving away in a wide arc – a pincer movement – so that once they were several hundred yards above the butts they could flush out the birds and drive them towards the guns. They moved stealthily at first, creating as little disturbance as possible, and far away from where they hoped the grouse would be feeding on the fresh shoots of heather that were the result of last year's burning.

It was a long walk, and both Charlie and Gordon were grateful for the chance to blow away the cobwebs. Gordon in particular seemed to have found a new seam of energy.

'Do you mind slowing down a bit? I'm very impressed with the new you but I'm beginning to miss the old lethargy,' teased Charlie.

'Best thing I ever did, giving up the booze,' replied Gordon. 'I feel like a new man.'

'In your case that could be taken the wrong way . . .'

'Very funny. Not much chance of that. Now don't spoil the moment, I'm enjoying myself up here, even if I am a bit preoccupied with the late Mr Adzic.'

'You've not heard anything then?'

'Not a peep.'

'Do you think he'll turn up?'

'Who knows?'

'Does it bother you?'

'Only from a point of view of the ramifications. Frankly I've had a bellyful of foreigners and their funny ways. Personally I don't care if I never set eyes on him again, and I suspect he feels the same.'

'How did you leave it with him then?'

'He was meant to meet me on the Woodstock Road so that I could drive him up here, but he didn't turn up – that's why I was late.'

'So he's not best pleased with you?'

'It's rather worse than that. He really laid into me at our last meeting. Said that it was all my fault he'd got into this unholy mess; that he should have never come to Britain but should have stayed in Yugoslavia where he belonged.'

'Nobody forced him to come here, did they?'

'No. Not exactly. But I've seen this happen several times now. These students come over here full of freedom-fighter fervour. They want nothing more than to take a pop at the unjust regime in their own country. They see the UK as the land of milk and honey, but before long they see that it has its own problems.'

'Yes. And 1974 wasn't exactly a good year, was it? Striking miners, power cuts, a three-day week – the worst times economically since 1926 . . .'

'Exactly. And yet you'd think that freedom of speech would compensate for all that, and it does for a while, but then familiarity breeds contempt. The novelty wears off. They take freedom of speech for granted and once you've said your piece, what else is there to say? The rebellious instinct has to have an outlet somewhere and it seems to turn on those who are closest to hand.'

'When did you last see him?'

'When he came out of a meeting with the man in black last week.'

'With who?' asked Charlie, incredulously.

'The man in black. We call him that because he always is.'

'And don't you know his real name?'

'Oh, it's Robinson, or Robertson or something, but we always call him the man in black. Well, I do. Somehow it seems better not to know.'

'But if the shit hits the fan, don't you really need to know who you're dealing with?'

'Alex does. That was enough for me. Anyway, it's academic now. I've had enough and I'm not going back.'

'Have you told them?'

'No. But I think Alex has an inkling.'

'Will he try to stop you?'

'I think he knows it's pointless.'

'But won't you be in any danger?'

'Oh, they'll probably put out feelers for a while, but then the fuss will die down. They have bigger fish to fry than me.'

'So surely Florin has no quarrel with you – it's your man in black who's to blame, isn't it?'

'Florin blames me for delivering him into the hands of the enemy. That's how he thinks of us now. I reckon he'll have buggered off back to Belgrade. Or been snatched. Over the past couple of months the Yugoslav embassy have been sniffing around; or at least people purporting to be from the Yugloslav embassy.'

'Why didn't you tell me this earlier?' asked Charlie. A worried note crept into his voice.

'Because I thought you had enough on your plate with Charlotte and her fancy man.'

'He's not her fancy man, he's her solicitor advocate.'

'So he says. Anyway, what's the latest?'

'Eleanor's dad has suggested we just keep our heads down and employ delaying tactics.'

'Are they working?'

'Well, Charlotte's been quiet, but it won't be long before she's back with a vengeance, I'm sure. It's been five months now since she dropped the bombshell.'

'I'd have thought you'd have wanted to resolve it, one way or the other. Isn't it worse to keep her hanging on?'

'The alternative is going to court and we just can't afford that.'

'What if she sends the bailiffs in or something?'

'She won't do that. I've been getting our solicitor to send letters every now and again just to make her think that things are moving. I never thought I'd be grateful for the slow-grinding wheels of the law.'

'And you can't afford to pay her off?'

'Not a hope, even with the income from the students and by raising the price of the guns at the shoots and the fishing beats. I've tried that, but it just doesn't make enough. And I'm buggered if I'm going to sell this place.'

'It's going to come to a head, you know. I'm surprised Eleanor's mum and dad haven't offered to help you out.'

'They would if they could, but they simply don't have that sort of money.'

'Aristocratic poor?'

'Sort of.'

'It strikes me that you need some sort of divine intervention.'

'If only.'

Their conversation was interrupted by a brief blast on a whistle. The beaters were in a long line now, perhaps a quarter of a mile from end to end. The mist was starting to lift, albeit gradually, when the line began moving slowly forward, each beater slashing to right and left with a stick or a crook to lift the birds and send them hurtling towards the guns.

They had been beating for about ten minutes, and perhaps a dozen birds had lifted – not a good start – when they came upon a thicker swathe of heather that had been sheltering a larger covey. Up they flew, a whirr of wings and their cries of 'go-back – go-back' echoing across the open moor as they did so. The guns sprang into action – cracking to left and right. Some birds were lucky enough to escape the shot; others came tumbling to earth, to be retrieved by four black Labradors and a couple of Springer Spaniels who snaked their way through the heather, picked up their quarry and scuttled back towards the butts, tails wagging, for deserved praise.

Then another covey rose with equal commotion as the beaters came to within a hundred yards of the butts. Crack and crack again went the guns, but this time a different sound rent the air amid the explosions of shot. It was the cry of a man; a man who had been hit. A long whistle blast followed and immediately the guns were silent. Two or three more birds made a bid for safety and flew unharmed over the butts.

Charlie looked across the moor in the direction of the cry and saw a figure falling to the ground. He ran as fast as he could, the tough stems of heather catching on his boots and impeding his progress. Eventually he reached the fallen figure who lay, face down, in the thick and aromatic rug of heather and ling. Charlie knelt down beside the body and with both hands pulled on his left shoulder so that the face would be clear of the undergrowth and the breathing passages open. He knew all the beaters by name, and his heart pounded heavily in his chest as he looked at the peat-smeared face that came into view. It was not Gordon, thank God, and it was none of the beaters either. The man who had been hit and felled to the ground was Florin Adzic.

37

Castle Sodhail

12 August 1975

'For what were all these country patriots born?
To hunt, and vote, and raise the price of corn?'
Lord Byron, *The Age of Bronze*, 1823

It was a relief to them all to discover that the Yugoslav was still alive. They ferried him down to the castle on a makeshift stretcher, cobbled together from jackets, baler twine and beaters' sticks. At first glance, Charlie had thought he was dead, but then Florin began breathing, stertorously at first and then more deeply. He opened his eyes and said something in Serbo-Croat that neither Charlie nor Gordon, who had come rushing over, could make out.

Once he had fully come round Florin made to get up, with every intention, or so it seemed, of running off. But when he realised that he had been hit – in the right shoulder – he sat down again and the blood drained from his cheeks.

They could get nothing further out of him until he was back at the castle. The shoot continued, with the gun who had peppered the interloper feeling especially guilty, but when it was pointed out that the man leapt straight out in front of them, seemingly intent on reaching the row of beaters, he was absolved from firing too low and allowed to carry on. The last thing Charlie wanted was for the shoot to be abandoned, but having flushed out most of the grouse from that particular section of the moor, the shooting party moved off to another row of butts further east.

Once Florin was propped up in the castle kitchen, the doctor was called and while Eleanor and Gordon waited for him to arrive, Charlie went back to the moor to help Murdo with the organisation and to calm things down. He was hopeful that the incident would be forgotten and his guests would have better reason to remember the Glorious Twelfth at Sodhail than the toppling of a foreign national.

The wound was not serious – just a light peppering of shot. Eleanor took off Florin's jacket with great care and eased the shirt from the right-hand side of his body before bathing the area in Dettol. She would leave it for the doctor to remove the shot – it would be a painstaking job – but she hoped that such a precaution might at least soothe the patient and help prevent the likelihood of any infection.

Gordon insisted on staying with Florin, but it was Eleanor who asked what the Yugoslav was trying to achieve by running out in front of the guns and putting his own life at risk.

'You could have been killed,' she said sympathetically.

Florin looked unconcerned. 'What do I care?' was his only answer. It was some time later – and after several cups of tea laced with condensed milk, something she knew he enjoyed – before he was more forthcoming.

'Why weren't you there yesterday?' asked Gordon. 'Where we arranged to meet? I waited for two hours.'

'Because I go back to my country.'

'But you didn't go back to your country. You came here. Why?'

'Because I think you get into trouble if I leave without telling you.'

'So why didn't you tell me down there? Why come all the way up here – and how did you get here, anyway?'

'I thumb lift. I decide to go home, then I change my mind. I know Robertson make you . . . how you say? . . . scapegoat . . . if I disappear without telling you.'

'Well, that's very good of you, but I don't think it's going to make much difference to Robertson whether you've told me or not.'

'I have written letter.' He reached in his inside pocket and pulled out an envelope, now spattered with blood. It looked nothing if not dramatic. 'Please read,' said Florin.

Gordon opened the envelope and took out the letter. It was written on two sides of the paper in rather better English than Florin chose to speak. Gordon read it silently before putting it back in the envelope and slipping it into his own inside pocket. 'Well,' he said, smiling ruefully. 'At least it's saved you a stamp.' Then he added, 'I think it would be better if you just went home.'

'But you—!'

'Don't worry about me. I'm going to disappear as well.'

Eleanor looked at him, her face the picture of alarm.

'It's all right,' Gordon reassured her. 'I won't be gone forever. Just long enough for the dust to settle and for nobody to care.'

'But why? What's all this about?'

'I can't really tell you, Eleanor. Well, I can, but it's better if I don't. There's never been any chance of you or Charlie being involved or implicated, but the foreign students you have been taking in during the holidays have all been helping us – helping the government – in all kinds of ways. That's all I can say, really.'

'But . . . the children. How could you ask us to be involved in something so risky when there are children here? What about the danger to them? Did nobody think of that?'

For the first time, Gordon noticed the fire in Eleanor's eyes and did his best to reassure her. 'You're not involved, don't you see? It's me who's involved and that's why I'm leaving. Florin will be the last of the students; there won't be any more. I'll make sure of that.'

Eleanor was angry now. 'Does Charlie know about all this?'

'A little. I assured him that there was no danger. His concern was for you and the children, but I knew that there was no real risk and that the money would come in useful.'

'To you as well, I suppose? I presume you were being paid?' she said bitterly.

'Eleanor, I am not remotely proud of what I have done; quite the reverse, but if I thought that there was any real danger being posed to you and the children—'

'But there was, wasn't there?'

Gordon looked ashen. 'I'll wait for the doctor to come and then we'll go. I'll see Florin safely out of the country and I'll just slip away myself.'

'But this is dreadful!'

'And it's all my fault. I'm really sorry. I shouldn't have been persuaded to get you involved. I realise that. But it's at an end now and nobody's come to any harm, have they?' He looked at Florin. 'With one exception.'

Eleanor got up and went to the window, digging her finger-nails into her hands. She was angry with him, but sorry for him, too. He was clearly troubled – had been troubled for some time – and she cared for him as well as worrying for her own immediate family. She could hear a child crying, but knew that Mrs Murdo would be taking care of her.

'Where will you go?' she asked.

'Who knows? I've some money saved. I can find a place to rent. Somewhere.'

'Will they follow you? I mean, are *you* in danger?'

'I shouldn't think so. Oh, they'll be angry for a bit, but I don't know anything really. They can't go around bumping off anyone who's been involved in intelligence gathering; if they did they'd certainly thin out the population. We don't live in Communist Russia, thank goodness. They'll be irritated with me but that will be all. Still; it'll be better if I'm out of the way for a while.'

A smart rat-a-tat at the oaken door of the castle interrupted their conversation. Eleanor opened the door to Dr Crawford and wished with all her heart that it had been anybody other than the man who had been happy to certify for Charlotte that her husband had been of 'unsound mind'. Until then she had always thought him a pleasant man – stocky and always smartly dressed in tweeds. As ever, today, his face was the colour of a Victoria plum, his pipe clamped between his teeth.

It took the doctor the better part of three quarters of an hour to extract all the shot from Florin's arm, then he bandaged it up and gave him an injection. 'Take the bandage off after a couple of days and try to keep the wound dry,' he said. 'You were lucky; I've seen worse.'

In the interests of his patient he had slipped his pipe into his pocket, but now he took it out again and lit it before making his final pronouncement. 'You'll have a bit of scarring I'm afraid, but at least it missed your face. Nothing to put off the ladies, eh?' The doctor grinned and sucked on his pipe; a cloud of blue-grey smoke assisted with the disinfection process.

Florin managed a weak smile and Eleanor handed him one of Charlie's shirts that was airing above the Rayburn. She took the bloody and shotgun-tattered one from him and rolled it up, with the intention of burning it.

'I'll be on my way then,' said Dr Crawford.

Eleanor showed him to the door, and could not resist asking him, as he stood on the doormat, 'Dr Crawford, why did you tell Charlie's stepmother that his father had been in a disturbed state of mind when he last saw you?'

'I'm sorry?' The doctor looked puzzled.

'Charlotte. Charlie's stepmother. You know she's trying to lay claim to half the Sodhail estate? She's disputing the will, saying that it was made when Angus's mind was "temporarily disturbed".'

'But that's a nonsense!'

'You mean you didn't say it, Dr Crawford?'

'I most certainly did not.'

'And you didn't write Charlotte a letter to that effect?'

'I really don't understand what you're saying. When Mrs Stuart – that is, Angus's widow – came to see me to ask if I thought that Angus's behaviour before the unfortunate occurrence could in any way be described as demonstrating serious signs of mental problems, I reassured her that he was nothing more than uneasy about moving away from the Highlands and pitching up in Edinburgh. I may well have said that much, but I certainly did not go any further and I have put nothing in writing.'

'You didn't give Charlotte anything at all in the way of a letter confirming that?'

'I did not. I gave her a prescription for sleeping tablets but that was all.'

'I see.'

The doctor still looked confused. Then he said, 'Eleanor if there is anything I can do to help . . . ?'

'Thank you, Dr Crawford. You've already been very helpful.'

Eleanor closed the door gently then leaned upon it and closed her eyes. A glimmer of hope. At least she would have something to tell Charlie that might lift his spirits. But what had Charlotte done? If she said she had a letter – and her solicitor claimed that that was the case – then presumably it existed. It could only be a forgery. But how could Charlotte turn a prescription for sleeping tablets into a letter purporting to question Angus Stuart's sanity? She shook her head to rid it of confusing thoughts and walked back towards the kitchen.

Mrs Murdo had put Lucy in a high chair, and Ellie was sitting on the floor, doing her best to scatter building bricks as far afield as possible. 'Is this for the laundry?' she asked, indicating the rolled-up shirt placed upon a chair by the Rayburn.

'No. No; it's for the fire. It's beyond laundering. There was an accident this morning; somebody got shot.'

'Good grief!' exclaimed Mrs Murdo. 'Tell me it wasnae serious?'

Eleanor was rather distant. 'No. No, it wasn't serious, fortunately. Just someone being rather stupid.'

'Well, thank the Lord for that. There are some very stupid people around nowadays.'

Looking out of the kitchen window at the brightening day, Eleanor confirmed, 'Yes, there are, Mrs Murdo, and some of them very close to home.'

The children had been put to bed. Charlie and Eleanor were sitting on either side of the kitchen table. He knew that something had upset her – Eleanor was seldom as silent as she had been over the last few hours.

'What's wrong?' he asked.

'Nothing. Nothing at all.' She carried on eating.

'There must be. You've barely spoken all evening.'

Eleanor did not reply.

'Tell me what's—'

'Were you going to tell me or did you just hope I wouldn't find out?' she said softly.

'Tell you what?'

She avoided his eye and looked at the food she was cutting up. 'About the students. About where they came from. About why they were here.'

'You mean—?'

'Gordon told me. He told me about them being involved in intelligence. About the ferrying to and fro. About us being a safe house.'

'Well, I . . .'

Then there came an explosion the like of which Charlie had never experienced at any time in their relationship.

'How could you? How could you put your family in such a situation? How could you expose your children – YOUR CHILDREN – to such a thing?'

'But Gordon said—'

'"Gordon said!" What about what you say? Gordon was a school friend. You – you're a father! And a husband! Gordon isn't. He has nobody to care about but himself – well, not until—'

'There really was no danger. He assured me that—'

'What? That we were just an innocent bed and breakfast?'

'Yes. And the money would come in—'

'Money? You did it just for money?'

'I have to keep a roof over our heads – all our heads. It was a source of income—'

'And what about the consequences? Is it all right to accept money from any quarter, even if it means compromising your family?'

'I didn't compromise my family. I knew that if I didn't manage to raise a bit more money we'd probably have to leave this place and then where would we be?'

'Safe?'

'But that's unrealistic. I weighed up the likely risk and came to the conclusion that there wasn't one. I wouldn't do anything to endanger you and Ellie and Lucy, you must know that. Of course I worried at first, but I really did my best to make sure that we were nothing more than a glorified B&B and that there really was no reason for us to be in any kind of danger.'

'Then why didn't you tell me this?' Eleanor put down her knife and fork, got up and walked to the window. She had her back to him as she asked, with a break in her voice, 'Why didn't you share it with me?'

Charlie got up and walked over to where she stood. He laid his hand on her shoulder and said, softly, 'Because I thought you'd say "no".'

'And so you just kept it to yourself.'

'Yes,' he murmured.

'I see.'

'And I'm sorry. It was wrong of me. I see that now. It was wrong of me to do it and it was wrong not to tell you.'

'It was cowardly.'

'Yes.'

She turned to face him. 'Promise me you won't do anything like that again!'

He nodded. 'I promise. But it was only because it seemed a way of keeping us together. Instead it seems to have driven us apart. But it's all over now. We won't be seeing any more students.'

'Good.'

'So where are Gordon and Florin?'

Eleanor shrugged. 'I don't know. I haven't seen them since Dr Crawford left.'

'Crawford?'

'Yes. He came to treat Florin's wounds.'

'Well, I hope he survives. I'm surprised you let Crawford into the house, bearing in mind what he said about Dad.'

'I think it's time for me to share a piece of information with you,' said Eleanor. 'A piece of information that you're going to like, though why I should be kind to you after all you've done, I don't know . . .'

38

Edinburgh
August 1975

'A guilty conscience needs no accuser.'
Proverb

'This is a very serious allegation, Mr Stuart.'

The smugness and self-satisfaction that Charlie had observed in Sebastian Brodie's demeanour the last time he had entered his office had vanished, to be replaced with a mixture of irritation and unease. It was something Charlie felt he could take advantage of.

'It is a very serious offence, as far as I am aware, Mr Brodie, to forge a letter that purports to be from a doctor, questioning the sanity of one of his patients. Especially when the purpose of that forgery is to extract money. I think they call it extortion.'

'Be very careful about bandying such words around, Mr Stuart; you might find yourself with a lawsuit on your hands.'

Charlie stood his ground and suspected that the merest hint of doubt had entered the solicitor advocate's mind. 'Do you have the letter in your possession, Mr Brodie?'

'I am not prepared to divulge that information.'

'Are you prepared to talk to Dr Crawford?'

'My client has assured me that the letter from Dr Crawford is genuine and that its contents are exactly as were explained to you.'

'But Dr Crawford says otherwise. He denies ever saying that my father was of a disturbed frame of mind, and he also categorically denies writing a letter to that effect.'

Sebastian Brodie forced a smile, but Charlie detected that it was not his most confident effort. 'Doctors are very busy men, Mr Stuart, I am sure they cannot recall every detail of every meeting with every patient.'

'Oh, I think any doctor would recall a letter which confirmed that one of his patients was losing his mind, don't you? It's hardly in the same league as a letter requesting a blood test, is it?'

The solicitor advocate got up from his desk; an indication that their discussion was at an end. 'Mr Stuart, if you are questioning the honesty of my client and the veracity of her claim then we open a very sordid chapter in this saga. By so doing you are not only bringing into disrepute the reputation of Mrs Stuart Senior, but you are also questioning the probity of this firm. This, I would have thought, you would have been reluctant to do, the situation already being complicated – and unpleasant – enough without adding an extra – and very inadvisable – dimension to the case.'

'Oh, it's complicated, I grant you, and it's most certainly unpleasant, but on both accounts that is down to your client, not to me. I make no accusations relating to your practice, Mr Brodie, but I do suggest you ask Charlotte about the letter and then get back to me when you are confident that she really does have a case. It would not do, would it, Mr Brodie, for a solicitor advocate with such a reputation as yours, to be basing a claim for such a large amount of money on what amounts to a forgery?'

With that, Charlie left the office and stepped out into the fresh air. His heart was thumping in his chest, but at least he had managed to keep his nerve. He was as certain as he could be that Charlotte was pulling a fast one, that Dr Crawford most certainly did not write the note. He also suspected that Sebastian Brodie had no idea that his client had lied to him. Patience; that's what they needed at the moment, and a steady nerve – just as Eleanor's father had suggested. They were not out of the woods yet, but the omens looked a great deal brighter than they had done a few days ago.

With a spring in his step – the first for some time – Charlie headed for Edinburgh Waverley station and the train to Strath Carron. He could not wait to tell Eleanor the news. It was also time to put Murdo and Mrs Murdo in the picture – now that he was more certain of a favourable outcome, he felt that he could risk letting them in on the affairs of the past few months.

Through the window of his office, Sebastian Brodie watched Charlie walk down the road, then he sat back behind his desk and thoughtfully drummed his fingers on the polished ebony surface before pressing a button on his intercom. 'Emma, would you get me Mrs Stuart on the phone please? Mrs Charlotte Stuart.' He waited calmly until the intercom buzzed, then lifted the receiver.

'I'm sorry, Mr Brodie, but there's no answer from Mrs Stuart.'

'Right. Thank you. Can you get me a Dr Crawford then, please? I assume he has a practice in Strath Carron; I think that's the nearest town to Castle Sodhail, isn't it?'

'I've no idea, Mr Brodie, but I'll see what I can find.'

The wait was rather longer this time, but eventually the secretary buzzed him back. 'I have a Dr Fergus Crawford listed as being in practice in Strath Carron. Would that be the person you were enquiring about?'

'Is he the only Dr Crawford listed for that neck of the woods?'

'I think so, sir.'

'Then it's likely that he's the man I want, isn't it? How many Dr Crawfords are there likely to be in a small Scottish town, for God's sake?'

The secretary made no reply. She was taken aback by Mr Brodie's sharp retort. Normally he was very polite. Clearly something had rattled him and she was not going to risk further inflaming his temper.

39

Loch Sodhail

September 1976

'Sweet is revenge – especially to women.'
Lord Byron, *Don Juan*, 1819–24

The year-long silence on the part of Charlotte and her solicitor advocate indicated to Charlie and Eleanor the likelihood that the claim against the estate had been dropped. But as far as Murdo was concerned, the situation was by no means resolved. 'I wouldnae put anything past yon woman,' he confided in Charlie one morning when, having worked long and hard for the better part of the month, the two men took a boat out onto the loch with the intention of catching a salmon for supper.

'She's a conniving termagant that's for sure. You just make sure that she's not cooking up some other way of getting money out of ye.'

Charlie was tying a different fly onto his line, having failed to interest the fish with a Lucky Charlie. 'I've called her solicitor advocate a couple of times but he hasn't returned my calls. I'd think that was a good sign, wouldn't you?'

'Nothing's certain until yon woman goes to join her maker.'

'Maybe not.'

'If I were you, I'd be wanting something in writing – some kind o' insurance policy. If ye dinnae have that ye'll be ever afeared that one day she'll pop up and start finding some other reason tae rob ye.'

Charlie looked at Murdo quizzically. 'This wouldn't be on account of you being thrown out of your house if she had succeeded, would it?'

Murdo was playing his line gently and drawing the fly across the water. 'It might have coloured my judgement more than a little, but it's you and the wife and the bairns that I'm most concerned aboot.'

'I'm very grateful.' Charlie cast his fly across the water. He felt lucky today, but it was Murdo who landed the salmon – a twelve pounder.

'I'll share it with ye,' he conceded.

'We'll celebrate with a fish supper,' grinned Charlie.

'Aye, well let's just hope it's nae premature.'

'Come on, Murdo; even you must admit that we'd have heard by now if Charlotte was going to proceed.'

Murdo shook his head. 'I learnt long since that there's nae predicting the motives of the female o' the species. They do their ane thing in their ane time, and anyone who thinks otherwise disnae undertand the ways and wiles o' women.'

Charlie sighed. 'Ah well. We'll see.'

'That much there's nae denying,' muttered Murdo, tucking the hook of his successful fly under the lowest ring of his rod and tightening the line. 'But if I were ye, I'd be seeking some kind o' assurance from yon advocate.'

'What was it then?' asked Charlie, indicating the fly that Murdo had been using.

'One o' my ane.'

'Does it have a name?'

'Aye. It's called a Black Widow.'

Their supper finished, the dishes washed and the children safe in their beds, Charlie and Eleanor lay side by side in their own divan, the moon glinting through the window and casting the objects in the room into sharp relief.

Eleanor, curled up beside her husband, asked, 'So Murdo thinks you should find some way of making sure that Charlotte has withdrawn her claim?'

'Yes. I've tried three times to talk to Sebastian Brodie now, but he simply doesn't return my calls.'

'I'd have thought that was a pretty good sign that they weren't proceeding.'

'That's what I said, but Murdo wasn't convinced. He thinks the female of the species is a wily beast and not to be trusted.'

'I bet that attitude goes down well with Mrs Murdo.'

'Mmm. Perhaps I should take another trip to Edinburgh. Actually go to Brodie's office and buttonhole him there. I could go and see Charlotte as well.'

'Don't you think it's best to let sleeping dogs lie?'

'Well, yes, in a way. I don't want to stir up a hornets' nest, but unless we hear something from one or other of them this is going to be hanging over our heads indefinitely. The uncertainty isn't much fun and I want to be able to get on with our lives, especially now that . . .' He stroked Eleanor's stomach. She was expecting again – twins, the midwife had said. 'With just three months to go, I'd like to feel settled.'

'That would be nice,' agreed Eleanor. 'For all of us.'

'I'll go in the morning,' said Charlie. 'Better done and got out of the way rather than left to chance.'

There was a pause before she said, 'I wonder what's happened to Gordon?'

'What made you think of him?'

'Oh, it's just that he's another loose end. Unresolved, I mean. We've never heard from him. That afternoon – after the shooting accident – I at least expected him to come and say goodbye. I hope he's all right.'

'He'd have been in touch if he wasn't.'

'You say that. I'd have thought if he was in trouble he wouldn't have been able to get in touch. I worry about him. And Florin.'

'Two Bob? I don't think you need to worry about him. He'll be back home in Yugloslavia, doing his bit for the resistance or whoever he supports. Is there anybody else you want to share your concerns about? It must be your condition – all these worries coming to the surface.'

'Yes. I'm sorry. It's just that it all seems so . . . well . . . complicated.'

'I know. But it will all turn out fine, honestly.'

'You do still love me, don't you?'

'What's brought that on?'

'Oh, just . . . things. You don't think I'm a wily beast do you – like Murdo suggested?'

Charlie pulled her close to him. 'You are the least wily beast I know. And another thing . . .'

'Mmm?'

'If I hadn't had you beside me I don't know how I'd have got through the last few years, what with Dad and Charlotte.'

'Sometimes I feel I just get in the way.'

'What?'

'Oh, you know. You're busy running the estate and generating income and all I do is stay at home and look after the children.'

'Now stop right there. We have these children because we want them – even the ones that haven't arrived yet. That's what I do it for. I know I love the castle and the estate and that I'm devoted to it, but that doesn't mean I'm not devoted to you and the children. If I had to choose between my family and the estate, there's no contest.'

'As long as—'

'As long as nothing. Now go to sleep and stop worrying. You're the light of my life, Mrs Stuart, and it's time you appreciated that.'

'Not wily?'

'Not even a tiny bit.'

'That's all right then.'

Charlie was aware that within a few minutes Eleanor had fallen asleep. It was some time before he drifted off himself. Half waking, half sleeping, through his mind there flickered mingled images of the castle and the loch, of his wife and children and of Murdo and Mrs Murdo. Among this confused melange of dreams, the image of Charlotte smiling and shaking her head featured as a leitmotif. He must go to Edinburgh in the morning and sort it out once and for all.

40

Edinburgh

September 1976

'Out of the crooked timber of humanity no straight thing can ever be made.'

Immanuel Kant, 'Idea for a Universal History with a Cosmopolitan Purpose', 1784

There were moments, on the journey, when Charlie wondered if he was doing the right thing. Would it not be better, as Eleanor had said, to let sleeping dogs lie? But if he did, how could he be sure they would not wake up later and bite him? Three times he was near to turning back, but resisted the temptation and finally climbed the steps to Sebastian Brodie's office and announced himself to the girl at reception. She refrained from using the intercom and instead got up and disappeared down the corridor. Charlie sat in a smart Barcelona chair of black leather with a polished chrome frame and stared at the William Scott painting on the wall behind the girl's desk. He wondered how large were Brodie's fees.

The girl was gone some time, and Charlie wondered if Sebastian Brodie were trying to get out of seeing him. He considered lifting the William Scott from the wall and walking out with it, but then dismissed the idea. Anyway, it would probably be alarmed. Stupid thought. Possible, though. He glanced at the copies of *Country Life* and *Interiors* on the low glass table. They were all relatively current – so unlike the dentist. His mind began to wander. After several minutes the receptionist returned and said, 'Mr Brodie will see you now, sir. You know where his office is, I think?'

With mounting apprehension Charlie walked down the corridor to the door he remembered so well – it was as black and glossy as everything else in this set of plush solicitor advocate's offices. He knocked – he hoped purposefully – on the door. There was no reply. Instead, after a few seconds, the door was opened and Sebastian Brodie motioned him to come in. His expression, on this occasion, was more amenable than on Charlie's last visit. He shook Charlie by the hand and said, 'I've asked Emma to bring us coffee – white with no sugar, wasn't it?'

'Yes,' said Charlie, unnerved a little by the unexpected civility and the fact that Brodie remembered how he took his coffee.

The jacket of the dark suit – worn like armour at their last encounter – was draped over the back of the chair. In shirt, tie and braces, the solicitor advocate bade Charlie take a seat in another Barcelona chair that was set at an angle of forty-five degrees in front of the desk. He opened the slim file that lay on the desk in front of him. As Charlie recalled, the last time he had been here the chair offered to him had been upright and hard and positioned at a ninety-degree angle to the desk – altogether more confrontational. Or was he imagining it? Had it just seemed that way?

'I am afraid I am at a loss as to what to say to you, Mr Stuart,' began Brodie.

Charlie waited for him to continue; unwilling to offer him anything like a lifeline lest it should weaken his own position. He wanted to know where he stood, once and for all, but he would rather play his cards close to his chest until he was forced to do otherwise.

'You see, I have had no instructions from Mrs Stuart Senior.'

Still Charlie refrained from asking, 'Does that mean she has dropped her claim?' In the event he did not need to.

Sebastian Brodie continued. 'Concerned by what you said at our last meeting, I confronted my client with your accusation and, much to my surprise, I am afraid she had no adequate explanation. From that moment on, Mr Stuart, I made it clear that this firm was unwilling to represent Mrs Stuart in her claim for part of the Sodhail estate.'

'So she has dropped her claim?' Charlie asked.

'That I cannot say. What I can confirm is that she is no longer represented by Brodie & Company.'

'I see.' Charlie thought for a few moments and then asked, 'Is it likely that she will be represented by anyone else?'

'No one with a sound business acumen, nor any law firm worthy of respect. We take a dim view of fraudulent activity, Mr Stuart, and have to safeguard our own reputation as well as endeavouring to pursue the interests of our clients.'

'So why haven't you been taking my calls?'

For the first time that Charlie could remember, Brodie looked uncomfortable. 'Mindful of the events which had led up to our last encounter, of your attitude when you visited these offices, and the revelations which transpired during the course of our meeting, I assumed that you were in some way about to take legal action.'

'So you chose to ignore me?'

'In common parlance, Mr Stuart, I was playing for time. I wanted to find out just what Mrs Stuart Senior was playing at and why she assumed that something so blatant as a forged letter could prove her entitlement to half your estate.'

'And have you? Found out, I mean?'

'Alas, I have been unable to.' Sebastian Brodie read the look of bewilderment on Charlie's face. 'Mrs Stuart has, in common parlance, done a bunk.'

'She's what?'

'She has disappeared, Mr Stuart. Without trace. Owing this company, I might add, a tidy sum of money.'

'But the house – in New Town . . . ?'

'Sold.'

Charlie sat back in his chair. 'But she can't just have vanished into thin air. What about her friends?'

'As baffled as you are – as I am – Mr Stuart.'

'But the estate agents who sold the house. Have they no forwarding address?'

'No. Believe me, Mr Stuart, we've done all we can to trace her.'

'When did she disappear?'

'About a year ago. Sometime around your last visit here. It seems that the house was already sold – she used another firm of solicitors for the conveyancing or we would have been able to keep a closer eye and maybe even sense that all was not as it should be. She had agreed with me that we would pursue the matter of her claim on your estate at a steady pace. That was what I advised her. You will forgive me, Mr Stuart, but often matters sort themselves out if allowed to run their natural course, rather than being rushed through. In such instances, mistakes can be made and oversights occur.'

'So you thought that if you just let me sweat a little I'd come to my senses and give in?'

'In a nutshell, and *sans* legal jargon, yes.'

'But I didn't "come to my senses"?'

'No. You, too, played the waiting game, which, in this particular instance, had the desired effect on Mrs Stuart. She began to suspect that she might be found out, so she sold up and left.'

'But what a stupid thing to do. I mean, to assume that we wouldn't question Dr Crawford.'

'Well, according to Dr Crawford your wife only questioned him by chance – when he was called out to some shotgun accident.'

'Yes. That's true. I mean, the thing is . . . well . . . I assumed that she was telling the truth. I didn't think to question her.'

Sebastian Brodie shook his head. 'I rather wish you had, Mr Stuart. And I rather wish *I* had. It would have saved us all a lot of trouble, and my firm' – he added as an afterthought – 'a considerable amount of time and money.'

'So what now?' asked Charlie.

'Well, you can keep your ears open and try to find out where she is, though, to be honest, I don't hold out much hope of her turning up. If it's any consolation to you, I feel rather more foolish than you do. I'm meant to be able to spot duplicitous people. On this occasion I failed and I can only apologise for any distress it has caused you and Mrs Stuart – the young Mrs Stuart, that is.'

For a moment Charlie actually felt rather sorry for Sebastian Brodie. He got up from his chair, with more than a degree of difficulty, so near to the ground did he find himself, and reached out to shake his hand. As he did so he said, 'There is just one thing . . .'

'Yes?'

'The first time we met.'

'Yes?'

'You were at Charlotte's house. And you weren't in a suit. You were dressed casually. In a yellow cashmere sweater.'

Sebastian Brodie smiled. 'You have a very good memory.'

'I was just wondering . . . did you know my stepmother socially before becoming her advocate?'

The smile disappeared and Brodie said, 'I don't think I have to answer that question, Mr Stuart.'

'Oh, I know you don't have to, Mr Brodie, but I'm just curious. I mean, I wouldn't want to think that she'd taken you for a ride emotionally as well as financially.'

There was no humour in the reply. 'That's very kind of you, Mr Stuart, but please don't concern yourself with my emotional well-being. In my line of work I can't afford much in the way of emotion.'

'No,' said Charlie, 'I've noticed that.'

As he walked down Castle Terrace, Charlie felt just the slightest bit guilty, but not for long. He walked down the Lothian Road, across George Street and Queen Street before turning right into the street where Charlotte and his father used to live. As he came to number thirteen he made to turn in, but was stopped in his tracks when the front door opened and a family of young children spilled out on to the front steps. 'Will you calm down!' said the mother, doing her best to marshal her unruly brood. The front door was painted bright red. That alone made it clear that Charlotte was no longer in residence.

'Excuse me?' he asked.

The woman looked up and smiled through the mayhem.

He asked the question to which the answer was self-evident. 'Does Mrs Stuart live here?'

'I'm afraid not.'

'You wouldn't have a forwarding address, would you?'

'Sorry, no. I'm afraid she didn't leave one. I think she went abroad.'

'But what about her letters; her post?'

'We just write "Not known at this address" on her letters and put them back in the post. Sorry, but I must get these kids to swimming.' She fielded a particularly wilful child by grabbing its arm and bundling it into the estate car that sat at the kerb. 'If you could tell me how to make children disappear as effectively as Mrs Stuart I'd be very grateful,' she said.

As the vehicle drove out of sight, Charlie turned to look at the house once more. It seemed now to bear no trace of his father, or of that former part of his life. It was a part of somebody else's life now. Charlotte had gone, and with her all trace of dark brown and dark green paint. For that he must be grateful.

He turned and began his journey home. As one chapter of life ended, so another began. Soon their family of four would be a family of six. It was that which must occupy him now; that which would enable him to look forward, rather than back, though something deep in his heart told him that this would not be the last he would ever hear of Charlotte Niven. That was how he would think of her; never as Charlotte Stuart. She might once have been a part of his family, but now there was every reason to hope that those days were over.

41

Fort William
December 1976

> 'It is the secret sympathy,
> The silver link, the silken tie,
> Which heart to heart, and mind to mind,
> In body and soul can bind.'
>
> Sir Walter Scott, *The Lay of the Last Minstrel*, 1805

The plan was for Eleanor to go into hospital a week earlier than her projected date of delivery, since after the complications of Lucy's birth, both the midwife and the doctor thought it a good idea. They could keep an eye on her that way. Monitor developments. Charlie could come and go as he pleased – managing the estate during the day, coping with Ellie and Lucy at night with the help – as always, of the irreplaceable Mrs Murdo.

So far, things had gone according to this plan and Charlie had made the long journey to the maternity unit several times. Not that there was anything he could do at this stage, except comfort Eleanor in her boredom.

'Do I have to be here now?' she asked. 'I mean, suppose they don't arrive for another fortnight, what then? You'll be worn out travelling up and down and I'll be bored to distraction.'

'It's all for the best,' Charlie had assured her. 'For you and the babies. If anything goes wrong you're in the right place. And I'll bring you plenty of reading matter. What do you want?'

'A couple of Georgette Heyers.'

'But you've read all the Georgette Heyers.'

'It doesn't matter.'

'What about that big fat history of art by the bed?'

'I'm giving birth, not writing a dissertation. I need comfort reading not intellectual stimulation. I want stories of dashing heroes and happy endings.'

Charlie stroked her tummy. 'And are these two all right?'

'Yes, they're fine. I'm not sure they want to come out into this world.'

'Well, it's a better world than it was a few months ago.'

'Safe to come out now?'

'I think so.'

'And you're sure you're happy with the names?'

'If you are.'

'What do you think? Boys or girls?'

'Or one of each? Wouldn't it be good if we could have known now?'

'No. Not natural. I'm happy to wait and see. Though it would be nice if at least one of them was a boy. For you.'

'When have I ever complained about girls?'

'Where shall I start?' grinned Eleanor.

'Oh, come on! I don't mean the day-to-day irritations – they'd happen whether they were girls, boys, dogs or ferrets. But I've never been bothered about not playing football, even if I'm not that brilliant with dolls and dressing up.'

'I know. You've been very sweet. I'm just sorry that the last few years have been such a trial for you. But I'm very proud of you, you know; proud of you for keeping it all – us all – together.'

From his seat by the bed, he leaned forward and kissed her on the forehead. 'I do love you,' he said.

'And I you,' she murmured.

★ ★ ★

Back at the castle, weary from the travelling and the daily organisation of the estate, from the rebuilding of stone walls and the thinning of woodland, Charlie was dozing in an easy chair by the fire in his study – there was no point in lighting the one in the hall which was so lofty that the flames seemed to have little warming effect at this time of year.

The girls were tucked up in their beds and he was halfway between waking and sleeping, telling himself that it would be better to go to bed and get a good night's sleep, rather than doze here and wake up with a stiff neck, when the phone rang. It was the hospital. Would he mind coming in now? It looked as though the babies were on their way.

Sitting by Eleanor's bed, he felt a strange sense of foreboding. Her face, spangled with perspiration and drained of colour, seemed pinched. He remembered from last time the agonised expression, the tension, the strain, and wished that somehow he could share it with her and be more useful. Standing by her, holding her hand, seemed such a pathetic contribution. He patted her forehead from time to time with a damp flannel, but she turned her head to one side as if to avoid contact and seemed barely aware of his presence. Her body went into ever more frequent spasms and her legs kicked and flailed as though she were trying to shake off some unseen hand that was intent on holding her down.

As Eleanor's labour progressed, Charlie became more aware of the concern etched on the doctor and the midwife's faces. A cold fear took hold of him and a feeling of being out of control and helpless enveloped him. Why could they not do something for her? 'Is she all right?' he asked.

They did not answer, but hurried around the bed doing he was not sure what. Then the midwife said, 'I think you should leave us for a while, Mr Stuart.'

'But I said I would be here.'

'All the same, it would be good if you left us just for a while. There are things we have to do. You'll be right next door. Not far away. We'll call you in when we're happy.'

He looked imploringly at Eleanor, who was now on the verge of delirium and unaware of anything that was going on around her, least of all the presence of her husband. Then he saw the growing pool of blood beneath her body. The doctor nodded his approval of the midwife's instruction, and with a student nurse's arm guiding him to the door Charlie was ushered out of the delivery room and deposited in a small side room where hard tubular metal chairs with taut fabric seats were positioned around the walls.

In his distress the posters on the wall were possessed of a nightmare quality – even though they were extolling the virtues of Scottish holidays, the magnificence of the Glenfinnan monument and the architectural delights of Edinburgh. The perspectives seemed distorted, the views harshly coloured and worryingly surreal. He tried to sit down; he tried to be calm. He picked up a magazine and flipped through its pages, though saw only confusing print and pictures that made no sense. He stood up again and paced the room – four paces this way, five paces that. Nothing registered except the muffled cries emanating from the room next door.

He glanced up at the clock on the wall every few minutes, but time ticked by so slowly. He wanted to be there, on the other side of the wall, holding her hand, telling her it would all be all right; telling her that he would sort things out, protect her, protect the children. But the longer he waited the less convinced he became that everything was going to turn out well. His fingernails dug into his palms as he repeatedly clenched and unclenched his hands, muttering prayers and promises to God that if Eleanor were all right he could forgive anything else that might happen.

After the better part of an hour – the longest of his life – the door opened and the doctor appeared. Charlie could tell from his expression that it had been a difficult delivery. His face bore a look of profound sorrow. How could that be? And then the reality of the situation dawned.

'Please tell me . . .' said Charlie, his voice breaking.

The doctor did his best to smile. It was the kind of sympathetic smile that Charlie knew came before bad news. His stomach churned and his throat tightened.

'Please sit down, Mr Stuart.'

Charlie felt as though he was in a trance. He could not move.

'It was a difficult delivery I'm afraid. Mrs Stuart suffered what we call a post-partum haemorrhage. I'm so very, very sorry. Your son and daughter are quite healthy but . . . I'm afraid we have been unable to save your wife.'

42

Castle Sodhail

1976–1985

> 'All the statues of Victory have wings: but Grief has no wings. She is the unwelcome lodger that squats on the hearthstone between us and the fire and will not move or be dislodged.'
>
> Arthur Quiller-Couch, Armistice Day anniversary sermon, 1923

Those first weeks and months after Eleanor's death found Charlie in some strange no-man's land, drained of all emotion except that of profound despair – a numbed, blank, bleak state that seemed to have little connection with life: the life that he had once known. The emptiness was excruciating and he could not help but blame himself for letting her down, for putting his family at risk. She had told him that herself, in her own words. 'How could you do it?' she had asked. And now she was gone and he was aware that towards the end of her life – although he had never for a moment seen it coming – he had let her down; had not been the man she thought he was, the man she so deserved.

He had never loved anybody else. Would never love again, of that much he was certain. The light that once burned so brightly had gone out of his life, and even on days when the sun shone, it appeared to do so through a thick gauze. He could not touch his inner emotions; they seemed to have been frozen by some unseen hand – locked away and denied him.

Day after day, in fair weather and foul, he would take himself up onto Creag Sodhail and stare out into space, often returning to the castle soaked to the skin and shivering or stiff and chilled to the bone. The connection with the earth seemed somehow to cauterise his pain, to take it to a place where he could learn to endure it, almost take it for granted.

He had never contemplated the fact that history might repeat itself. Why would he? Why should it? And now he had some inkling of how his father must have felt when his own mother had died. At the age of twenty-six, Charlie was now a single parent with four young children. How could this possibly be? What had he done to deserve this ever-worsening chain of events?

Why had he listened to Gordon, a school friend, rather than putting his wife and children first, which was the right and proper thing to do? Why was he so obsessed with not letting people down? His feelings towards Gordon were coloured now – coloured by a tragedy which was not of his friend's making but which was nevertheless inextricably entwined emotionally with that relationship. If he never saw him again he would not worry. It was over, though it could never be forgotten.

Mrs Murdo moved into the castle, taking on the role of mother, though she had never been one herself. Charlie marvelled at her capabilities, and was grateful for the way in which she tolerated his introspection and the long silences when he seemed disconnected from life itself.

The children learnt to read their father's moods; knew when to be quiet and make themselves scarce. Charlie reproached himself for being withdrawn, but as the years passed he opened up a little, ever conscious of the distance between his own father and himself and of the fact that it was something he did not want to replicate with his own children.

On summer afternoons they would all walk up the hill behind the castle with a picnic to eat while they watched the eagles and the ravens. Charlie found solace in sharing his love of nature with the children. Ellie and Lucy, though only in single figures themselves, became mothers to Sarah and Rory, the twins; helping out Mrs Murdo when they came home from school in Strath Carron. He knew that soon he would have to send them away to board. How he hated the prospect. But as a single parent there was little option if he were to keep the estate going. He could not rely on Mrs Murdo's good grace indefinitely; could not concentrate on looking after the children on a daily basis as well as managing the estate, and Eleanor's parents had insisted on paying the fees. The alternative was to move out and become a full-time child minder or else hire a nanny and have someone else living in and taking care of his children, and he could not reconcile himself to that state of affairs. Nor would Eleanor have wanted that. She, too, had become proprietorial about this place – it had become her home every bit as much as his; he felt she was still here, somehow, in spite of the endless void. And yet he chastised himself for the compromise he was having to make. He hoped she was looking down on him and watching their children grow. The prospect often moved him to tears during those long dark nights when he lay alone in his bed, reaching out to where she would have lain and feeling the emptiness.

Even the Fitzallans had suggested, two years after Eleanor's death, that it would be a good idea if he got out and met other people – perhaps with a view to marrying again – and although he understood the perceived wisdom of widening his horizons, he knew it was not really an option, certainly not in terms of finding a wife.

No, his place was here and he must make the best of the hand that life had dealt him. His girls brought a welcome degree of happiness into his days, though he struggled to hit it off with Rory. Perhaps he expected too much of him. But so determined was Charlie to have a better relationship with him than he had had with his own father that he continued trying to do things that the boy would appreciate, even if sometimes it seemed he could do nothing right.

In Murdo he had seldom found an outlet for his frustrations, a ready ear for his admissions of guilt and sorrow, and after several years the old ghillie was beginning to lose sympathy with Charlie's introspection. It was, he said, time that Charlie had new interests; time he took on new challenges. Charlie felt that his current life presented challenges enough.

By the mid-1980s, all four children had outgrown the little establishment at Strath Carron and were away at boarding school. It was a double-edged sword; their absence allowed him to run the estate more efficiently, and to adjust his work-load so that when they were at home in the holidays he could be with them as much as possible. But it also condemned him to lonely nights in term time – periods during which Murdo and Mrs Murdo did their best to make his life more eventful than he seemed capable of doing himself. Murdo would take him out at least one night a week to the local hostelry, where the locals would jolly him along; he even consented to go to the occasional Scottish country dance and, for a couple of hours, he could lose himself in the reels and strathspeys and enjoy company other than his own.

'What you need is to be taken out of yersel,' explained Mrs Murdo. But in spite of his best efforts, and those of the locals, he still did occasionally 'sit on yon rock and mope'.

It was on one such day during the summer holidays, when the children were at Invergarry House with their grandpar-ents and Charlie was 'sitting on yon rock', that he experienced an epiphany that gave him the will and the courage to move on. He could not be sure how it had happened, only that he had been gazing down on the waters of the loch and watching a lone swan dabbling in the reeds that bordered the water. The light was strange that day; it had an amber quality that reflected off the ripples and turned the feathers of the swan to pure gold. Charlie rubbed his eyes, as if to clear them, but the golden swan remained. Then the silence was broken by a distant honking. Charlie turned in the direction of the commotion and saw a flock of swans flying low over the water. They were soaring over the centre of the loch in 'V' formation, like some heavenly battalion intent on . . . what? The golden swan turned its head to look at them and then, flapping its wings, beat a path across the water, splashing and running across the surface until it became airborne. As it did so, it joined the formation of birds at their outer extremity, and then the whole flock wheeled around and flew towards Charlie, passing directly overhead, so low that he found himself ducking to avoid being hit. He could hear the whistling of the wind in their feathers, could feel the down-draught from the beat of their wings and then, within seconds, the swans were gone and the air, and the afternoon, was still once more.

Charlie got up, his heart thumping rapidly, and leant against the rock upon which he had been sitting. He felt somehow different. As though a weight had been lifted from his shoulders. At first he thought it was fanciful; that in a moment the black cloud would descend again. But it did not. He walked down from the hillside towards the castle with a lightness in his step that he could not remember experiencing for many a year.

That evening, as the children returned from their grandparents and sat with him on the sofas in front of the hall fire, he told them of his experience. Unused to their father expressing such a depth of emotion, their reaction was one of rapt attention. Only Rory looked uneasy, but he said little and kept his thoughts to himself. It was Lucy who asked, innocently, 'The golden swan; do you think it was Mummy?'

Charlie could not speak, but nodded and smiled, and they could see that his eyes had filled with tears. The girls came and kissed him one by one and made their way up to bed. Rory smiled at his father and said softly, 'Goodnight, Dad. Sleep well.'

For the first time in many a year, Charlie did.

43

Castle Sodhail

July 1995

> 'Tell me, Muse, of the man of many devices, who wandered far and wide after he had sacked Troy's sacred city, and saw the towns of many men and knew their mind.'
>
> Homer, *The Odyssey*, 8th century BC

Charlie had been working with Murdo, clearing ditches and wondering if, at the age of forty-five, he should be letting one of the estate lads do more of the heavy stuff. Then he reminded himself that Murdo was not far short of seventy and it didn't seem to be worrying him. But Murdo had long since learnt to pace himself. Time that he did the same. He stood up to stretch his back muscles and noticed a figure walking along the track towards them. At first he assumed that it was a hiker, but the male figure carried no backpack. He was a tall and balding man with a shambling gait; he reminded Charlie of someone. Then the spoken words removed all doubt: '*Hic itur ad astra*!'

'I don't believe it!' murmured Charlie. 'What the . . . ?'

Murdo clambered out of the ditch to get a better look at their visitor.

'Well, bugger me!' he muttered, half to himself. Then, more loudly, 'We never thought tae see ye again!'

Gordon Mackenzie grinned at the two mud-caked men. 'I can see that you still like getting your hands dirty.'

'And I can see that you're still a stranger to the laundry,' countered Charlie, observing the state of his old friend's clothes.

'No, no! I'm much more hygienic now. I've just come on a long journey, that's all.'

The two men walked towards each other and shook hands warmly. For a brief moment Charlie felt that he wanted to hug his old companion, but distant memories of their parting, and of Eleanor's disappointment, prevented him from such an open display of affection.

'Where on earth have you been?' asked Charlie.

'To the ends of the earth and back again.'

'But it's been . . . years. How many?'

'Twenty, less a month. "*Tempus volat hora fugit*" and all that.'

'Twenty years . . . Good God! Where's the time gone?'

'I've just told you – it has wings.'

'We waited to hear from you but—'

'I know; rotten correspondent. But then I kept thinking, the best thing to do would be to come and see you. Every year I said it to myself; every summer, when the Highlands would be looking at their best and the heather would be colouring up, I said, I'll go and see the Stuarts. And then I wondered if you'd still be here. If that old bat would have got her way. But I entrusted you to the vicissitudes of fate, thinking that she could not possibly take away your birthright, and' – he spread his arms wide and indicated the landscape – 'here you still are.'

Needing no further excuse to stop work, and after telling Murdo to go home and have some lunch, Charlie walked Gordon back to the castle and over a pasty and a pint of local beer at the kitchen table, related the events of the past twenty years as fully as he felt able. It took some time. Gordon listened attentively: the shock of Eleanor's death seemed to hit him hard, but he expressed palpable relief at the withdrawal of Charlotte from the fray and incredulity at her disappearance.

'What a time you've had,' he said softly.

'Yes. What a time,' confirmed Charlie. 'And I'm afraid I blamed you for a while.'

Gordon looked confused.

'Eleanor and I had a row. A few weeks before she died. We so seldom rowed that it really shook me. Shook both of us, I think. She said I'd let her down – not telling her the full story about the students.'

'Oh God!'

'Oh, it was a long time ago. I've never been very good at nursing grudges. It's better that you've been away so long. Water under the bridge and all that . . .'

'And the children? What are they doing now? How old are they?'

'Ellie is twenty-four – a willowy blonde. Bright, level, sensible. She works in Edinburgh, in a bank. Lucy is twenty-one – she's the one who looks most like her mum, and she has her cheekiness, too. She's not as tall as Ellie. She's studying accountancy but I don't know for how long. She seems to have fallen in with a farmer's son, down in the Borders. Nice boy, but a bit dull. Still, you can't choose your children's other halves, can you?'

'Or express an opinion?'

'Heavens, no! They're talking of getting married next year. It's a tense subject but I've tried to keep my own counsel and mutter nice things from time to time, even though I'm convinced it will all end in tears. Then there are the twins – Sarah and Rory – they're eighteen years and seven months. I always know their ages exactly,' he confessed softly. 'Anyway, they're thick as thieves.'

'Too young for any long-term relationships there, then?'

'Sarah has a new boyfriend – a lawyer. A bit of a high-flyer.

She's just started working for a law firm in Fort William. Rory is at Auchincruive – my old college – doing his best to keep his mind on agriculture, and failing.'

'Will he take over from you?'

'I hope so. But I'm not giving up just yet. Another twenty years and I might think about it. Mind you, Rory's a willful blighter. A mind of his own.'

'A bit like his dad.'

'You think so?'

'Oh yes. Stubborn as a mule – but in a nice way.' Then, seeing that Charlie was about to contradict him: 'Tenacious perhaps, rather than stubborn. Unwilling to let go of something you intend to see through. Like hanging on to this place.'

'That's a good thing, surely?'

'In your case I suspect it's been your salvation.'

'Yes, I suppose it has.'

There was a short pause before Gordon asked, 'Are you lonely?'

'Sometimes. When the kids are away and I'm here on my own. They come back at weekends when they can, to keep an eye on me I suppose. The last thing I want to be is a liability. It was good when they were at boarding school; then we had long holidays here together. I think they liked that. They still love this place – even Rory – and say they couldn't think of anywhere else as home. That's nice.'

'What about the Murdos? He's still working here, I see.'

'Yes. I'm not sure he wants to retire, even though he's pushing seventy. When he does, the cottage is supposed to revert to the estate, but I haven't the heart to turn them out, not after all they've done. Mrs Murdo has been a godsend – surrogate mother to the kids, really. And they both try and get me out of myself when they see I'm a bit low. But I've always been happy in my own company, even though not as happy as I was when . . .' His words tailed off.

'No. She was very special.'

Charlie nodded but did not speak.

'And you've never been tempted to . . . to start up another relationship?'

'No. It could never be as good as the one I had with Eleanor. What would be the point in settling for second best?'

'Company? Companionship?'

'This place is company enough. I don't know what I'd have done without the castle and the loch and the mountains. Weird to some folk, I know, but it suits me. And the kids offer me companionship – when they're home. Lucy is very good at marshalling me; marshalling us all.'

'But there's no . . . intimacy. No one to talk to at night.'

'I've come to terms with it. I'm alone but I don't feel lonely. Eleanor is still here. I talk to her a lot.'

'Where is she? I mean where . . . ?'

'She didn't want to be buried. I scattered her ashes on the loch, from the rowing boat. That's what she said she wanted when we fell to talking about it by chance one night. I never thought I'd be doing it at twenty-six.'

'But you feel she's here somehow?'

'I know she is.'

Charlie found himself telling Gordon the story of the swan. He half expected him to scoff at the very idea. Instead he nodded and said, softly, 'How lovely. How wonderful.'

'You don't think I'm being fanciful?'

'No. "There are more things in heaven and earth, Horatio, than are dreamt of in your philosophy."'

Charlie smiled. 'Still a quote for every occasion?'

'No. Not always. There are times when a quote is hardly enough.'

'But what about you?' asked Charlie. 'We've talked about me for an hour and I've not learnt a thing about you: why you're here, where you've been, what you've been doing.'

'Put the kettle on, old bean; it's a long story.'

Charlie did so, and made two large mugs of coffee. Then he said, 'Come and sit by the fire in the hall.'

'You still have the fire lit? Even in July?'

'These are the Highlands of Scotland, the castle walls are very thick and, anyway, Eleanor liked a welcoming fire. I try not to let it go out, except at night.'

'The eternal flame?'

'I suppose so. It keeps the place alive – especially when I'm the only one here.'

They sat at either end of one of the long sofas that were positioned in front of the hall fire and Charlie asked, 'So where did you go when you disappeared? We seem to have had more than our fair share of disappearing acts around here.'

'Where do you think?'

Charlie shrugged. 'No idea. I mean, you slipped away with Two Bob but that was all I knew. When I got back from the shoot they said they didn't even see you go.'

'Two Bob! I'd forgotten you called him that. Well, we went to Yugoslavia.'

'We?'

'Florin and I.'

'You made sure he got back safely?'

'In a manner of speaking.'

Gordon saw the puzzlement on Charlie's face and continued. 'Do you remember when Florin – Two Bob as you persist in calling him – was shot? He pulled out a letter in a bloodstained envelope and handed it to me?'

'Yes. Yes I do.' The memory was returning. 'You read it and put it in your pocket saying that he wouldn't need to send it now . . . or something? Who was it addressed to?'

Gordon looked away for a moment, as though gathering his thoughts. Then he said, 'It was addressed to me.' Seeing the blank look on Charlie's face, he continued. 'I suppose you would call it a love letter.'

'What?'

'There had always been . . . feelings between us. Unspoken; unresolved, not acted upon. I suppose neither of us knew if they were reciprocated by the other. He even threw a brick at me when I was punting down the river because he was angry that I didn't seem to care for him in the same way he cared for me.'

'But I always thought he had a bit of a crush on Eleanor!'

'Only because he used her as a sounding board.'

'What? She never said.'

'No. Your wife was very discreet. Even with her husband.'

Charlie looked crestfallen.

'She would probably have told you, one day, but Florin asked her not to say anything to anybody. It rather proves that he was right to trust her when she wouldn't even tell her husband.' Gordon saw that Charlie looked disappointed.

'It's to her credit that she didn't let him down. She wasn't being disloyal to you; rather, she was being loyal to Florin.'

'But she always denied that there was anything—'

'And there wasn't. Not between the two of them. And back then there was nothing between me and Florin either, except unrequited . . . whatever.'

'Bloody hell!' murmured Charlie. 'So you went off to Yugoslavia together?'

'Yes.'

'And?'

'Well, put it this way, if you were young and in love I wouldn't suggest you make a bee-line for Belgrade.'

'It didn't work out?'

'Not in Belgrade. And I think Florin realised that his dream of being a patriot had lost something of its gloss by then. He'd grown up a bit. Become more realistic.'

'So what did you do? Where did you go?'

'Various places. We ended up in Italy. On the Amalfi coast. Living together.'

'You were lovers?'

'Of course we were lovers. I wouldn't have stayed with him out of a feeling of loyalty to a misplaced foreign student, however much my conscience was pricked.'

'Sorry. Yes. Obvious. But how did you earn a living?'

'I taught English to foreign students – clearly I couldn't get away from them – and Florin painted.'

'What? Pictures?'

'No, dear heart, sitting rooms . . . yes, of course, pictures; oils of the Amalfi coast. There seemed to be a continuing demand for them from tourists.'

'Goodness. All a far cry from espionage.'

'It was.'

'Past tense?'

'Alas, yes.'

'What happened?'

'What happens in so many love stories? Love palls. The attraction fades. Someone else comes along. Someone younger, more exciting and . . . pop! That's it.'

'Two Bob – sorry – Florin went off with—'

'A toy boy. Yes. A twenty-two-year-old Italian stallion who looked like James Dean – but not blond.'

'Oh dear,' said Charlie sympathetically. 'When did it happen?'

'About five years ago. I stuck around, thinking that something would happen, that someone else would turn up. But nothing did – and no one did – so I decided to cut my losses and up sticks. And here I am. You catch me on the cusp of a new phase of my life.'

'So what do you intend to do?'

'Who knows? I shall keep my eyes open for opportunities.'

'And a new partner?'

'If it happens, it happens, but truth to tell, old bean, I am in the same situation as you. And having loved not wisely but not too well twice in my life I am less inclined to bother any more. I just don't think it's worth the trouble. I am coming around to Malcolm Bradbury's way of thinking.'

'What's that?'

'Genitals are a great distraction to scholarship.'

'But it wasn't just the sex, was it? With Florin?

'No. I really loved him.'

'They're a defence mechanism, aren't they? The quotes.'

'They take my mind off the tragedy of my life.'

Charlie tried to jolly Gordon along. 'But there were good times, surely?'

'Oh, the best. And I cling on to them. Memories of a time when all the world seemed golden. When the wine was sweet and the company sweeter, but as we've both come to know, nothing lasts forever.' He looked Charlie in the eye and said, 'Your memories will remain forever untarnished. Be grateful for that. No one can take away from you the pureness of your love and the knowledge that love never died. Mine did –well, not mine, but my other half's – and that's hard to come to terms with. Almost as hard as losing the one you love to . . . Well, almost. But perhaps not quite.' He patted Charlie on the hand and said softly, 'What a pair, eh? Who could have predicted where we would have found ourselves and in what state, back then in the 1960s.'

'No. Perhaps it's as well we didn't know what lay ahead.'

Gordon got up from the sofa and walked to the fire. He turned round, his back to the flames, and said, 'Well, we can't keep looking back, can we? We need to look forward.'

'I guess,' murmured Charlie unconvincingly.

'Can I ask you something?'

'Of course.'

'Could I stay for a while? I mean, not long, just to get my breath back. I'd try not to get in the way. I could even offer you an extra pair of hands – for digging ditches and suchlike.'

'You? Digging ditches? But you're a wordsmith.'

'And you're a qualified estate manager with a collar and tie and a tweed sports jacket and those bobbly Turk's head cufflinks, but you still dig ditches.'

Charlie threw back his head and laughed. 'All right then, Gordon the Gopher, you're on.'

'Gordon the Gopher?'

'Yes. Oh, I forgot; you've been away. He was a TV puppet. The kids used to love him when they were little.'

'Ah, well I clearly fit the bill on two counts then: I've been a puppet for years, and kids love me. Well, most kids. Perhaps yours might be an exception.'

'You'll soon find out. They'll all be here next weekend, without their other halves, mercifully.'

'So I can stay then? For a short while?'

'You can stay as long as you want.'

'*Deo gratias!*'

'Yes, well I still hope you're thanking God at the end of it.'

44

Creag Sodhail

July 1995

> 'Children: You spend the first two years of their life teaching them to walk and talk. Then you spend the next sixteen years telling them to sit down and shut up.'
>
> Anonymous

Charlie decided that a picnic was the best way of introducing Gordon to his children. He prayed for fine weather and was not disappointed. If nothing else, the glorious day that dawned would remind them of the beauty of this place – their home and their birthright. That was how he thought of it; though he was always chary of droning on about it, aware that they might feel too pressured into taking on responsibility for the place.

The initial introductions, over breakfast on the Saturday morning, were cordial enough. In fact, all four children, having had a long journey to reach their father the night before, were a little out of it. But Gordon, breezing into the kitchen wearing an orange hoodie and a wide grin, soon woke them up.

'Morning all. I'm Gordon. Your father and I grew up together.'

The stunned silence was broken by Charlie. 'This is Gordon Mackenzie; the Gordon I was at school with.'

'The Gordon who disappeared?' asked Rory, with his head on one side as if to size up the apparition that had unexpectedly presented itself.

'The very same. Unreliable, capricious; a fair-weather friend if ever there was one, now down on his luck and putting himself at the mercy of his old school chum.'

'That's not how Dad puts it,' said Lucy, curled up in an armchair, spooning cornflakes into her mouth.

'Really?'

'No.' She swallowed a mouthful and continued. 'He says you're the best friend he ever had, after Mum and Murdo.'

'Oh. That's not bad then. The third best friend.'

'He meant it as a compliment,' said Ellie softly. She walked over to where Gordon stood and gave him a peck on the cheek. She was wearing a pair of floral pyjamas, her fair hair pulled up into a knot behind her head.

'Oh! Thank you.'

'You're welcome,' replied Ellie, flashing him the kind of smile that melted hearts. She had thought occasionally of the man that she had known when she was just four years old. She could remember him, vaguely, as he was then – one or two episodes had engraved themselves on her mind. He was much older now, with very little hair, but his character seemed every bit as engaging as it was in her infancy. She had always had a soft spot for him, not least because her father had thought so highly of him.

Rory and Sarah were seated at one end of the table. 'We're the twins,' they chorused.

'I rather suspected as much,' replied Gordon. 'Process of elimination.'

'Are you staying long?' asked Sarah abruptly.

'Sarah!' cried Lucy. 'Don't be rude.'

'I'm not being rude. I was just curious.'

'Till the wind changes? Like Mary Poppins,' added Rory, grinning and tucking into a bacon sandwich.

'You're welcome to stay as long as you like, as far as we're concerned,' said Ellie. 'Dad's often talked about you and I should think he'll be grateful for the company.'

'Good idea,' mumbled Rory, endeavouring to speak through an over-ambitious mouthful of wholemeal bread and bacon at the same time as thumbing through *GQ*. 'Take him out of himself.'

Charlie cleared his throat. 'Excuse me! Do I get a say in any of this?'

'Certainly not,' replied Lucy, getting up from her seat and taking her bowl to the sink. 'Just you leave everything to us, Pops, and we'll make sure your life runs as smoothly as clockwork.'

'That'll be the day,' muttered Charlie. 'Anyway, are you all up for a picnic later?'

There were collective words of agreement from all four children, with the proviso that they would not set off too early. Various reasons were given – hair and make-up, choice of wardrobe, calls to boyfriends or mates – but the assembled party reckoned that they could probably be ready to leave by one o'clock.

'A late lunch then,' said Charlie, looking at Gordon.

'Oh, about right for Italy.'

'Italy? Have you been in Italy? How romantic,' said Ellie.

Gordon needed no further encouragement. Before they knew it, all four children were drawn into the world of Gordon – his adventures and disasters (with emphasis on the adventures since their acquaintanceship was a little too fresh to warrant delving too deeply into the trials and tribulations of his catastrophic relationships).

Within an hour the Stuart clan felt they had known him all their lives, and he had teased out of them as much as he needed to know for the time being about their own characters and their various lovers. Only Rory was cagey about his current love, because, said Ellie teasingly, 'Rory doesn't really do love. He's sort of got stuck at lust.'

At this, Rory threw his copy of *GQ* at her and Charlie suggested it was time they all went and got themselves ready for the climb up the hills. Rory's disappointment at the lack of a Land Rover led him to leave with a frown, but the girls went off to their rooms in high spirits, having clearly decided that Gordon was, as their father had often put it, 'a good egg'.

Gordon remained at the breakfast table, gazing into his empty coffee mug.

'So there you are,' said Charlie. 'You've met the Addams Family. Are you still sure you want to stay?'

Gordon looked up and smiled, and Charlie was surprised to see that his eyes bore a misty faraway look. 'Oh yes,' he said. 'I'm sure.'

The picnic became a continuation of their morning conversation, with Gordon speaking conspiratorially to the children about their father's behaviour as a schoolboy. Rory slowly warmed to him, especially when Gordon let slip that his father had never really appreciated *Lady Chatterley's Lover*.

'You mean Dad actually read it?

'I don't think he ever got to the end. He said it was all a bit tame.'

'Tame!' For the first time, Rory seemed to be impressed by a part of his father's history. 'Blimey, Dad! What was your own sex life like?'

At this, the three girls collapsed in hysterics.

'Never you mind. If you really want to know, it was like the sex life of all schoolboys, including you – fifty percent imagination and fifty per cent frustration. In other words, nonexistent.'

'Speak for yourself,' muttered Rory, to cries of derision from his sisters.

'Can we move on?' asked Charlie. 'It can only be a matter of time before this conversation becomes embarrassing enough to cause me to leave.'

They lay among the heather in a loose circle, Ellie and Lucy leaning on one another, Sarah and Rory, as ever, sitting side by side, each, from time to time, getting rattled with the other and administering a playful tap or a heavier swipe, depending on the general tenor of abuse being dispensed at the time.

Gordon watched and listened, chipping in occasionally, until Rory asked him, 'Did you meet Charlotte? Dad's step-mum?'

'Oh, I did.'

'Was she as unpleasant as Dad says?'

'Rory!' admonished Lucy. 'Dad's always careful never to slag her off. Well, most of the time. But she does seem to have been a real battleaxe.'

Charlie chipped in. 'I think I preferred the conversation when it revolved around sex, and that's saying something.'

'I'll say nothing about her,' said Gordon, 'except that your father was an absolute saint.'

'Did she really drive Grandpa to take his own life?' asked Sarah, revealing a degree of candour matched only by her brother.

'Oh, I don't think we should talk about that,' said Charlie, getting up from the mound of heather in which he'd made himself comfortable. 'Not on a day like this. Look at the view. How far do you think you can see?'

'Twelve miles,' said Rory. 'That's the maximum.'

'Are you sure?' asked Gordon. 'I've stood under the copper horse at Windsor and seen the centre of London, and that's twenty-two miles away.'

'You know everything, Gordon,' said Lucy.

'I wish,' replied Gordon. 'There is an awful lot I don't know. Like how your dad put up with Charlotte, for a start. But this is too nice a day to go into all that. Suffice it to say that a day without Charlotte is worth a dozen in her company.'

'Do you think she's dead?' asked Sarah.

'Come on, you lot,' said Charlie. 'Time to head back home. Things to do, places to go, people to see.'

With the skill of a ringmaster taming lions, the head of the family managed, without too much irritation on both his part and theirs, to round up his brood and their adopted uncle and herd them back down the hill to the castle.

It was the beginning of an episode in their lives that was to last for rather longer than any of them had intended, and one that was to culminate in circumstances that none of them could have foreseen.

45

Loch Side

31 December 1999

> 'Every position must be held to the last man: there must be no retirement.
> With our backs to the wall, and believing in the justice of our cause, each one of us must fight to the end.'
>
> Earl Haig, order to British troops, 1918

'Of course, you know it's really a French word – Hogmanay?'

'What?' Charlie was clearing up the last of the supper plates before he and Gordon sat down by the fire for a warming drink – in Gordon's case, what he referred to as a rather cheeky elderflower cordial with particularly fierce bubbles.

'Yes. There's no record of it being mentioned in Scotland until around 1604.'

'Perhaps that's why I'm not wild about it.'

'I don't know many folk over the age of twenty-five who are.'

'I did wonder about having a party here every New Year's Eve – for the estate folk, and some of the village – but Dad warned me off it.'

'Why so?'

'He said that most people like to do their own thing at New Year and that if we muscled in and expected them to spend every Hogmanay with "the laird", relations might sour. The Scots have enough prejudices against landowners without exacerbating the problem.'

'That seems a bit harsh.'

'Oh, it's true. So rather than having a "drinks do" on the night when everybody else does, we stick to that one we give in summer.'

'Yes; they were a rum bunch last year, as I recall. But isn't there still a likelihood of people thinking you're a bit grand with a summer drinks party?'

'Oh, a few do. But Dad said that if we didn't they'd complain about the lack of hospitality.'

'So either way, you can't win.'

'No. Still; just time for a quick one before we visit the Murdos.'

Charlie had begun his own tradition – that of walking down the track to Loch Side and delivering a large bottle of single malt to Murdo, and one of Harvey's Bristol Cream to Mrs Murdo, by way of 'first footing' on New Year's Eve. He knew that the only time Letty Murdoch ever drank was at Christmas – on Hogmanay she would abstain, the better to support Murdo on his way home from whatever party they had attended. But Charlie was also aware that Mrs Murdo did like to offer one or two ladies from the village a glass if they turned up at the appropriate time – 12.30pm on a Sunday or six o'clock in the evening during the week. The New Year's Eve gift would take care of that eventuality for a good few months.

The custom had altered just a little over the last five years. Now it was Charlie and Gordon who delivered the gift – 'The Odd Couple', as Mrs Murdo had come to call them. Gordon's stay had proved indefinite. Its length had never been discussed. He had never enquired as to whether he might continue to lodge with Charlie, and Charlie had never asked when he planned to leave. It was an open-ended arrangement that seemed to suit both of them. Gordon proved invaluable on the estate, once Murdo – never given to verbosity when it came to conversation during the working day – had got used to the Latin badinage. At first he rather grudgingly tolerated Gordon's presence, but over the months and years he had come to appreciate the extra helping hand – and Gordon could never be accused of being work shy.

As for Gordon Mackenzie, his countenance took on a hitherto unseen roseate glow. His cheeks were flushed, there was a light in his eye, and his sense of humour was, if anything, enhanced by being in an environment where he felt both unthreatened and completely at home. The sherry decanter remained untouched. He was a changed man.

The last year had been an eventful one. All three daughters had married on the same day in January. They told their father it would be cheaper that way, and the hall of the castle would cost less than a marquee so a winter wedding would be fine. While Charlie knew he could not say anything untoward about their choices of men, he did hope that things would turn out rather better than they promised. He loved his daughters – as different from each other as they could possibly be – and wanted the best for them. Now he could do no more than make sure that he was always there for them, and let them know that the castle and the estate would be a bolt-hole whenever they needed it. They were marrying young, but then so did he. How could he suggest that they were not ready?

For their part, they had become used to the presence of Gordon – always affectionately known to the four of them as 'Gay Gordon', though they had certainly never seen any evidence of male friends in the time that he had been living with their father.

The two men picked up, in a way, where they had left off at school; each completely different in tastes – and predilections – from the other. To preserve their respective sanities, as he put it, Charlie gave Gordon his own rooms – sitting, bed and bath – in one wing of the castle, even though, most of the time, their evenings at home would be spent in each other's company. When they did need to be alone, they could do so without fear of offending the other – that much was established early on.

They talked, on these 'nights in', about anything and everything, and although at the heart of it they knew they were two men who had been disappointed in love – albeit for different reasons – they came to terms with their situation and made the best of it.

'You know we're weird?' asked Charlie as they walked down the track to Loch Side on that frost-rimed New Year's Eve, carrying a bottle apiece.

'I do. But why especially?'

'Because most men wouldn't settle for what we have. They'd decide that life should be better than this and go off and find some dolly-bird or toy boy half their age and shack up with her – or him.'

'Until they got knackered.'

'Or the dolly-bird or toy boy got bored.'

'Which probably wouldn't be long. It's called a mid-life crisis.'

'Ours or theirs?' asked Charlie.

'Both. It's just that we've chosen to handle it differently.'

'Have we chosen it, or has it chosen us?'

Gordon sighed. 'The thing you have to remember is that life finds you out. If you let it. So many people spend their time battling away to no avail. If only they'd let fate take a hand they'd find themselves much more content.'

'Not happy?'

'Happiness is evanescent. It doesn't last. Not like contentment.'

'And you're content?' asked Charlie.

'More than I've ever been.'

'But you were in love. I was in love. Isn't that better than this?'

'Of course. At the time. But times change.'

'And you think we should change with them? Make the best of it?'

'Yes. And not confuse it with second best.'

'Even if it is?'

Gordon shook his head. 'Nothing ever lasts. We are where we are now, and even that won't last. *Carpe diem* – live for the day. There's a lot of wisdom in that.'

'You know, if I were your wife I'd probably be screaming at your Latin phrases by now.'

'And you're not?'

'Oh, yes. Inwardly. But at least I'm not your wife.'

They arrived at Loch Side, rapped with the heavy and highly polished brass knocker on the varnished front door and were let in by Murdo. The sight of him off-duty had always made Charlie smile, for instead of the deerstalker he habitually wore while working, his head was furnished instead with a generous endowment of iron-grey wavy hair, evenly parted in the centre and flattened down with a particular brand of brilliantine that Mrs Murdo had to travel to Fort William to buy. Nothing else would tame it, he claimed.

Their party had clearly been a good one; Murdo's countenance was akin to that of a beetroot. He had taken his jacket off now and wore a smart tweed waistcoat and trousers and his National Association of Gamekeepers' tie –his 'Sunday best'. Mrs Murdo, in a woollen two-piece best described as 'heather mixture', had had a 'rinse and set' at 'McHair' in the village especially for the evening.

Charlie admired the way that both of them treated such occasions as special; loved the scrubbed skin and the scent of brilliantine and Johnson's Baby Powder that seemed to emanate from Loch Side on evenings such as this – though at this time of night on this particular day there would also be the faintest overlay of Scotch whisky fumes. The Murdos exemplified the kind of folk who dressed up to go out rather than dressing down. Dressing down, albeit in clean clothes and appropriately turned out, was what they did during the working week, and Charlie always appreciated the way they honoured their host or hostess during their leisure time, when others would pull on any old garment. It seemed to him to be the supreme compliment.

As ever, the bottle of malt was broken into – Murdo insisting that they share the first nip from the bottle, rather than him keeping it for himself. 'We Scots may be regarded as tight, but that'll nae happen in *ma* hoose.'

Mrs Murdo, as ever, could not be tempted to have even a drop of sherry. 'No, no, noo! I'll jist have a bitter lemon with Mr Gordon.'

Charlie – and now Gordon – went to the Murdos' a good hour before midnight. There was the old year to chew over without the children being in the way – scattered to the four winds, they seldom appeared nowadays on New Year's Eve. They had their own celebrations to attend – these last few years safe in the knowledge that their father would not be spending the evening alone. As long as they came to the summer drinks party, Charlie was content to let them do their own thing. The sooner that Hogmanay was past, the better.

On this particular evening, Murdo seemed strangely reticent. The welcome was warm enough, but Charlie detected an unusual undercurrent. Then, the pleasantries and compliments of the season having been exchanged, and the four of them sitting around the small fire in the Murdos' front parlour, Murdo himself broached the subject that had clearly been troubling him for some time.

'I dinnae want to let ye down, ye know that. But I'm no gettin' any younger and, seein' as how this is yon new millennium, I think t'would be a good year tae step down.'

'What?' asked Charlie, unsure that he had heard correctly.

'Tae retire.'

'But you always said you would never retire.'

'Aye, I did, but this estate is nae getting any cheaper tae run, and I dinnae want to be takin' up a place that I cannae fulfill tae the best of my ability. I'm seventy-one now, after all; even if I do feel younger inside.'

Gordon sat silently, sipping his bitter lemon, knowing what Charlie's reaction would be.

Charlie glanced at Mrs Murdo. She smiled weakly and said, 'He's been mitherin' aboot it for some time. I tellt him he should tell ye noo and not drag it oot. We appreciate that this cottage goes wi' the job and we'll no make your life difficult. We'll look for somewhere in the village and, even if we have tae rent, we'll get oot o' your hair.'

'Right,' said Charlie. 'Let's get one thing straight. Retirement is never a good idea . . .'

Murdo made to interrupt, but Charlie silenced him with a look and continued: 'I know that some of the heavier jobs – ditching and suchlike – are too much for most of us over the age of forty-five, and this year I shall be fifty. You certainly shouldn't be doing them at seventy-one. So from now on you will not. But do you plan to stop fishing in your retirement? Or shooting?'

'Nay; I were hopin' tae have more time fer that.'

'Exactly. So you might just as well do it and get paid for your trouble as do it and have to pay for it yourself. You're a great draw here, Murdo – all the regulars love you . . .'

The old man demurred and looked embarrassed, as did Mrs Murdo, whose face turned the colour of her heather-mixture two-piece.

'Without you, I couldn't hope to get as many folk to come here shooting and fishing. You're an asset and not one I intend to forgo. So just you focus on those things and let me handle the rest. Gordon isn't getting any younger, and neither am I, but between us we can get through the work and with Rory coming on board now that he's finished his stint at the Boultbees' place in the Borders, he'll be able to do a lot of the heavy work that you did.'

'But he'll be managerial, will he not?' asked Murdo.

'Partly, yes. But we all have to muck in on this estate; I've told him that and he knows what he's in for. So, you see, there really is no excuse for giving up.'

'But the cottage,' said Murdo. 'Ye'll be needing that for Rory.'

'No I won't. To be perfectly honest, I'm tempted to put Gordon in here just to get him out of my hair, but the castle is large enough for the three of us not to get under each other's feet, and we've still got room for the girls and their husbands – when they turn up. Rory can have the west turret. He'll be out of the way there.'

Mrs Murdo asked softly, 'So we can stay?'

'For as long as you want. I know my father agreed to let you live here for as long as you worked on the estate, but I reckon you've earned more than that.

I could not have brought up four children without you. You've been a godsend to me – as you were to Eleanor – and the cottage is yours for as long as you want to live here, even when you don't want to shoot and fish anymore.'

Both Murdo and Mrs Murdo seemed lost for words. Charlie raised his glass. 'It's the start of a new millennium. Here's to the three people who got me through the last one. Gordon, Murdo, Mrs Murdo, your very good health. Here's to us and whatever the future holds. A happy New Year.'

They raised their glasses and sipped from them, and then Mrs Murdo said, 'Well, I have tae say that I'm relieved.'

'I'm glad,' said Charlie. 'And glad you're pleased, too, about the house and the job.'

'Och, it's no just that,' confessed Mrs Murdo. 'It's him; Murdo.'

'What do you mean?' asked Charlie.

'Well, retirement means twice as much husband on half as much money, and I've always been a great believer in the wedding vows.'

She could see the puzzled look on Charlie and Gordon's faces, and made to clarify her meaning. 'For better for worse, but not for lunch. I'm very grateful to you, Charlie, for getting my husband oot the hoose!'

46

Castle Sodhail

June 2000

> 'The divine will manifests itself in many forms, and the gods bring many things to pass against our expectations. What we thought would happen remains unfulfilled, while the god has found a way to accomplish the unexpected. And that is what has happened here.'
>
> Euripides, *Bacchae*, 5th century BC

The day of the summer party dawned brightly – Charlie knew that, because he was up early to make sure that Rory rose in time to sort out the drinks tables: the glasses and bottles that would provide the sustenance for the great and good of Sodhail and a few from Strath Carron – everyone from the young and enterprising grocer who dispensed comestibles to the aged Dr Crawford, who once dispensed medication and who now dispensed sage advice, and from Henry Dundas, the solicitor whose days of delivering legal advice were long gone, to Aileen Bell, no longer able to ride a bicycle in a straight line and deliver papers. The air, it seemed, in this part of the world, prolonged active life, a fact no better exemplified than by Sir Robert Fitzallan, now in his ninetieth year and still 'rubbing along' with the woman he introduced as 'my young wife Davina', now a sprightly eighty. Their continued presence at Invergarry House proved a godsend to Charlie on those days when his children exasperated him or he simply needed to sound out Robert on some thorny issue or other. They had been good grandparents, and Ellie, Lucy, Sarah and Rory had found them a reliable safety valve when their father's introspection had left them either bewildered or frustrated.

Rory, still reluctant to settle down at the age of twenty-four, in spite of his father's frequent protestations, had finally agreed to share the running of the estate. He wanted to see a bit of life, he said, and though his father feared the worst, he knew it was unreasonable to demand otherwise. There were days when he bit his lip so hard that it bled.

Charlie had worried that their relationship, which was strained at the best of times, might break down altogether if they lived under the same roof. He had not taken into account Rory's ability to live in a world of his own (neither had it dawned on him that the trait was inherited) – when that world was not populated by some attractive girl.

Rory had proved surprisingly useful on the estate in the six months that he had worked there, and Charlie's disapproval at the way his son ran his love life was tempered with a respect for his ability to get stuck in and to get on with Murdo. The old man teased his great-nephew mercilessly, but a bond of profound respect had grown up between the two – Murdo well aware of the father's expectations of the son and sympathetic to the son's need to plough his own furrow. He had seen it all before; history, as it so often did, was repeating itself.

Mrs Murdo was as fond of Rory as was her husband. He was bright; would help her solve crossword puzzles in a way that no one else seemed capable of, and when he discovered that his great-aunt had once been offered a place at university, was lost in awe and admiration. 'But that was when very few women went there. Wow!'

Mrs Murdo appreciated the compliment and did her best

to live up to Rory's renewed academic expectations of her. 'It was a very long time ago. And, anyway, I didnae go.'

'But you can still do the crossword in the *Scotsman*?'

'Aye, I can, but it's nice tae have a wee bit o' help now and then.'

The two of them worked together on this particular day – Mrs Murdo instructing Rory as to what should go where in the way of bottles and glasses, and Rory attentive and obedient of her every suggestion.

'Have you got the logs in?' asked Charlie of his son, looking across at the fire in the hall and noticing that the basket was empty.

'Not yet.'

'Well nip off and get them, will you?' asked Charlie of his son before stepping out of the front door and looking up at the sky.

It had clouded over, and the hope that drinks would be served outside receded – it would be more sensible to dispense them in the hall and allow folk to spill out onto the drive and the apron of green under the old yew tree if the fates were kind and the sun ventured out once more. Fearing the worst he came back indoors.

Gordon was charged with seeing to the canapés – sent in the first van of the morning by the young grocer in Strath Carron, who had decided the only way to build up trade was to raise both expectations and the standard of service as well as producing a more adventurous product. Canapés were regarded as an exotic dish by many in this part of the Highlands. On this occasion he had wisely stuck to mini Yorkshire puddings with roast beef and horseradish sauce, and 'little smoked salmony things', as Gordon called them. When Charlie criticised Gordon's lack of culinary vocabulary

– surprising in someone whose command of language was seldom found wanting – Gordon insisted that if they had been serving pasta he could have told everyone the difference between *farfalloni* and *conchiglioni* and explained why he preferred *ricciolini* to *creste di galli*.

Charlie did his best to look impressed. 'Italian?'

'Yes. But I can't see the gastronomic delights of Amalfi taking root in Sod-all. Best stick with Yorkshire pudding.'

Their idle banter was broken up by Rory, who pushed open the heavy door of the hall and asked, 'Dad, are you expecting some old biddy from the airport?'

'Which old biddy? As far as I'm aware, all the old biddies I'm expecting are from no further away than Strath Carron.'

'She's wearing a fur coat. Just getting out of a taxi with heaven knows how many suitcases. She says she's not expected but that you'd know who she was and why she's here.'

Something in the innocence of Rory's remark caused the blood in Charlie's veins to run cold. He glanced over at Gordon to see the colour draining from his cheeks.

'Not . . . ?' was all Gordon said.

Charlie did not reply, but strode through the open door and stepped outside. As the grimy airport taxi chugged back down the drive, its light once again touting for unlikely trade in this part of the world, it left behind a solitary woman standing amid a circle of Louis Vuitton suitcases and hold-alls. The last twenty years had not been kind to her, but there was no mistaking the fur-clad figure of Charlotte Niven.

'Hello, Charlie,' she said. 'I've come home.'

47

Castle Sodhail

June 2000

'Revenge is a kind of wild justice, which the more man's nature runs to, the more ought law to weed it out.'

Francis Bacon, *Essays: Of Revenge*, 1625

Charlie made sure the door of his study was firmly closed behind him and Charlotte.

Rory carried the half-dozen suitcases into the hall and stacked them in a neat pile. He looked at both Mrs Murdo and Gordon, neither of whom was forthcoming with information.

'Right,' said Mrs Murdo. 'Let's get on. We've barely an hour before they all turn up and we'll need more wood for yon fire. That small basket ye brought in will no last long.' She nodded at the dying embers in the grate, and Rory knew that meant another trip to the log shed down the track past Loch Side.

'I'll take the Land Rover and bring a load,' he said, and left through the door leading to the kitchen. He could tell that something strange, something uncomfortable was going on, but was not sure that he wanted to be a part of it. It would be a relief to escape for a while.

'Well!' said Mrs Murdo to Gordon. 'Here's a turn-up for the books. I think you and I should make ourselves scarce, too.'

'No,' said Gordon, 'I don't want to leave him alone with her.' And with that he walked across the hall, tapped softly on Charlie's study door and, without waiting for a reply, let himself in.

The two of them were standing in the middle of the room, Charlie with his hands placed defiantly in his pockets and Charlotte remonstrating with him. She took off her fur coat and flung it onto the chair of the desk, the better to indicate that she was here to stay. It was clear to Gordon that she had come with the intention of making trouble.

'Charlotte, it's been twenty years!' exclaimed Charlie. 'Twenty years without a word. You can't just storm in here and say you've come home!'

'Why not?'

'Because this isn't your home. Your home is . . . well, I don't know where. You left without leaving a forwarding address when you realised that you weren't going to get your own way.'

'That's very unfair and very cruel!'

'But true. You tried to get me out of the castle and when you found that the only way to do it was to lie you had no hesitation in doing just that. Pricking of conscience is alien to you, Charlotte. You tarnished Dr Crawford's reputation, you left your solicitor in the lurch along with unpaid bills, you sold the house Dad had left to you and you buggered off. It's no use coming back here and expecting to be welcomed.'

'I was distraught! I had lost my husband. I wasn't thinking straight. I admit I did those things but that was twenty years ago. Things are different now.'

Charlie sized her up. Her dress, of a tight-fitting jersey, did not flatter the fuller figure that had developed over the years, delineating with crystal clarity the amplitude of her waist and bosom. She had lost the beauty she once had; age had not been kind in the way it had to Davina Fitzallan. His mother-in-law had become, if anything, prettier as she had grown older; had developed a kind of serenity that shone from within. His step-mother had a pinched look about her, in spite of her voluptuous figure and what appeared to be a tropical tan. Her unfortunate aspect had nothing to do with wrinkles; there was a hollowness to the eyes, a tightness of the lips that owed less to age than to disposition. Charlotte Niven's mean-spiritedness had clearly manifested itself in her complexion, aided and abetted by a fondness for sunshine and, he suspected, alcohol.

'So where did you go?' asked Gordon.

Charlotte swivelled round and fixed him with a cruel eye. 'What's it to you? Who are you? What are you doing here?'

'I live here . . . well, at the moment.'

'Oh, I see. So strangers can come and live here but not family.'

Charlie cut in. 'Gordon *is* family now. You're not. You chose not to be when you left.'

'No. That's not true. I married into this family. You can't take that away from me. I'm still your stepmother. I've spent the last twenty years in Cannes trying to make a new life, but that's all over. The money your father left me has run out and I've come home to spend the rest of my days here.'

'Once and for all,' insisted Charlie, 'this is not your home. You know nothing about me – us – Charlotte. You have no connection with this family – it was your choice to go away, nobody else's.'

'I know about Eleanor,' she whispered dramatically. 'I'm very sorry.'

'That was a long time ago.'

'And the children. I know their names.'

'You must have done your research.'

'That's very cruel.'

Charlie winced. 'You'd know all about that, Charlotte. Now, I think it would be best if you left. We have a lot of people arriving soon and I have to look after them.'

'Everyone . . . everyone except your stepmother.'

'Everyone who means something to me, Charlotte. I did my very best to accommodate you after Dad died, in spite of the way you treated him. You were having none of it. You did your best to get me out of here and now you want to be allowed back. Are you seriously expecting me to let you move in here?'

'Not here. Not into the castle. Into Loch Side. It was the Murdochs' for as long as Murdo worked here; that's what Angus said. When they retired it reverted to the estate. It would suit me to live there.'

'Out of the question. My father had that arrangement, but I've chosen to let the Murdos live on there in retirement. They've done a lot for this place and for the family – it's the least they deserve.'

'That's a wicked, wicked thing. What's to become of me? Where am I to go?'

Charlotte reminded Charlie of the Wicked Queen in *Snow White*. Her fury was pantomimic in its intensity. Gordon found himself suppressing a smile, but then recognised the tell-tale traits of an alcoholic – irrationality, over-dramatisation, self-pity and a general disconnection from the real world.

'I'll run you down to the station,' he offered.

'You'll do no such thing!'

Gordon moved to usher her out, putting his arm around her shoulder. 'We'll put you in the Station Arms in Strath Carron until you find somewhere to go.' He looked questioningly at Charlie, hoping that his intervention would be seen as helpful rather than interfering.

Charlotte was having none of it. 'Take your hands off me, you bastard! No stranger is going to see me off the premises.' She swung round, at the same time raising her right arm and slapping Gordon hard across the face. He staggered back; for an older woman she had surprising strength.

For a moment he was both off-balance and taken aback. 'I'll go and get the car,' he said, and slipped out, closing the door behind him.

Charlie was stunned into both silence and inaction, then Charlotte turned her fury on him. 'Are you going to let him do this to me? Are you as spineless as you've always been?'

Charlie had seen and heard enough. He moved towards Charlotte in an effort to restrain her – her arms were flailing wildly now with the intention of raining blows upon his head, and he could smell the alcohol on her breath. As he closed in, she swung again, but Charlie sidestepped the arm and, as a result, Charlotte was thrown off-balance. She fell sideways towards the desk and before Charlie was able to intervene her head hit its sharp corner with an ominous thud. Her heavy body twisted on impact and fell to the floor.

Charlie braced himself, amid the gin fumes, expecting a tirade of abuse. It did not come. Instead, Charlotte lay motionless at his feet, her mouth and eyes wide open.

Recoiling at first, he then stood transfixed at the sight of the unmoving body. Then, marshalling his senses, he knelt down to feel her pulse. Try as he might, he could not find one. He turned and made for the door of his study. He opened it enough to put his head out and saw Mrs Murdo on the other side of the hall.

'Has Dr Crawford arrived yet?' he asked.

'Yes; just. You know Hamish Crawford; never late when it comes tae a free drink. Has Mrs Stuart gone?'

'Yes. I think she has. In fact, I'm sure she has. Can you ask Dr Crawford if he'd come to my study for a quick word?'

Charlie closed the door and looked again at the crumpled

heap on the floor. Charlotte was not breathing. Something told him he should call an ambulance. Another inner voice told him there was no point. For several seconds he stared at the body, then heard a tap at the door and Dr Crawford's voice asking, 'Shall I come in?'

'Yes please, doctor. I think we have a bit of a problem.'

48

Castle Sodhail

June 2000

'God and the doctor we alike adore
But only when in danger, not before;
The danger o'er, both are alike requited,
God is forgotten, and the Doctor slighted.'
John Owen (c.1563-1622), *Epigrams*

Hamish Crawford listened as Charlie gave him a brief account of what had happened. There was no rush, said the doctor, Charlotte was quite dead. There was no earthly point in sending for an ambulance. Not just yet. Better that Charlie go out and see to his guests for now – they were snaking up the drive, dozens of them in a state of high excitement at the prospect of a glass or two at the laird's expense. The problem in his study could be dealt with when they had all gone home.

'Nothing is going to spoil,' said the doctor, which Charlie thought was such an odd choice of phrase. He would talk to Charlie afterwards, he said, when he had got his thoughts straight. Then he could give a full account of exactly what had gone on.

'We all know what small villages are like when it comes to gossip,' said Dr Crawford, 'and I think you have enough on your plate without putting yourself through all that.'

'But she's dead!' said Charlie softly. 'She was in here with me and there were no witnesses. I've hated her all my life.

She's done her best to turn me out of house and home – I have every possible reason for killing her.'

'I think you are jumping to conclusions. Let's discuss all this later. I'll stick around. Can you lock your study door?'

The doctor's calmness stunned Charlie. Why was he not making more fuss? Why did he not call an ambulance instantly? The party would have to be cancelled; there was no alternative. The guests would be told there had been a dreadful accident – that somebody had been bludgeoned to death.

'Who?' they would ask.

'The laird's stepmother,' would come the reply.

'Who killed her?'

'Why, the laird hisself – in his study with a paperweight, most likely.'

It had all the makings of a game of Cluedo, except that this was no game but bitter, horrifying reality. There was no Colonel Mustard in the library with the lead piping, only Charlie Stuart in the study with a paperweight. The black humour seemed only to make things worse. Why could he not put back the clock? Why had he allowed himself to be alone with her? It was asking for trouble.

His head swam. He could hear the guests arriving.

Dr Crawford's voice cut through them.

'Give me the key,' he instructed in his soft Scottish burr.

Charlie reached into his pocket and handed over the key to the door of his study as if in a trance.

The doctor placed a hand upon Charlie's arm. 'Charlie; listen to me. Go out there and welcome your guests. Say nothing of this to anybody. Not a word. There is nothing you can do here. We will attend to it when you are finished. I'll stay behind, and when they've all gone home we can work out the best course of action.'

Charlie did his best to play the role of host. It was never one that had come easily to him, and today of all days it was nigh on impossible. He tried not to be impatient when the likes of Nessie Mackintosh asked inane questions; tried not to look too distracted when his daughters came across and gave him a hug and a kiss; tried not to be more irritated than usual with the two out of the three husbands who had turned up.

But who was he to cast aspersions in their direction? He was a father-in-law who would now be facing a murder charge. What earthly chance did he have of proving that he had not killed the stepmother he had always loathed, when absolutely everything seemed to point to exactly that? He had felt alone when Eleanor had died; so dreadfully alone that he could not imagine an outlook any bleaker. If only he had seen what was on the distant horizon. Perhaps if he had he would have found a way out of it all.

As the family went back inside the castle, and the last of the guests departed, he walked steadily towards the door, then stopped and looked up at the sky. Several seconds passed before he raised his arm and, with considerable force, threw his glass at the wall of the castle and watched it smash into little pieces.

For a moment he stared at the shards of glass that lay at the foot of the granite wall. Then he buttoned his jacket and went indoors.

He walked across the hall towards the kitchen – the hub of the household where he knew the family would be gathered. He could hear them laughing and talking on the other side of the door. He paused before entering. What was he to do? There was only one thing he could do: he would tell them, calmly, exactly what had happened. He would also make the consequences of his actions quite clear to them: that there would be a trial: a trial in which he would almost certainly be accused of murder. There had been no witnesses; it was his word alone that it had been a dreadful accident. He had every reason to believe that no judge and jury could possibly find him innocent 'beyond all reasonable doubt'. He shuddered at the prospect of the girls' reaction. He had tried so hard to bring them up well; knew that he had not been the best of fathers; that so often his thoughts had been on other things, on keeping the estate together, on providing them with an education, on . . . But what was the point? Fate had taken a hand, yet again, and his world was about to crumble away. It would not be the first time, but it would very likely be the last.

He reached for the handle of the kitchen door, and as he did so the door on the other side of the hall opened. He turned. Gordon Mackenzie came out of the study and said, steadily and quite brightly, 'There you are, Charlie! Dr Crawford would like a word. Have you a moment?'

Silently, Charlie walked across the hall and entered the study. Gordon followed him in and closed the door behind them.

Dr Crawford stood with his back to a roaring fire. Several logs were spitting in the grate. Charlie looked about him. At first he thought that he must have misremembered the precise spot where the body had fallen, but no. There was the corner of the desk and there was where Charlotte had lain. But her body had gone. They must have called the ambulance. That was it. She had already been taken to hospital – even though it would be too late for them to do anything. The police would be on their way and would arrive at any minute, now that the party was over. He must go and speak to the children before they were alerted by the wail of sirens.

'The police; I must go tell the children before they arrive.'

'No need,' said Dr Crawford.

'No need,' said Gordon.

'But they need to know from me before they know from anybody else.'

'Sit down, Charlie,' said Dr Crawford, indicating the chair behind Charlie's desk.

Charlie did as he was bid, his mind a maelstrom of confused thoughts.

'You gave me an account of what occurred,' said the doctor. 'I have had a long conversation with Mr Mackenzie here, and he has also explained to me in his own words exactly what happened.'

'But he can't have done; he wasn't here.'

'Not at the precise moment the fatality occurred, no; but until just before that very moment, yes. He explained how Mrs Stuart – Charlotte Niven as we used to know her – lashed out at him. I explained to him what you had told me about her behaviour towards you, and the fact that she lost her balance and hit her head on the desk.'

'But no court of law is ever going to believe that. They don't know me from Adam. As far as they're concerned I'm an angry stepson with a grudge who has killed the woman who drove his own father to suicide. What chance will I have?'

'Very little. There were no witnesses, except those who can testify to a life which had been blighted in so many ways, not only by personal loss and tragedy, but also by Charlotte Niven's existence (you will forgive me, I hope, if I refrain from calling her Mrs Stuart. I am afraid I find that particular appellation grossly offensive). On the face of it, Mr Stuart

– Charlie – you have very little going for you when it comes to proving your story.'

'Exactly.' Charlie leaned forward on the desk and supported his head in his hands. His father's desk. What would his father think if he were here today?

But Dr Crawford had not finished. After a few moments of silence he continued: 'Mr Mackenzie agrees with me that of all the people he has ever known, you are the most honest, trustworthy and generous-spirited man he has ever encountered.'

Charlie lifted his head and managed a weak smile. 'That's very kind' he said.

'I myself have no cause to disagree with him.'

'Thank you.'

'I have watched you grow up, Charlie. I have ministered to your father and your mother, your late wife and your children. I have attended to you for nigh on fifty years now – even though for the last twenty I've not been in full-time practice. If I don't know you well enough to be absolutely certain that there is not a bone in your body or a thought in your head that would make you capable of killing someone – even someone you have every cause to hate – then I am not much of a general practitioner. Oh, and before you say it; there have been mistakes from time to time, I admit. Your father-in-law will never let me forget that I once confused a broken corset bone with angina in Lady Fitzallan's case, but that was a long time ago and he has never forgiven me for being a year younger than he is and carrying on working far longer.'

Gordon coughed, by way of reminding Dr Crawford of the matter in hand.

'In short, Charlie, you have no need to worry. Charlotte Niven has left your life as quickly as she came into it; rather more speedily if anything.'

'But . . . but that's against the law, surely? I mean, there will be a post-mortem; an inquest. Questions will be asked. We can't get round that.'

'There will be a post-mortem, yes, and an inquest. Neither will concern you. What happened to Charlotte Niven was a nasty accident that occurred in a room at the Station Hotel in Strath Carron. It is a rather down-at-heel establishment with very loose-fitting rugs in its rooms. I'm sure you know it. The Rotary Club meets in the function room there – albeit reluctantly. Apparently, Charlotte Niven was making herself a gin and tonic in the privacy of her own suite, which is what the Station Hotel is pleased to call a room which has a bathroom attached. She was fond of a dram or two by all accounts – her taste for 'mother's ruin', as we used to call it, was picked up among the ex-pats in Cannes where, if you ask me for my doctor's opinion, rather too much sun is taken and too much alcohol imbibed.'

Charlie listened to the doctor with mounting incredulity.

'She was dropped off there by Mr Mackenzie, who had picked her up at the airport. She was doubtless invited to the party at the castle but, alas, died before she could attend.'

'But the people at the Station Hotel; the proprietor—'

'Is a very long-standing patient of mine who is about to retire. He was naturally amazed that someone of Charlotte Niven's standing should want to stay there, but as he is also a man of very impecunious means he cannot be choosy about his guests. Over the years I have had to waive many bills in order to maintain the health of him and his late wife. He was happy to . . . accommodate Mistress Niven.'

Charlie slumped back in the chair.

'The body has already been removed from the Station Hotel to the mortuary in Strath Carron and doubtless the police will be questioning the landlord, as we speak, about the dreadful accident that occurred within his establishment. I doubt that he will be too concerned, since his plans to retire to Oban appear to have been given a boost by an unexpected pension scheme that has matured.'

'But this is criminal!' muttered Charlie, unable to believe his ears.

'Not nearly so criminal as incarcerating a man for a murder that his friends *know* he did not commit and which a mean-spirited solicitor advocate would have little trouble in proving beyond reasonable doubt.'

Charlie tried to make sense of the thoughts that whirled in his head; tried to think of something that Gordon and Dr Crawford had forgotten; told himself that this was all wrong and yet . . . the alternative was what? Life imprisonment for a crime that he alone knew he did not commit. But then, it seemed that Gordon and the doctor did not believe he had committed murder either.

'The cases; where are Charlotte's cases?'

'At the Station Hotel,' replied Gordon. 'I carried them up to her suite myself when I dropped her off. They were even heavier than she was. There was a heavy table in the room, too. It appears she fell on it while preparing herself a gin and tonic. There was a glass with the gin already poured, and a lemon, not yet . . . er . . . sliced.'

'But, I mean, who knows about this? The proprietor of the hotel – Sandy Whatsisname – does he know?'

The doctor shook his head. 'Only the three of us in this room know what really happened. Sandy Murchison asked no questions when I explained to him what had clearly happened in the room he let to Mistress Niven. The post-mortem will confirm it. I know the pathologist and he and I are likely to agree.'

'But Rory! Rory saw her in the drive and let her into the castle.'

'Rory had no idea who she was. We told him she was a tourist who had lost her way and got confused; thought she was coming home. He smelled the alcohol on her breath and took us at our word.'

'And Mrs Murdo?'

'Mrs Murdo says she can't remember when she last set eyes on her,' confirmed Dr Crawford.

'So you see, old bean,' said Gordon, 'all eventualities are covered. Charlotte came to the Highlands with the intention of renewing old friendships but, sadly, never made it as far as the castle. Such a shame.'

'I don't know what to say,' said Charlie, softly.

'No need to say anything,' said the doctor. 'And now, I must be on my way. It's been a fine party, Charlie. I look forward to coming again next year. Give my love to your daughters, especially the cheeky one.'

He walked towards the door and, as he made to pass through into the hall, he turned and said, 'There's just one thing, Mr Stuart.'

'Yes?' answered Charlie, fearful that the worst was yet to come.

'I wouldn't want you to think that Charlotte Niven's forging of my signature all those years ago on the note that questioned the balance of your father's mind had anything to do with today's events. Is that perfectly clear?'

'Perfectly,' answered Charlie.

49

Creag Sodhail

July 2000

'Your children are not your children.
They are the sons and daughters of Life's longing for itself.
They came through you but not from you
And though they are with you yet they belong not to you.
You may give them your love but not your thoughts,
For they have their own thoughts.
You may house their bodies but not their souls.'

Kahlil Gibran, *The Prophet – On Children*, 1923

Charlie knew that he would never fully come to terms with the events of that fateful day in June. The whole episode he would have to bury deep inside him if he were to stand a chance of returning to a normal life – or what passed for one.

A month after the event, high up on Creag Sodhail with Rory mending yet another broken-down shooting butt, the two fell into conversation. Such discourse was not, in itself, unusual, but it had about it a rare quality. The morning was fine and fair, the air clear and pure, and the warming rays of the sun released from the heather moorland that sweet-and-sour aroma unique to the Highland terrain. It was, for both of them, the smell of home. The sun warming their necks, the skin of their hands chafed and torn by the rough lumps of granite they had stacked into some semblance of a low wall, they sat with their backs to the completed arc of stones to catch their breath and enjoy the view. Charlie opened a flask of coffee and poured a plastic cupful for each of them.

Neither of them said anything for a while; they just sipped at their refreshment, breathing heavily; the climb had been steep and the rocks heavy. After a while, Charlie asked, 'Are you getting on all right? With the job? And Murdo?'

'I think so.'

'Are you enjoying it?'

'Yes.'

'I'm glad. I was a bit worried that we might not get on. That working at home might irritate you. That I might irritate you.'

'Who's to say you don't?'

Charlie was surprised at his son's candour. Then he turned to see that Rory was grinning.

'That's what dads are for, isn't it? To irritate their sons; to nag them and chivvy them along?'

'Well . . . if you put it like that . . .'

'I expect I'll be the same – when I have kids.'

'There's not much chance of that if you keep chasing every bit of skirt in the vicinity is there?'

Charlie could have bitten his tongue the moment the words came out. Here he was, sitting on his own land with his own son – the man whom he hoped would one day take over from him, the sun was shining on the shimmering water of the loch, the sky was clear and blue, the grouse were calling, and all he could do was criticise his son for . . . doing what sons did. He half expected Rory to get up and walk back down to the castle on his own. But he did not. He sat silently, occasionally sipping at his coffee and looking down upon a skein of geese that were skimming across the water far below them.

'I'm sorry,' offered Charlie. 'I shouldn't have said that.'

'No. It's all right. I know how it must seem to you.'

'It's really none of my business how you run your love life.'

'But then you're my dad. And fathers of sons have expectations, while fathers of daughters have worries.'

'Where did you get that from?'

'I read it somewhere.'

'Well, it's true,' confirmed Charlie. 'However hard you try as a father you do worry about your daughters. And you do – rightly or wrongly – have expectations of your sons. I suppose it was true of my father as well.'

Rory was silent for a while and then said, 'You didn't let him down, Dad.'

'Oh, I wonder sometimes. Not that he would ever have said much, either way. We had very little in common, my father and I – apart from a love of this place – and we only ever had a handful of real conversations. I'm sorry about that. I never really knew him.'

'Do you think you know me better than he knew you?'

The frankness of the question was unexpected.

'Well, I really don't know. I mean, I hope so. What do you think?'

'I think you don't approve of the way I live my life – as far as girls are concerned, anyway.'

'Mmm,' was as much as Charlie felt able to offer by way of a reply.

'It's only because I look at you and see how lonely you are.'

'Me?'

'Yes. I admire what you've done enormously, Dad, but I'm terrified of being in the same situation. Supposing I commit to one person and something happens to her, what then? I couldn't go through what you've gone through; I haven't the strength.'

'So you'll just carry on playing the field?'

'For a bit. They might think I'm a commitment-phobe, but there is a reason. I've seen what can happen when people commit. It can all go horribly wrong.'

'But that's no reason for not doing it. Yes, it's a risk, but the rewards are far greater.'

'Even if you end up alone?'

Charlie turned to face his son. 'I loved your mother like I've never loved anyone else. We had just six years together as a married couple but they were the best six years of my life. How can I possibly regret committing to her? Not least because it brought me Ellie and Lucy and you and your twin sister.'

'But you lost Mum all because of me and Sarah.'

'That's not true and there has never been the slightest accusation from me that your survival may have caused your mother's—' He failed to finish the sentence.

'I know. You've always been brilliant about it. But there's no getting away from the fact that the day you gained Sarah and me, you lost Mum. What we can't understand – and what we rate you for - is that you've never once mentioned the two things in the same breath.'

'Because I really don't associate them. It's as simple as that. I know the one thing might be regarded as leading to the other but I really can't go there. I won't go there. I lost your mum – the one person I loved more than any other – but I gained you and Sarah; I've never felt the slightest bitterness towards either of you. If I thought that you were reluctant to commit yourself to someone you really loved for fear of losing them, then I've taught you nothing at all.'

'But the grief—'

'The depth of grief is a measure of the depth of love. You can't separate the one from the other. Grief is the price we pay for love.'

'Is it worth it?'

'Every moment. I wouldn't have missed those six years for anything.'

'Even though it's meant you've been alone for so long?'

'I haven't been alone. I've had you four nipping at my heels the whole time.'

'But don't you miss . . . closeness?'

'Yes. Very much,' said Charlie softly. 'But there are other things in life.'

'Like this place?'

'Yes.'

'And Gordon?'

Charlie laughed. 'Yes; and Gordon, bless him. I don't know what any of us would have done without Gordon.'

'Do you think he'll stay?'

'Who knows? Until something else captures his imagination, probably, then he'll be up and off in search of pastures new, tilting at windmills and following his bliss.'

'That's a nice expression – following his bliss.'

'Yes. You should try it some time.' Charlie got up and stretched, his back stiff from the exertion.

Rory, too, got to his feet, but with rather more speed than his father. 'I don't have to look very far though, do I?'

'What do you mean?'

'For my bliss. It's here – this place. Where we all grew up.'

They began to walk down the heather-clad moor towards the castle.

'Don't worry about the girls, Dad. I'll find one – one day. The right one. When I'm ready.'

'And how will you know she's the right one?'

'Easy. I'll fall in love with her and she with me. Then she'll fall in love with this place.' The two of them stopped to admire the view – of mountain and loch and castle.

Rory turned to his father and smiled. 'Then I'll bring her home.'